LEGACY OF A LAWMAN

LEGACY OF A LAWMAN

A Western Story

Johnny D. Boggs

CHIVERS

British Library Cataloguing in Publication Data available

This Large Print edition published by AudioGO Ltd, Bath, 2012.
Published by arrangement with Golden West Literary Agency

U.K. Hardcover   ISBN   97814713 1110 9
U.K. Softcover   ISBN   97814713 1111 6

Printed and bound in Great Britain by
MPG Books Group Limited

For Cotton and Sonya Smith

PROLOGUE

June 8, 1902

She slapped him hard across the cheek.

I saw it. Heard it, too, the sound so much like a gunshot that I instinctively pushed back my coattail, and gripped the butt of the double-action Smith & Wesson holstered on my right hip. Pushing open the gate with my left hand, I stepped into the cemetery, and waited, staring. What followed was the longest, hardest silence I had ever experienced until her lips started trembling, finally parted, and released a piteous, heartbreaking wail that had me longing for silence.

Her whole body shook, yet her cries stopped as suddenly as they had started. Rage took over. She flung herself at him, hammering his broad chest with tiny fists.

Bass Reeves just stood there, an unmoving mountain of granite, big black hat in his left hand, not defending himself, not saying a word, not even bothering to wipe away the spit sliding down his face through gray-ing beard stubble. Exhaustion overtook her at last, and she turned away, saying something I couldn't catch, and staggered, likely would have collapsed had not a white-haired colored man and the Negro preacher come up at that moment, followed by four other Negro men. The preacher and the white-haired gent caught her, whispered something, and each took one of her arms, steering her toward the covered bench they had set up for the family alongside the freshly dug grave. That left the four men, and they didn't speak, just stared at Bass with malevolent eyes, telling him without words that he had no right to be here. They didn't move.

Neither did Bass.

I did. Those gents weren't armed. Who went heeled to a funeral? So I released the .44, and walked to Bass's side. For a moment, the four men turned their attention to me, and I pulled back my coat to let them see the badge pinned to my vest's lapel. I kept quiet, and they gave me the same look. I didn't belong there, either — only I knew it.

Another thing I knew. They might have challenged Bass Reeves even though he wore a badge same as I did, but they would never try anything with me, a white man. Some things, even in Muskogee, you just don't do if you're a Negro. Assaulting a white federal lawman likely tops that list.

Did Bass have any business at the Union Agency cemetery that morning? That's hard to say. They were burying his daughter-in-law — I assumed it was her mother who had slapped Bass — but there wasn't one member of the Reeves family there, except for Bass, and I'm not rightly sure he was really there. Physically, sure, but he stayed a few rods from the gate, far from the crowd of mourners. Mentally I'm not sure where Bass was, but I knew my place had to be right beside him, even if I was the only white man in a cemetery for coloreds and Creek Indians.

Everything a peace officer could see in Indian Territory I figured I had seen, and much of that I'd witnessed riding alongside Bass Reeves. For thirteen years, back when I first pinned on a deputy marshal's badge in 1889, I'd known him, and. . . . No, that's not altogether truthful. I can't honestly say I *knew* Bass Reeves.

We covered the same territory, sure, had worked closely together those past five years. I lived across from his house on West Court Street, but Henrietta, my wife, and I had never been over to Bass's for supper. I don't think I'd ever set foot inside his house, just stood on the porch. When Bass had married Winnie Sumner, a Cherokee freedwoman, two-and-a-half years ago, Henrietta and I hadn't attended the wedding. His first wife had died in Fort Smith in '96.

He was a man of color, and I was a white man.

Over the years, I had saved Bass Reeves's life, and undoubtedly he had pulled my hide out of some fierce shooting scrapes with outlaws, but know him? I'm not sure anyone really knew Bass Reeves, least of all a white man like me. Come to think of it, we had never even shaken hands. Yet, next to Henrietta, I considered Bass Reeves my closest friend. That's why I stood beside him on that warm June morning in 1902. That's why I'd be with him when he made his toughest ride in the coming weeks, to make his toughest arrest.

CHAPTER ONE

June 8, 1902

"Let's go, Dave."

The preacher was leading the mourners in "Ride Up in the Chariot" when Bass Reeves spoke. I hadn't been sure if Bass even knew I was there, at his side, till he called me by name, pulled his hat onto his closely shaved head, and went through the gate. The coloreds kept on singing that spiritual, but I could feel their stares on our backs as we left the agency cemetery. Bass swung onto his sorrel, I mounted my bay, and we trotted our horses away from the funeral. I didn't rightly know where we were bound, though I should have known. It wasn't a surprise when Bass reined up at the federal courthouse, dismounted like a man on a mission, tethered his horse, walked up the steps, and pushed through the doors.

A big man, six-foot-two and one hundred eighty pounds, quick as a catamount, he had

11

reached the third story before I caught up with him outside the office of United States Marshal Leo E. Bennett. Over the stammering protests of the owlish-looking secretary in the antechamber, Bass went right through that door, too.

"Sit down, Poindexter," I told the sweating, paling secretary, and the freckle-faced lawyer muttered something. When I closed the door behind me, he was sinking into his chair.

Inside the office, Marshal Bennett stood at the window, a warrant in his hand, talking to Deputy Grant Johnson, another colored marshal who usually worked out of Eufaula. Both men stopped, turned, stared.

"Bass," the marshal said, lowering the warrant he was about to hand to Grant Johnson. "I thought. . . ." The words died. He didn't know what to think.

Leo Bennett was a fine man. He had five children just cute as buttons, and his second wife, Anna, a white woman adopted by the Cherokees and the mother of Doc Bennett's two youngest daughters, had to be one of the most beautiful women I'd ever seen. They say she had even mesmerized the late President McKinley on their trips to Washington City. I knew that, because, unlike with Bass Reeves, I'd supped with the marshal at his house maybe a dozen times over the past five years. In his mid-forties, Bennett had been a doctor — still was; often enough, he'd come downstairs to the jails to treat sick prisoners — first in Fort Smith, Arkansas, before moving to Eufaula in 1883 and then settling in Muskogee. The man had more energy than a bolt of lightning. He had started up a newspaper in Muskogee, the *Weekly Phoenix,* in the late '80s before he landed the appointment of U.S. Indian Agent. He resigned as agent in '92, and had been appointed marshal of Indian Territory in '97.

I know what you're thinking. United States marshals are political appointments, with as much brains as the pettifogging idiot — in this case, the late President McKinley — who gave them the job. Doc Bennett, however, surely didn't fill that bill. He could care less who had appointed him, Republican or Democrat; he was just out to do his job, and he did his job well. As marshal, Bennett didn't just sit behind a desk in a third-story office and have his secretary, Preston Poindexter, keep visitors and, especially, deputy marshals, out of the marshal's office. Doc Bennett had gone after a few felons himself, and brought more than his share to jail, or the morgue. The man had the most piercing blue eyes I'd ever seen.

Those eyes held Bass Reeves's for only a second, then studied the floor.

" 'Mornin', Reeves," Deputy Johnson said. "Adams."

Bass lifted his right arm and pointed a thick finger at the paper in Doc Bennett's hand. "That for Bennie?"

The marshal sucked in a lungful of hot air. Even with the windows open and a breeze blowing, Doc Bennett's office always felt a furnace in the summer months, and the marshal tossed the paper on his desk, and ran his long fingers through his wavy, graying brown hair.

"Grant didn't want to take it," Doc said, and those blue eyes revealed determination again.

"That's right." Grant Johnson reached inside his vest pocket for a cigar. Another warrant had been shoved into the opposite pocket.

"Who you going after?" Bass jutted his jaw toward Johnson's warrant.

"Cherokee Bob." Johnson bit into a Famous K. of P. cigar, spit the end into the nearby spittoon, and fished out a match.

"Dozier's boy?"

"Uhn-huh." He struck a match against his

gun belt, and, as soon as he had fired up the smoke, he said: "Followin' in his daddy's footsteps. Robbed the Katy north of Eufaula yesterday. Killed the express man. Crushed the conductor's skull. Ain't expectin' him to live through the week. Made off with six hundred dollars and some." The cigar went back to his mouth, but only for a moment. He was looking at me now, pointing the cigar in my direction. "You want to come with me, Adams?"

My eyes held his for a moment, then fell on the warrant on Doc Bennett's desk. That's when I straightened, feeling suddenly uncomfortable, knowing what had brought Bass Reeves here. "I'll have to pass, Grant."

"Figured. I'll pick up Paden in Vinita, if that suits you, Marshal."

"You'll need more than Marshal Tolbert to assist you, Grant," Doc Bennett said.

"Won't be hard getting some Cherokees, 'specially with the reward I'm certain sure the Katy's gonna offer. Might be able to talk Bud Ledbetter into comin' along if he ain't got no pressin' concerns as city marshal. We'll be fine, Doc."

Clamping his yellowing and gold-capped teeth on the cigar, Deputy Marshal Grant Johnson grabbed his hat off the rack in the corner, and walked to the door, but stopped when he was shoulder-to-shoulder with Bass Reeves. "I wasn't gonna take that bench warrant, Bass," he said tightly, the cigar still in his mouth. "Want you to know that. Sorry that had to happen to a man like you."

He gave a slight nod, and pulled open the door.

"Good luck, Grant," Bass said, but I don't think Johnson heard because the door closed, and Grant Johnson was gone, leaving behind only the foul smell of his cigar.

Bass removed his hat, and I followed suit, and we both looked across the room at Doc Bennett, who motioned at the two jury chairs in front of his desk.

"Reckon there's no time to sit, Marshal," Bass said. "I'll take that bench warrant for Bennie, sir."

"Bass," the marshal said, "shouldn't you be with your wife at a time like this?"

"Winnie ain't the boy's mother," Bass said. "She's fine. But I'm Bennie's pa. He's my responsibility."

"It's the law's responsibility."

"I am the law." He looked down at the badge he wore. His next words were hushed. "Been a lawman for better than twenty-five years. Don't know nothin' else."

Doc Bennett's head shook, and he turned

away, pressing his palms against the window sill, staring down at the streets of Muskogee. "Bass," he said softly, "Grant Johnson was telling the truth. He wouldn't take this warrant. No deputy I have, colored or white, will, not voluntarily. Because of you. They think that much of you, Bass. Thought I might have to go after him myself, but . . . well . . . Bass . . . I can't ask you to. . . ."

"You ain't doin' the askin', Marshal. I am. I'm beggin' you, sir. I can't let no peace officer risk his life to go after Bennie, especially you. Bennie killed his wife. Shot her down in cold blood. Then took off like he wasn't nothin' better than a swamprunnin' nig—" He stopped, turned, walked to the territorial map hanging on the wall. "Give me the writ," he said.

I did it. Doc Bennett just stared out that window, and Bass Reeves looked at the map, so I walked to the marshal's desk, found the warrant, opened it, saw Ben Reeves's name on it, saw the words *MURDER* and *DEAD OR ALIVE* written in bold, black capital letters. I refolded the paper, and put it in my pocket.

"I'll go with you, Bass," I said.

"Dave . . . ," Bass began, still in front of that map.

"No." Marshal Bennett turned from the

window. "Deputy Adams is right. You want to go after your son, Bass Reeves, you go, but we do this by the book. You'll need someone to drive the tumbleweed wagon, too."

A long silence followed, with Bass Reeves turning around from the map, staring hard across the room at Doc Bennett, but our boss won that round. Bass sighed. "I'll hire out Erskine again," he said. "If he's sober."

"Is that enough?" Doc Bennett asked.

"Bennie's twenty years old. This ain't Cherokee Bob I'm going after."

"He's a murderer, Bass."

Well, as hot as that office was, those words lowered the temperature substantially. I felt chilled. After another hard silence with nobody and nothing moving, Bass wet his lips, and nodded at Doc Bennett.

"I'll bring him in, Marshal," Bass said. "Dead or alive."

CHAPTER TWO

June 9, 1902

The country kept changing, and Muskogee boomed. What had once been a dusty little village south of the Three Forks and hadn't been incorporated until 1898 now sported a population of more than four thousand. The city claimed three newspapers and better than twenty grocery stores, nigh a half dozen banks, a couple of photographers, five blacksmiths, and four billiard halls, not to mention more attorneys than preachers, and we had practically every religious denomination there was. We had an honest-to-goodness fire department, and the Adams Hotel boasted of its very own electric enunciator, even though about the only places a guest could telephone were the federal courthouse and St. Mary's Hospital. No saloons, though. Not anywhere, legally. Prohibition was the law of the land in the Indian Territory, but rum-runners kept lawmen like Bass Reeves and me busy.

Hard to fathom, all this change.

It seemed that people kept moving in every single day. White folks like me comprised a minority, though I reckon we outnumbered the Indians. That had always been the case, even before the Missouri, Kansas, and Texas Railroad — the Katy — reached town back in 1872. Most of the Negroes were freedmen of the Creek Nation, but since Congress' Dawes and Organic Acts had opened up the Indian Territory to settlement, more and more whites flocked into the country. The Twin Territories, Oklahoma and Indian Territory, were full of plenty of good, God-fearing folks, but many others not worth spitting on — and people were already talking about statehood. Why, Indian leaders were trying to turn Indian Territory into the state of Sequoyah, and I didn't know what that would mean for a white man like me or a black man like Bass, if that ever happened.

Talk also went around Muskogee that folks might start drilling again for oil in the next year or so, and I didn't like that thought at all. Cowboys, whiskey peddlers, and rowdies kept me busy enough as it was. Times kept changing, I thought, watching the city's one horseless carriage, a steam-powered Locomobile owned by a white banker, sputter down Court Street, causing my gray gelding to stamp, and damned near break his tether out front of Bass's home. The Runabout disappeared after turning onto Fourth Street, and, when my horse settled down, I shook my head, removed my hat, and knocked on Bass Reeves's front door.

My broadcloth suit of the previous day had been changed for trail duds: duck trousers tucked inside stovepipe boots, a blue and yellow checked cotton shirt, brown vest, calico bandanna, and wide-brimmed gray hat. I wore my gun belt and badge, with an extra revolver in my saddlebags and a '94 Winchester .25-35 sheathed in the saddle scabbard.

For a big man, Bass always seemed to go for tiny women. Winnie answered the door, a petite gal in her forties with hair beginning to show streaks of silver. Same as my hair, and Bass's, only we both had a few years on Winnie. She looked tired, looked as if she had been crying, but, same as her husband, she put up a strong front. Bennie might not have been her own blood, but she loved the boy. So did Bass. This had to be hard on the entire family — Winnie's daughter from her first marriage, and Bass's two other sons, in their late teens or early twenties, still living there, Homer and Bass, Jr. Bass and his first wife, Jennie, had reared close to a dozen kids, but some died young. Like I've said, I don't think I really knew Bass or his family, but they always struck me as close-knit. There had been another son, Robert, a brakeman for the Central Arkansas & Houston line, who had been killed back in '93 while coupling cars. When we rode the trail, Bass often spoke of him, always quietly, always reverently.

" 'Mornin' Marshal Adams." Speaking in an accent flaked with Cherokee, Winnie held open the screen door. She tried to smile, but soon gave up.

"Ma'am." I was just budding with conversation. I nodded.

No sound but the birds chipping.

"How you managing?" I asked.

"We're all right." Finished with small talk, Winnie turned, and raised her voice: "Bass! It's Marshal Adams!"

Spurs chimed, boots pounded the floor, and Bass Reeves appeared, squeezing past Winnie, loaded down with Winchester, war bag, and saddlebags. He wore a striped tan shirt of buckskin cloth, badge pinned over his left breast pocket; ragged bandanna, once red, now faded to pink, almost white;

navy woolen britches with the seat and thighs reinforced with brown cowhide; calf-skin boots I'd seen advertised in the Sears, Roebuck and Co. catalog, and that omni-present big black hat, which he pulled onto his head once he reached the porch.

His eyes were blacker than the ace of spaces.

"You ready?" he asked.

My head bobbed.

"I'll pick up my horse at Birchfield's, swing by the courthouse to get Erskine and the tumbleweed wagon. Meet you there." He turned back to his wife, removed the hat, leaned down to kiss her cheek, then was telling me something while Winnie vanished inside the house, the screen door slamming, the wooden door being pulled shut and bolted.

When he finished saying what he wanted me to do, my mouth had turned to sand. "You want me to interrogate Wadly?" My voice cracked.

"Likely Wadly saw which way Bennie run. The boy's got a two-day start on us. If we want to catch Bennie, that's something I got to know."

I pursed my lips. Bass just stared.

"You don't think you should talk to Wadly?" I asked.

23

After pulling on his hat again, Bass turned, strode down the steps, and headed across the yard toward Court Street. "I might kill him," was all he said.

"I'm not here to arrest you." I spoke at the crack in the doorway to the little shanty on the hill where most of the coloreds lived.

When the crack didn't widen, my patience ended. "But if you don't open that damned door, Wadly, and step out here, I'll whip the bitter hell out of you, then haul your sorry arse to the calaboose."

The door opened, and John Wadly's mulatto face appeared. Wide eyes looked past me, up and down the street, in the shadows, even on the roofs of his neighbors' homes before he slipped outside, and kept his back to the house's frame walls.

"What you wants, Marshal?"

"Tell me what happened."

"I tol' the city constable."

"Tell me."

"That boy kilt her. Shot her dead."

I raised a finger at a scab over his right eye. "He do that, too?"

Wadly's lips flattened. At last, he nodded.

"You were with her?"

Another long pause. My eyebrows narrowed, and he got the message.

"We wasn't doin' nothin'. We was at her cousin's. Bennie come along and. . . ."

"Bennie. You mean her husband."

That stopped him. A mean thing to say, I reckon, but I wasn't in a charitable mood, thanks to Bass Reeves. Beads of sweat bubbled on Wadly's forehead, and he shifted his feet — the boy was still in his stockings — restlessly on the clapboard porch.

I let out a breath. "I don't plan on arresting you for adultery."

"Naw, Marshal, me and her, we ain't, we hadn't. . . ."

"Don't play me for a fool, Wadly." I leaned into his face. He stank of scared sweat and Choc beer. I tried to remember the funeral yesterday, couldn't place him, and decided he hadn't attended. Likely he had been here, drinking beer and hiding from the entire Negro population of Muskogee. "What happened?"

"Bennie come up," he said at last. "We was at Emma's home. Emma Solomon, like I done tol' you, like I tol' that other white marshal, like I tol' that newspaper reporter. We was just sittin' there, talkin'. Wasn't doin' nothin'."

"Where's Emma Solomon live?"

His eyes shot down the street, then his jaw jutted in that direction.

"Let's go."

"I can't. . . ."

"You will. One way or the other, you will."

Kneeling on the warped doorsteps, I fingered the dried blood.

"That's where she fell," John Wadly volunteered.

Emma Solomon wasn't home, but that didn't matter. With a heavy sigh, I rose, removed my hat, and wiped away the sweat. It would be another day of living in a furnace, but my body wasn't leaking out rivers of sweat the way John Wadly's was.

"You were inside?"

His nervous head bobbed.

"Bennie just barged in?"

Now the head shook. "No, sir, he knocked. Emma, she let him in."

A cat suddenly shot across the porch, and I thought John Wadly might soil his britches. His eyes darted, wondering what had spooked the cat, likely figuring I had led him here so Bennie, or maybe Bass, could kill him. When a dog came trotting down the street, he managed to catch his breath, and pull out a rag, mop the perspiration off his face.

"What happened then?"

"Nothin'. He just shot her dead."

26

My head shook. "You said you were inside. That blood on the steps, you said, was where she fell."

"That's right. We talked some."

I pointed to the scab. "Did more than talk."

"I slipped. Hit my head on the corner of the pie safe."

"You told me Bennie gave you that."

His head bobbed. "He was reachin' for me. I tried to get up, turned, and fell. Then she leaped up, got in Bennie's face."

"Emma?"

"No." The head shook violently. "Not Emma. It was. . . ."

"Bennie's wife."

Silence. His head bowed. "Yes, sir," he murmured.

Sometimes, it's best to let the silence run its course. Wadly was crying now, tears streaking down his cheeks, catching up the sweat, spilling onto the porch. He put the rag to his nose, and blew, then stepped away from the wall he'd been hugging the same as he'd done back at his own home.

"When he comes through the door, she was holdin' my hands, callin' me somethin' sweet." He looked up. "We loved each other, me and her." He couldn't even say her name. "Bennie comes in. We hadn't ex-

27

pected him. He was supposed to 'a' been workin' at the barbershop. I gots up, tried to, but Bennie lunged at me, pushed me. I slipped, hit my head. Thought Bennie might kill me dead with his own hands, but . . . she stood, started yellin' at him, and Bennie stopped, just stood there, starin' at her."

His eyes closed. "He tells her . . . 'I thought you said it was over.' And she tells him . . . 'I got more love for John's little finger than I got for your whole body.' And walks right past him, right out the door. She was holdin' the screen door open, tellin' me to come on, and Bennie turns toward her. That's when I seed the pistol. Big ol' Forty-Five Colt. And he's bringin' it up . . . like he was hardly even movin' . . . . and thumbin' back the hammer, and then there's this deafenin' roar. My ears start ringin', the smoke a-stingin' my eyes. And I see the blood just a-sprayin' from the back of her head, and she's fallin', and Emma's screamin', and Bennie's shootin' at her again as she falls on the porch, her legs there, the rest of her on the steps. And Bennie's got that gun, and I seen he's cryin', and, swear to Jesus, I fear he's a-gonna kill me, but, no, he puts the gun to his own head, and pulls the trigger, but the barrel's slippin', and the bullet just grazes his head.

Plows into the ceilin'. And then he's walkin' away, blood a-leakin' from where the bullet grazed his head."

I saw the brown drops leading out the door, down the steps, toward the street.

John Wadly kept talking. "He's walkin' right past her . . . like he don't even see her no more . . . and then he's climbin' onto his horse. And he just rides away, reins in his left hand, Colt in his right, hangin' at his side."

I let the tears run their course. No longer was John Wadly standing. He had slid down onto the porch, pulling his knees up, rocking back and forth, head bowed, sobbing.

When he looked up, he repeated: "I swear, Marshal, sir, swear to Jesus Christ hisself, I thought he was a-gonna kill me."

I said: "He had a horse?" Needed to make sure.

Wadly barely nodded.

"Saddlebags? War bag? Bedroll?"

"I . . . I couldn't see. Not through all that white smoke."

"Damn it, Wadly, you just told me you saw him plain as day. Reins in his left hand, and revolver in his right. Now think, Wadly. Saddlebags? War bag? Bedroll? Anything like that?"

A full minute passed, though it seemed

29

like an eternity. "No," he said, shaking his head. "No, sir. No saddlebags. Don't think there was a bedroll, neither."

"That's good, Wadly. Real good. Now think clearly," I said. "One more time. That Colt. Was it belted?"

His eyes turned glassy. "No, sir," he said after a moment, "he just pulled it out of his britches."

That might be a bit of good news. Maybe Bennie didn't have any extra shells. He had fired three rounds, which would leave him with only two shots — unless he was crazy enough to put six beans in the wheel. He had tried to kill himself, and, when he couldn't manage to do that, he had left town. But where?

"Which way did he ride?"

The head shook. "I can't remember."

"Come on, Wadly! Which way?"

He looked toward the street, still rocking, mind working, and I let him think. Biting his bottom lip, he at last gave a nod, and tilted his head in one direction. "Had to be that way," he told me. "I was lookin' out that screen door. Front door was still open. I wouldn't spied him ridin' by if he'd gone t'uther way. Yes, sir." He pointed. "Had to go that way."

That way would have led down the hill,

out of town, toward the Texas Road. That was a start, although not much of one. My eyes returned to the petrified Negro rocking on Emma Solomon's porch. "How long had you been seeing her?"

He shrugged. I thought he might not answer, but after a moment he said: "Off and on, 'bouts a year. We'd stopped for a while. Bennie and her tried to make things work. He got another job, stopped porterin' for the Katy, went back to barberin', wasn't travelin' so much, and I jus'. . . ." He wet his lips again. Snot dribbled onto his shirt front. He looked up again. "We loved each other, Marshal. It pains me somethin' fierce that she's dead now, that I seen her brains get blowed out."

"By her husband." I let the meanness stay in my voice.

His head fell. I stepped off the porch, and looked down the street. A dog barked. A mule brayed.

"Bennie Reeves," I whispered, "you damned fool." My head shook. Times like this I thought that maybe I had been packing a star for too many years, that I would be happier sweeping out the mercantile or emptying spittoons in the Adams Hotel.

A jealous husband had killed his unfaithful wife. A white man would have known

31

not to run, would have turned himself in. Maybe, maybe, he would have been charged with manslaughter, but a jury most likely would have acquitted him. Or if Bennie had killed that sniveling coward rocking on the porch. Or shot the both of them. I doubt if any white jury would have convicted a white husband. Most grand juries would have brought in a no bill. I'm not saying that's right. Far from it. I couldn't imagine what I would have done had Henrietta betrayed me like that, but I know I could never have shot her down like Bennie Reeves had done his wife. Or course, Henrietta wouldn't have cheated on me, nor would I ever have considered such a sin. Had I been in Bennie Reeves's place, maybe I would have spit in my wife's face, and her lover's, too, and left them sitting at the table at Emma Solomon's house. Yeah, that's what I would have done. That's what Bennie should have done.

Bennie Reeves, however, had let jealousy enrage him, and shot his wife in the head. The coroner's report said another bullet — the second one, according to John Wadly — had been a flesh wound, and completely unnecessary. She had died instantly.

Bennie hadn't turned himself in, though. He had run, and, by thunder, no matter how much his father was respected in these parts, Bennie Reeves was a Negro.

That's why I had a bench warrant for Bennie Reeves in my vest pocket. That's why that warrant stated *Dead or Alive.*

CHAPTER THREE

June 9, 1902

It's right pretty country.

Cottonwoods, live oaks, even some walnut and pecan trees, lined the banks of the Verdigris and Grand Rivers, and tall grass, interspersed with sunflowers and Indian paintbrushes, waved along the rolling hills where the two rivers joined the sandy Arkansas River. That's how this place got its name, Three Forks.

Erskine Jones cursed the mules, pulled on the lines, and halted the tumbleweed wagon at the Texas Road's cattle ford near where the Grand flowed into the Arkansas. He whipped off his porkpie hat, slapped it on the spring seat beside him, stopped swearing at the mules, and cussed out Bass Reeves instead.

"Damnation, Bass, you said we was goin' to Marshall Town. How the hell do you expect me to get there iffen I don't cross this river?"

Bass rode alongside the prison wagon on his sorrel. "We'll camp here tonight."

"Hell's bells, Bass!" Erskine Jones slammed his hat again. "There's plenty of daylight left."

"Make camp," Bass said bluntly. "Over yonder."

"You act as if you want that boy of your'n to get away. Hellfire and ruination, I knowed Doc Bennett was makin' a serious error of judgment sendin' you after that kid."

I spurred the bay and shot past Bass, who was turning in the saddle, toward Erskine Jones. "You best shut up," I told our tumbleweed wagon driver and cook, "and just do as you're ordered."

Muttering a few foul oaths, he slammed the hat back on his head, gathered the lines, and turned the tumbleweed wagon around, talking to himself while first clucking at the mules, then singing a song, all the while easing the wagon off the Texas Road. Erskine and I followed Bass to a long-dead and uprooted cottonwood several rods from the banks.

Erskine Jones was part Choctaw. Mad as a hatter. His gut looked like a balloon, his hair thinning on top but with a salt-and-pepper beard thicker than the canebrakes that once dominated the banks of the Arkansas. That beard stretched down to the lowest button on his pull-over muslin shirt. He had, maybe, six teeth left in his mouth. His right pinky was minus the first two knuckles, and, when he walked, he favored his left leg. "But you should 'a' seen the panther after we tangled," he would often say when someone noticed his limp.

He carried no bedroll, no war bag, no change of clothes, no razor — his beard was proof of that — and no soap. I doubt if his body had felt water since the last thunderstorm. Nor did he carry a firearm, or, rather, was not supposed to. The latter was on Marshal Bennett's orders. The rest could be chalked up to personal preference.

Doc Bennett had followed the late Judge Isaac Parker's directions. When Judge Parker first arrived at Fort Smith, with jurisdiction over the Western Judicial District of Arkansas, he would send out his marshals, usually numbering four or five, with a tumbleweed wagon. The wagon's driver went unarmed, to keep the prisoners from being tempted to snatch the weapon. When a cook was also hired, he, too, went unarmed, although, at night, the cook and/or driver would help guard any prisoners.

A jail house on wheels, the tumbleweed

wagon had two high-spoked wheels on the rear axle and smaller wheels up front, along with iron bars secured to the reinforced wooden floor, where chains could hold down the rowdiest prisoner. Two steps in the back of the wagon led to a padlocked door, and a roof kept the sun from baking the prisoners too much, and even extended to provide the driver some protection from the sun or rain, as well. The wooden exterior was painted white and red, with orange capital letters on the sides reading *U.S. COURT.*

On this afternoon, the jail cell, of course, was empty of any human cargo.

Bass had dismounted, wrapped the reins to his sorrel around the stub of a cotton-wood branch, and was unsaddling the sorrel when Erskine stopped the wagon and set the brake.

I slid from the saddle, pulled the small Winchester from the scabbard, and led the bay to the fallen cottonwood. My eyes scanned the road and the rivers before I leaned the rifle against the cottonwood, and began loosening the cinch.

Truth be told, Bass's actions had perplexed me almost as much as they had propelled Erskine Jones into a cussing fit. The sun said it wouldn't be dark for another two hours, and we could have easily made Marshall Town instead of making camp, or at least crossed the Arkansas River. I wasn't even sure why we were going to Marshall Town.

The town was located a short ride just northwest of where we were, on the Military Road near the old Creek Agency between Love's Trading Post on the banks of the Verdigris and McIntosh Town. That area between the Verdigris and Arkansas was chock full of little settlements, schools and missions, and more than its share of wanted criminals.

Back in Muskogee, when I had met up with Bass and Erskine at the federal courthouse and had informed both men what John Wadly had told me, Bass had merely said: "Marshall Town."

"He could have turned south," I had suggested, "tried for Texas." The Red River lay some one hundred and forty miles away, and I knew that Bennie likely had friends down in Paris. Bass had operated out of Paris when he had been working for the U.S. Court for the Eastern District of Texas in the early 1890s, before he had been transferred to Muskogee.

"Marshall Town," was all Bass had said, shaking his head, so we had ridden toward the Three Forks.

"Damnation, Bass," Erskine Jones was complaining, "if this was as far as we was comin' today, why in the hell didn't we just spend the night in Muskogee and light out tomorrow morn?"

"Just unhitch the team, Erskine." Bass had begun rubbing down the sorrel's back.

"We just got back with a load of prisoners the other day," Erskine said. "Would 'a' enjoyed sleepin' in my own bed one more night."

"Your bed's an empty cell in the courthouse," I reminded him.

He glared at us over a mule's back. "But it's my damned bed!" He started singing "There Is a Tavern in the Town" at the top of his lungs.

Shaking my head, I slid the saddle off, set it down, and removed the blanket, which I placed on top of the saddle so it might dry. "I hope," I told Bass over Erskine's out-of-key screams, "you hadn't planned on sneaking up on anyone."

Bass didn't acknowledge me, or Erskine's bellows, for a full minute. At last, he lowered the brush he had been working over the sorrel's back, and said: "You know Marshall Town?"

Sure, I knew Marshall Town. Any deputy

marshal working Indian Territory undoubtedly knew about Marshall Town. It had been doing business since before the allotments had started in '98, opening up the region for white settlement.

Back in 1866, treaties required that freedmen of the Five Civilized Tribes — the Creeks, Choctaws, Cherokees, Chickasaws, and Seminoles — be accepted onto tribal rolls. Many of those recently freed slaves formed all-black towns in Indian Territory. Marshall Town was one of the first.

And among the worst.

Although in the Creek Nation, the settlement lay close to the Cherokees' country, and bitterness flowed like illegal whiskey between those two tribes. A lot of Negroes had ridden for the Creek Lighthorse Police, and there had been more than a few clashes between those blacks and Cherokee cattlemen. A black Lighthorse man had been killed in 1876. John Vann, a Cherokee cattle rancher, had been murdered, maybe in revenge, three years later. More blood spilled, and Marshall Town earned a reputation as a wild and woolly place. A hang-out for rustlers, thieves, whiskey runners, whores, and killers, of all races.

Since the late 1880s, things had settled down, but just an itsy bit. It wasn't a place I ever cared to show my badge, revolver, or face.

"I got a notion," Bass said, "that Bennie will be there."

"Why?"

Bass grimaced. "It's where he . . . awe, hell . . . it's where we buy our liquor."

He ducked behind the sorrel, and was down there a long time. When his face finally reappeared, I couldn't help but grin.

"Introducing and selling intoxicating spirits is a federal offense, Deputy Reeves," I told that big, black face, which hardened.

"Where do you buy yours?" he asked, not smiling.

"I don't," I said over Erskine Jones's maniacal singing. "Mine's impounded from peddlers I happen to arrest."

"That's dishonest." Still no smile. I hadn't expected one. We were trying to make light of the situation, but, by grab, that was Bass's son we were chasing. For murder.

Bass stepped around the back of the sorrel, crossed the cottonwood, and, with Winchester in his right hand, strode toward a cluster of brush and saplings.

After hobbling the bay, I turned back to the tumbleweed wagon and yelled at Erskine Jones to shut the hell up.

Filthy and profane, Erskine Jones was a terrible cook, too.

Since the tumbleweed wagon was *sans* prisoners, he had stored our supplies in the traveling jail, which he fished out after hobbling the mules, and then set to getting a cook fire started. Bass had stashed an extra saddle in the wagon, which had prompted an explosion of curses from Erskine Jones that it was *his* wagon, for *his* stuff, and damned if Bass Reeves was a-gonna hog it. Bass hadn't bothered replying, but the saddle remained.

The coffee was weak, brackish, and I spent most of my time spitting out sand from the Arkansas and grounds from the chicory. Erskine had burned the salt pork, and the beans were hard as pebbles. But he relished over his plate, like a hog.

Bass ate in silence, then took his dirty dishes to the river to wash them. When he returned, as fireflies sparkled in the gloaming, he deposited the tin cup, plate, and spoon beside the fire, and returned to the saplings and brush. This time, he carried not only his .44-40 Winchester, but the war bag.

Looking up from his plate, coffee and beans dripping into his rough beard, Erskine Jones mumbled: "He pissin' or crappin' again?"

I didn't answer. I had a pretty good idea, however, that what Bass was up to had nothing to do with answering Nature's call.

Finally when he returned to the firelight, Bass Reeves had changed, not only his clothes, but his appearance. He dropped the gun belt and Winchester on his bedroll, along with the war bag. Now he wore clothes that would make Erskine Jones's duds resemble Sunday-go-to-meetings. His woolen britches were frayed and patched, held up by a pair of canvas suspenders stained by tobacco juice. The hat was a brown floppy number, the front ripped where crown met brim. Three bullet holes ventilated the crown. His shirt was home-spun, untucked, the left sleeve ripped and repaired poorly with sinew and needle, and he had removed the heels of both of the brogans he wore.

Plate and cup slipped from Erskine's hands, clattering on the ground. Our wagon driver had just returned from washing, or perhaps pretending to wash, his supper ware. "Hell's bells!" Jones cried, and shook his head.

43

Ignoring him, Bass Reeves knelt beside the bedroll, and opened one of the saddlebags. He pulled out a .41-caliber Remington Derringer, opened it to check the loads, then snapped it shut and slipped it into one of the mule-ear pockets on his threadbare trousers. Then, as if his clothes and appearance weren't dirty enough, he reached over and scooped up sand, splashing the grains and débris across his shirt front and down his trousers, before powdering his face with dust and grime.

An owl hooted, and coyotes began singing across the river.

Without a word, Bass strode across the camp to the tumbleweed wagon, pulled open the door, and stepped inside. When he exited, he was carrying the saddle, as rawhide-looking a McClellan — the two stirrups didn't even match — as you'd ever see.

"I'll be ridin' into Marshall Town," he said, "alone." His eyes found me when he finished that sentence. Then, to Erskine he announced: "I'm borrowin' one of your mules."

"The hell you say." Erskine had found time to bite off a wad from a twist of tobacco, softening the quid with his teeth and gums. "Ride your own damned horse."

"That sorrel's too fine a mount for a colored boy like me to be ridin'," he said, thickening his accent, raising his voice a couple of octaves, and slurring his words.

I grinned.

Erskine cussed. He spat. When Bass began unhobbling one of the jacks, he strode toward the fire. "That's Lucifer, and I don't want him a-gettin' shot."

"He won't."

"I don't want him a-gettin' stole, neither."

Bass couldn't assure Erskine of that.

Erskine started to argue more, thought better of it, and spit again, the juice sizzling on a stone rimming the fire.

After throwing on saddle and hackamore, Bass swung onto Lucifer's back. His long legs practically touched the ground.

"How do I look?"

His eyes locked on me when he asked the question, but it was Erskine Jones who replied.

"You look like some old colonel's pet darky."

Tugging gently on the hackamore, Bass grinned as he turned the mule toward the river.

"Used to be one," he said, and the night swallowed him.

CHAPTER FOUR

1838–1875

From humble, unjust beginnings, Bass Reeves rose out of bondage, pulled himself up by the boot straps, and became a feared and respected officer of the court who has delivered justice to various malefactors: women, Negro, Indian, and White, alike.

That is the opening sentence in a biographical article published by the Oklahoma City *Weekly Times Herald* in 1907. Rarely moved to talk much about his past, Bass — usually with the aid of John Barleycorn — on occasion would step out of character and surprise me. Since the events I am relating in this narrative, I have been obsessed with learning more about the man I rode with in the Indian Territory for many miles, many years.

Bass was born into slavery. That much I knew. I cannot attest to the complete veracity of the *Weekly Times Herald* article, but

46

much of it rings true to what my own investigations have revealed. I quote from the newspaper:

Named after a grandfather, Bass grew up as the chattel of a wealthy Arkansas planter named William Reeves, and spent his early boyhood fetching water and later working in the cotton fields of Crawford County. When he was eight years old, the Reeves clan emigrated to Grayson County, Texas, and Bass left the cotton fields to work with the livestock. That's where he had learned to handle horses so well. William Reeves soon learned not to limit the boy to feeding and watering mules; instead, he let Bass train and care for prize stallions. Even before Bass had reached his teens, the young slave worked with the blacksmith, although he spent more hours with the horses than ever with anvil and bellows.

His master gave Bass as a twenty-first-birthday present to his son, George Reeves. That proved fortuitous for the young slave because in 1850, George Reeves was elected sheriff of Grayson County.

This much I know is absolute. While sharing a bottle of bourbon in a wagon yard one

47

night in Paris, Texas, Bass told me about riding in Sheriff George Reeves's posse. I remember Bass's words, spoken with such clarity, as if the scene had happened only yesterday. The story has stuck with me, perhaps, because Bass so rarely felt like talking. Maybe it was the bourbon.

"Wasn't no more than knee-high to a grasshopper, 'bout twelve, thirteen years old, but growin' up mighty fast," Bass said. "Didn't let me do much more'n hold the horses, take care of 'em, feed 'em, water 'em, chores like that. 'Course, I was mighty good at chores like that.

"In the summer of 'Fifty-Four, George had to bring in a man-killer named Browne, Greene . . . some kind of color. Me and George and a deputy named Hoffer was ridin' down a woods road to Browne or Greene-whatever-his-name-was's shack in the thickets along Jack Branch, when that desperado fired a round.

"Deputy went on one side of the road, his horse dead, and me and George took to the other, lettin' our mounts skedaddle.

"Two quick shots clipped a saplin' over my head, and George, he's yellin' somethin' to the deputy across the road, and then he's handin' me his musket.

"Scared the hell out of me. Not the fact

that that fellow was tryin' to kill us, but on account that George was givin' me his musket, shot pouch, and powder horn, and tellin' me . . . 'Load it.'

" 'Mister George, I can't load your gun,' I says, then tries to burrow myself into the ground once another bullet kicked up a fountain of leaves that rained down on us.

" 'You've seen me load that piece many a time!' George had drawn a Paterson Colt from his jacket pocket. 'Just do it, Bass! And you know better than to call me mister. It's George.' He pulled off his hat, slid down into the bar ditch where we had taken up fort, and asked . . . 'You seen his smoke?'

"My head shook violently.

" 'He's on the other side of the road,' George says as he's pointin' at a clump of blackjacks. 'You can tell from where the bullets have been hitting.' I rammed a ball down the barrel, fingered a percussion cap on the nipple, pulled the hammer to full cock.

"George smiled. Says he . . . 'That's good, Bass. Perfect. I been watchin' you. Now, you watch 'em blackjacks. Just keep an eye on those trees. Watch for smoke. When you see it, shoot at where the smoke's risin', but shoot below it. Shoot low. Always shoot low. And keep your head down.'

49

"Afore I can speak, George had done started down the ditch, not up the road, but back the way we had come, where the elevation was slightly higher. I wanted to follow him, but another bullet sung over my head, and I just hugged that ditch's side, and peered over the bank.

" 'I can't see where the son-of-a-bitch is!' the deputy yelled.

"Well, I sure could. Arms shakin', I aimed toward the driftin' white smoke, rememberin' to lower the barrel, and pulled the trigger. The kick of the musket practically slammed me into the leaves, and my shoulder's throbbin', and I see I've dropped George's musket, see it slidin' down the embankment. But I grabs that musket and powder horn and starts reloadin'.

"Sweat's almost blindin' me. My heart's racin'. Ten gallons of water wouldn't have slaked my thirst. I don't know.

"Ten minutes must've passed. No more shots come, and Mister Hoffer, he yells . . . 'Reckon he's lit a shuck?' Right then, I hear a twig snap, I turn to see that man-killer sneakin' down the ditch, right toward me, long gun in his left hand, revolver in his right. Don't rightly know who was more scared. Me, seein' that beady-eyed, bearded gent with a couple of guns . . . or him, spyin' a colored boy holdin' a musket. I was sixteen years old. Figured I'd never live to see seventeen.

"Only then, I hear George yellin' . . . 'Charlie.' Charlie *Burgundy* . . . Burgundy, that was the name! Well, Burgundy turns toward George's voice. George had doubled back. Reckon he had Charlie Burgundy figured out to a T. Well, George don't give him no more chance, but busts Burgundy's arm at the elbow with a pistol shot, and that black heart's writhin' on the ground, cussin', cryin'. And George is tellin' me . . . 'Good work, Bass!' *Good work?* I didn't see that I'd done nothin'. Anyhow, two weeks later, they hanged that fellow from the gallows tree in Sherman."

That was the most Bass ever talked to me about his life in one sitting. Perhaps it was because we were in Texas, relatively close to his old stamping grounds where he had been a slave. Then again, the bourbon wasn't the rotgut usually associated with the region, but was quite exceptional.

The capture of Charlie Burgundy made George Reeves a hero, so Reeves left the sheriff's office in '55 and was elected to the House of Representatives. He didn't take Bass with him to Austin, but when war broke out, George took Bass with him into the 11th Texas Cavalry.

Bass was in his early twenties when the 11th rode into Fort Smith, Arkansas, shortly before Christmas 1861. The day after Christmas, as Colonel George Reeves's manservant, he rode with the Texians into the Osage Nation. The 11th saw the elephant in the battle of Chustenahlah.

"Don't think I reckon I'd ever really thought about what 'em Texians was fightin' for," Bass once said. "Till I was gallopin' behind George. Most of those Union troopers was Indians . . . Creeks and Seminoles . . . but they had men of color with 'em. Rebels run 'em down. Crushed 'em. Wasn't much of a fight, but it left a mark on me. Made me bitter."

After the 11th made camp in Indian Territory, the horse soldiers celebrated, playing cards and drinking forty-rod.

"I always had thought of George as a friend," I overheard Bass telling some colored men at a barbershop in Guthrie. "We rode together, had fought together. Never really considered him my master. George never laid a hand on me, till we was playin' cards in his tent, and began arguin'. Lots of those colored Union troops had been tryin' to surrender when those damned

Texians rode 'em down, slashin' at 'em with sabers, riddlin' 'em with bullets. George stood up . . . well in his cups by then . . . and told me to mind my manners. I told him didn't seem that those Texas cavalry boys he was commandin' had any manners, him included. He called me 'an uppity nigger.' First time he'd ever called me that. Then he frowned, shakin' his head, sayin' that was a mistake, and he held out his hand, offered to make peace."

When Bass accepted the handshake, George sent a left hook into his manservant's temple.

"But he didn't knock me down." Bass had grinned as he recalled this. "I had four inches and forty pounds over George, and when I walked out of that tent, his nose was busted, maybe some ribs, and he wasn't goin' nowhere for a couple of hours."

According to the report in the *Weekly Times Herald,* Bass ran. Took to the rivers, the hills, made his way into the Cherokee Nation and joined up with the Keetoowah. Pins they were called as they wore crossed pins on their lapels. Abolitionists fighting the Rebels. Pretty much bushwhackers. Irregulars. That's where Bass learned more about tracking, learned to know Indian Territory

53

like the back of his hand. Learned to speak some Indian tongues, too — Seminole, Creek. Learned to hide from the white Rebs searching for runaways, for Unionists. Learned how to shoot better than George Reeves had ever taught him. Learned to be a man.

The war's end brought Bass Reeves emancipation. A big word, but I guess Bass had been free, or at least living free, since '61. He married a girl, took up working on farms, learning to read and write and cipher at a Freedman's Bureau school. Started raising a family. By 1870 or thereabouts, he had bought a farm outside of Van Buren, Arkansas, and brought his mother there to live with him, his wife and the kids — four or five by that time.

In those days, the U.S. marshal's office was headquartered in Van Buren, and the lawmen started coming to Bass's farm, hiring him out as a tracker, a scout. Pretty soon, he had stopped farming, and was living in town, although every once in a while someone would hire him out to help with horses. He lived in the First Ward — Colored Town, the whites called it, or, more often, something less polite — across from the Little Rock and Fort Smith Railroad tracks. He didn't spend much time with his family. Wanted to, but it seemed that every time he came home from helping a marshal trail some criminal who had fled into Indian Territory, another deputy would be knocking on his door.

In 1871, the federal court for the Western District of Arkansas moved out of Van Buren down the road to nearby Fort Smith.

"First judge I recollect was a fellow named Story," Bass once told me. "They made him quit after he taken money from some people who didn't have no business with the court."

Story was replaced by Isaac C. Parker, and I don't have to tell you much about him. They would call him "Hanging Judge" — he surely sent plenty to their doom on those huge gallows he had constructed next to the big courthouse. Judge Parker instructed his marshal to hire two hundred deputies. Sounds like a lot, but not when you consider those deputies would have to police an area covering seventy-four thousand square miles. A lot of those lawmen hired were on the wrong side of that badge.

Tully Griffin was one.

Griffin had ridden with Colonel George Reeves in the 11th Texas Cavalry, and he remembered Bass when the tracker showed up at the courthouse around the spring of '75.

"Man kept starin' at me when I rode in with four of Judge Parker's deputies," Bass would later testify in court, "but I didn't think nothin' of it. I am a man of color in a white man's world. I'd gotten used to looks like that."

From trial transcripts, newspaper reports, and correspondence with individuals living in Fort Smith at the time, I have pieced together what happened.

Griffin followed Bass to Second and Vine. While Bass was scrubbing trail dust off his hands and face, getting ready for supper with his family, Tully Griffin knocked on the door.

"Jennie answered it," Bass related to Deputy Marshal Grant Johnson. "I'm on the back porch. Next thing I hear is Jennie screamin', and my children cryin'."

Bass raced into the house. His son Robert, maybe ten years old, was slugging the white man. Then Tully Griffin saw Bass. Grinning, Tully Griffin slapped the boy with his hat, and sent him sprawling on top of his mother, whose nose was bleeding.

"You remember me, boy?" Tully Griffin said, and reached for an Arkansas toothpick sheathed in the uppers of his left boot.

"Truth be, I didn't remember him," Bass testified. "Bunch of ex-Confederates lived and passed through Van Buren, Fort Smith. I knowed to try to keep shy of 'em. Didn't want no trouble with nobody. But this man come lookin' for it. Come into my house. Hit my wife. Slapped my boy."

Before the knife was out of the sheath, Bass had launched himself across the room, and the two men crashed through the door, onto the porch, and rolled down the street. The knife blade slashed as Bass tried to stand. Sliced through his shirt. Blood trickled. Tully came up, feinted, then drove the blade, but Bass stopped it with both hands, and Tully Griffin screamed as the bones in his wrist were crushed. The knife fell into the grass, and Tully flew into the street, hit a passing carriage, breaking his collar bone, and rolled over. Bass was straddling him, knocking out Tully's teeth, breaking his jaw, ribs, damned near tearing off his right ear when two lawmen pulled him off.

"Had to buffalo me with a revolver," Bass said. "When I come to, the manacles was on both my hands and feet, and I was in that hell on the border."

Hell on the border. That's what folks called the jail at the federal courthouse, but, indeed, it felt worse than hell. Light sometimes managed to creep through the barred windows of the basement beneath a two-story brick building that housed the court-room, jury rooms, and offices for the marshal, clerks, and attorneys. Toilets were buckets placed in the old chimneys. Coal-oil barrels that had been cut in half served as washtubs. The stench would turn the hardest stomach.

A charge of resisting a federal peace office would land Bass a year's stay in prison. Assault with intent to kill would add length and labor to his sentence.

"They fetched me one morn," Bass said. "Light damned near blinded me when I stepped out of that dungeon. Still had the iron on my wrists, and my ankles was shackled. Them two trusties wasn't takin' no chances. Led me to Judge Parker's chambers. I was just an ignorant colored man. Didn't know a thing about the law. Not really. I thought this was how I was bein' tried, that I'd just stand before Judge Parker like a man stands before God Almighty and learns his fate." Bass laughed. "Come to think of it, lots of people in Fort Smith thought Judge Parker was God Almighty."

We picture Isaac Parker as an old man, view him as a white-bearded Moses bringing down the wrath of God, but in 1875, I

58

doubt if the judge had seen his fortieth birthday. He was a young man, but when he spoke, you listened. His dark hair was neatly combed, and he wore a well-groomed mustache and large goatee. His eyes seemed to reach into your soul.

According to a letter I received from Judge Parker's secretary, the judge told Bass: "You face serious charges, young man."

"Yes, sir." Bass stared at his dirty boots.

"You almost killed Deputy Griffin."

"That's what I was tryin' to do, sir."

"So you plead guilty."

Bass shrugged.

"Good, I take that as a not guilty plea." Now, Bass looked up, and Parker was scribbling something on a paper. When the judge raised his head, he didn't look at Bass, or the two trusties, but nodded at a man in a gray suit standing in the corner.

Marshal John Fagan came over and removed the iron bracelets on Bass's wrists and ankles. As Bass massaged his wrists, wondering what on earth was going on, Judge Parker said: "When Tully Griffin gets out of the hospital, John, put those very same cuffs on him." Judge Parker's eyes found Bass. "Understand, sir, that you still must face trial. You have been charged, and the state is demanding prosecution. Be that as it may, I am convinced that you will be acquitted. Raise your right hand."

Bass blinked. "Huh?"

"Raise your right hand."

Even before Bass started taking the oath, Marshal Fagan had pinned the six-pointed star, stamped *Deputy U.S. Marshal,* on the front of Bass's filthy shirt.

"Did George Reeves ever know you followed in his footsteps and became a lawman?" I once asked Bass while camped in the Winding Star Mountains.

I'll never forget the look Bass gave me, as he looked up from cleaning his Winchester rifle — like I was an imbecile. "I didn't follow nobody's footsteps," he said. "I made my own way."

CHAPTER FIVE

June 10, 1902
"Why the hell didn't you go with Bass?"

Ignoring Erskine Jones, I shifted my legs, set the Winchester on the ground, and leaned closer to the fire, fished my key-wind Illinois watch from a vest pocket, and checked the time. At my age, reading the hands on a watch in the middle of the night proved a challenge, even though Jones kept the campfire roaring like we were the Donners in December.

"Three-Oh-Seven." I snapped the case shut.

"Didn't ask you what time it was," Jones said. "I asked you why the hell didn't you go with Bass?"

That I knew. I wasn't senile. Bass had been gone a good seven hours. I hadn't slept at all. Erskine Jones's sleep had been fitful, and, about thirty minutes earlier, he had finally given up on trying to get

61

any shut-eye.

I looked over the fire toward Jones, who was rolling a cigarette, his back resting against the downed cottonwood.

"He didn't ask me to."

"Ain't that against Doc Bennett's rules?"

My head shook. There were few rules in Indian Territory, especially when it came to hunting down a murderer.

"Shouldn't he be back by now?"

I shrugged, and suddenly smiled. "By grab, Erskine, you're worried."

With a snort, he spit into the fire. "Horse apples. But you might start to worryin'. What if Bass rode into Marshall Town, found his son, and the two rode up toward Kansas? You ever think of that?"

"Bass wouldn't do that."

"No?" He let out a chuckle. "I've rode with that son-of-a-bitch longer than you. You mean to tell me you wouldn't do whatever it taken to keep your son off the gallows?"

Bass wouldn't do that, I told myself a little more forcefully. To change the subject, I repeated my earlier deduction that Erskine Jones was worried. Certainly I was.

"Only thing I'm worried about is Lucifer," he said. "He's a damned good mule." He crawled out of his sougans, reached into the fire, withdrew a burning stick, and fired up his smoke.

"Should you go lookin' for him?" Erskine asked after a few puffs on the cigarette.

"If he's not back by first light."

"How come Bass rode off dressed like that?"

"You know why. Disguise. It's why he took your mule, too."

Bass was good at that. Where he had learned to make himself look like some black character out of *Uncle Tom's Cabin,* I couldn't fathom, but disguises like that had helped him track down and arrest dozens of wanted men. He could make himself look like some waddie, or a farmer, even an outlaw or circuit-riding preacher.

Wasn't *that* hard. Most white folks in the Territory never really noticed a Negro's face, at least not so they'd recognize him. Indians weren't much more observant. They looked at the cut of a rider's clothes, at his saddle, at his horse. Over the years, I had lost count of how many eyewitnesses I had interviewed about a crime only to be told: "He looked like any ol' darky." They knew they had seen a black man, but that was about all they could tell me about the suspect, yet they'd be able to describe his horse in great detail. Marshall Town, however, was a colored settlement. The people who lived there wouldn't find Bass Reeves as invisible as some white or red man would.

A big man, Bass had picked up an old Indian trick of making himself look small in the saddle — at least from a distance — as long as he wasn't riding a fine mount like the sorrel with the white-blazed face hobbled out in the grass beyond the cottonwood along with my bay and Erskine's other mule. Usually, when we rode out on a scout, Bass would take a couple of extra saddle horses with us. Unshod ponies, more common among the farmers and outlaws of Indian Territory than the barrel-chested runners federal peace officers usually rode.

Erskine spit again. "Marshall Town's pret' close to Muskogee for him to be tryin' to fool somebody with that get-up he had on. 'Sides, didn't he say that's where he buys his liquor?"

I had thought about that, as well, but Bass Reeves knew what he was doing. Anyway, that's what I kept telling myself.

A mule snorted, and water rippled in the Arkansas. Immediately I rolled away from the campfire until the darkness enveloped me. Thumbing back the Winchester's hammer, I brought up the carbine and aimed over the fire, staying low. Erskine Jones rooted in a war bag, and hugged the cotton-wood.

A nighthawk called out.

I answered with an owl's hoot.

The water rippled again, then splashed. I rose, telling Jones that everything was fine, that Bass Reeves was coming in.

He rode the mule straight into camp, sitting far back in the saddle, a large bedroll draped over the pommel. No, not a bedroll. When he reined in the mule, Bass pushed his cargo off the mule, sending his prisoner, covered by worn woolen blankets, into the dirt. The tall figure dropped into the grass, rolled out of the blankets, and uttered not a sound. Iron bracelets cuffed his hands. A light-colored hat flew from Bass's hands, hit the blanket, and rolled toward the fire.

"He dead?" Erskine Jones asked.

"Not yet." Bass slid from the saddle. He stood there the longest while, gripping the horn for support, head bowed. For a moment, I thought he might collapse, but, as soon as I stepped into the light, he straightened and handed the reins to Erskine Jones.

"Thanks for the loan," he said without any feeling.

I lowered the carbine's hammer, laid the Winchester over my saddle and blankets, and walked over to the unconscious prisoner while our cook led the mule toward the other stock.

Bass pulled off the floppy hat from his head, and found the coffee. "More fire here than there was in Chicago in 'Seventy-Two," he muttered.

"Yeah, but my bones get cold, damn it!" Erskine yelled.

"It's too big a fire!" Bass's temper flared.

"Wasn't sure you'd be able to find your way back to camp, old-timer, lessen we gave you a lighthouse full of hell's fires to guide your way!"

Bass emptied the coffee pot on the fire, and flung the pot under the tumbleweed wagon.

I put my fingers on the knot above the prisoner's left ear. Felt to be the size of a Mexican spur's rowel.

"Leave him be," Bass said. "He don't need no doctorin'."

Well, Bennie Reeves was breathing. There was also a wicked cut near his temple, scabbing over, having cut a furrow up his head. He stank of blood, vomit, forty-rod whiskey, and fear. The eyes fluttered under the lids, his lips parted, and he gave a little moan. The cuffs bit into his wrists so deeply, I was sure that, if I could see better, I'd spot blood. Another odor assaulted my nostrils.

He'd pissed his pants.

I rose. "Where'd you find him?"

"Drunk," he said. "Roostered on that lightnin' Hoss Mike serves." He reached behind his back, pulled out a .45-caliber single-action Colt and tossed it on my bedroll. "Evidence," Bass announced, "for the territorial commissioner."

"He pull that on you?"

"He never got a chance."

"You didn't have to hit him so hard, Bass."

"The hell I didn't."

Best drop it, I told myself, and listened to my own advice. Erskine Jones had returned to camp, and Bass started railing on him, demanding he make some coffee, get breakfast started, that we were burning daylight, though it was too dark even to saddle our mounts — especially since Bass had doused much of the fire. This time Erskine Jones knew better than to argue with Bass, or pick a fight.

As Bass grabbed his war bag and walked into the night, I moved to the bedroll. The Colt felt heavy in my hands as I opened the chamber gate and spun the cylinder, ejecting the cartridges. Three empty casings, fired, two live rounds. I slid all of the shells into my vest pocket, examined the revolver, which I slipped into my saddlebag.

"He's crazy, Dave," Erskine said from the fire he was bringing back to life.

Wouldn't you be? I thought. Again, I held my tongue.

The skies were graying, and the birds singing. Salt pork sizzled in the skillet, and the coffee smelled something like coffee was supposed to smell. Bass busied himself hitching the mules to the wagon, while I fastened his spare saddle and other items onto the cell's roof.

When I climbed down, Bennie Reeves had just begun to stir.

Gingerly he tested the knot his father had given him and, with a grimace, tried to move his legs. He didn't attempt to stand, and I dropped by the coffee pot, filled a cup with steaming black tar, and brought it to him. I could feel Bass's eyes boring through my back.

Bennie was tall, though two or three inches shorter than his father, and weighed around one seventy, one eighty. His skin wasn't as dark as Bass's, either, and he had eyes the color of slate. His short hair was black, and, when I leaned forward and handed him the cup, I could see where the black powder had gotten underneath his skin when he had tried to kill himself. The wound was puffy, ugly, ragged.

"Remember me, Bennie?" I asked.

His eyes showed fear, looking past me, not at his father, but at the prison wagon. He didn't answer, didn't reach for the cup, and I set it beside him and rose.

Finished with the mules, Bass had started saddling the sorrel.

"Jones!" he barked while tightening the cinch. "Load the prisoner."

"What about our damned breakfast?"

"We can eat in Muskogee."

Well, there was the start of some rather sulphurous language before Erskine Jones bit his tongue, and began muttering, setting aside the skillet, shaking his head, and roughly tossing the relatively clean cups, plates, and forks into a canvas sack.

I left Bennie with the coffee cup, gathered my tack, and stepped over the cottonwood. Saddling my horse in silence, sliding the Winchester into the scabbard, I tried to think of something worth telling Bass, but suitable words escaped me. I'm not sure I could have found any even in a Webster's dictionary.

Erskine tossed his sack into the driver's boot, returned to the fire, head still wagging, and looked at the two of us. "You want coffee?"

Bass answered without looking up from the sorrel. "No."

"Well, I do, damn it," Jones announced, and filled a cup. "And I want my damned breakfast, too." He reached over and brought up a piece of pork, tossing the hot slice of meat in his hands, spilling the coffee, letting the greasy meat slide onto the ground. Undeterred, he picked it up, not even bothering to brush it off, and managed to bite off a mouthful with what few teeth he still had. The rest of the pork he flung toward the river.

"Get that fire out, Jones," Bass barked, "and load the prisoner!"

Furiously Jones kicked sand over the fire, drenched the flames and coals with the rest of the coffee, and hurled the empty pot toward the wagon. The pot hit the rear wheel, sending the lid one way and the rest of the blackened, bent enamel the other.

"You spook those damned mules and I'll haul your hide to the dungeon, too!" Bass roared.

"The hell with you, Bass Reeves!" Erskine fired back. "I ain't makin' no damned nine hunnert dollars a year. You pay me ten bits a day and. . . ."

"Start earnin' your pay, then."

I led the bay into camp. Bass had busied

70

himself cleaning the sorrel's hoofs with a pick.

After ground-reining my gelding, I gathered the busted coffee pot, deposited it in the wagon's boot, shot Erskine Jones a glare that told him to keep his trap shut and do what Bass Reeves said. His head shook, but he strode over to Bennie Reeves, and jerked him to his feet.

Bennie towered over the cook. The hat on his head was tan, a cheap woolen style with a high crown and narrow brim, curled up on the sides. His shirt was striped, stained, bloody, torn, and he wore brown pants tucked inside cheap boots. His full lips were flattened into a frown as Jones pushed him toward the wagon.

"The cuffs stay on him," Bass said from the sorrel.

"I wasn't plannin' on takin' 'em off!" Erskine snapped back. Then, softer, to Bennie: "Come on, boy. Best not keep the damned hangman waitin'."

At least this had been a short trip, I tried to tell myself. Bass was bringing Bennie in alive. He could hire a good lawyer. Plead to manslaughter, not murder. Get off with a light sentence — a few years in the federal penitentiary at Leavenworth, Kansas. Be back home before he knew it, cutting hair again, like nothing bad had ever happened.

Funny what even an experienced lawman will try to convince himself.

Just as I gathered the reins to the bay, Erskine shouted, but his words were cut short by a loud thud, and I was coming up, jerking the Winchester from the scabbard, shouting out a warning to Bass as Erskine Jones dropped to the dirt, and rolled under the wagon, holding his head, writhing between the wheels like a rattlesnake.

Bennie Reeves came up with what we called a whore's pistol. The small revolver shook uncontrollably, though he held it with both manacled hands, aiming in the general direction of his father.

"You ain't takin' me in, Daddy!" he yelled. "Ain't nobody takin' me back to Musko-gee!"

A gunshot sent the singing birds into flight.

CHAPTER SIX

June 10, 1902

The shot didn't come from the pistol Bennie held. It roared from out of the timbers, the bullet splintering an outstretched branch from the dead cottonwood.

A second later, a half dozen riders whipped their mounts out of the woods, charging toward us, spraying our little camp with bullets. A mule screamed, fell, kicked. I started to raise the Winchester, thought better of it, and, dropping the carbine, I reached for the reins to my bay, latched onto the leather, pulled myself close. A bullet clipped my hat. Fright filled Dutchy's eyes. Kneeling, hands against his neck, I began pushing, raising, yelling: "Down, Dutchy, down!" That horse dropped, protected by the cottonwood, and I lay down on top of him, cooing: "Good boy, Dutchy. Good boy. Stay down." Slowly I slid off the bay, reaching for my Winchester.

In an instant, Bass was kneeling beside me. Out of the corner of my eye, I glimpsed his sorrel loping back toward Muskogee. Bass ratcheted his rifle's lever, raised up over the dead trunk, pulled the trigger. My ears rang. Thick smoke burned my eyes. Bass had fired twice more before I ever got up my carbine. My first shot echoed his fourth. Bullets thudded into the cotton-wood, and dug up grass behind us. Drop-ping behind cover, we hugged against the fallen cottonwood.

"How many you see?" he asked, cocking another shell into the rifle.

"At least six." I swallowed, shot Dutchy a nervous look, but that bay of mine had no intention of standing up now. For that, I had to thank Bass Reeves. He had trained that gelding himself, and sold him to me when the horse was four years old.

On my back, I slid a few yards away, till I was next to Dutchy. I wet my lips, jacked the carbine's lever, and came up quickly, firing once, working the lever again, swing-ing the barrel toward another target, pulling the trigger, sending the lever down and up once more, and fired again. And again. Then dropped back behind the shelter of the cottonwood as bullets tore over my head. One ripped across the trunk, and I cursed as I felt the splinters tear into my cheek.

"You all right?" Bass yelled.

"Yeah!" I doubt if Bass heard my answer, because his big rifle sounded like a cannon.

"Come on, boy!" a voice called out from the campsite. "Grab my hand. Light on behind me."

"*¡Muy pronto, hijo!*"

A horse whinnied. More shots rang out.

I fired till the carbine was empty, then drew the .44 double-action.

Hoofs pounded. The riders thundered down the agency road, heading west. That gave them clear shots at us, but they sat bouncing on galloping, frightened horses, and nary a bullet came close. They were too far away, and riding too fast for me to do any damage with my Smith & Wesson, but Bass raised up, cocked the rifle, took careful aim, and his Winchester roared. A rider clutched his side, gripped the saddle horn, then tumbled into the dust after going another twenty yards. The horse kept running. None of the downed man's companions stopped or even glanced back.

Dust swallowed them up, and they were gone, out of range.

Although it felt as if an eternity had passed, all of this happened in less time that it has taken me to put it on paper.

"Seven of 'em." Bass leaned the smoking Winchester against the cottonwood. "Not six."

After holstering my revolver, I grabbed Dutchy's reins, and let him rise to his feet, then I stepped over the cottonwood.

I tasted blood, and remembered the splinters in my cheek. As I walked toward the tumbleweed wagon, I worked two pieces of the wood out. The rest would have to wait. I dabbed my face with a handkerchief, then shoved it back into my pocket.

Erskine Jones crawled from under the tumbleweed wagon. Blood streaked down his dirty face, into his dirty beard. I could make out the gash atop his skull. Weaving like alfalfa in the wind, I thought he might fall, but he staggered toward the wagon tongue, dropping both hands at his sides.

"My mules . . . ," he choked. Tears welled in his eyes as he turned toward me. "Sons-of-bitches kilt my mules!"

They were dead, all right, a lake of crimson pooling underneath their bodies.

Hoofs sounded, and we both turned to watch Bass Reeves loping down the Texas Road on my bay.

"Where the hell's he goin'?" Erskine asked.

"Catch up his sorrel."

"Horse of his is likely in Muskogee by now."

I shook my head. That horse would have galloped maybe a couple hundred yards, then stopped and waited for its master.

"Best get off your feet, Erskine." I gripped his arm, steered him away from the dead mules. He collapsed into a seated position, resting his head against the rim of the wheel, and I gently fingered the gash on his skull.

"You might have a concussion," I said. I'd heard Doc Bennett say that a few times, once when he was examining a knot a man-killer had left atop my big head.

Jones wiped his nose, shook his head, and sniffed. "Sons-a-bitches kilt my mules," he repeated.

"I'll take care of them," I promised him, but that was a lie. There would be no time to burn or bury those dead mules. A bullet had singed his right side, and yet another had clipped the heel of his boot. He was lucky I wouldn't be burying him along with those two dead mules.

As I knotted my bandanna around his head, I noticed a pistol in the dust, a little double-action number, a Forehand & Wadsworth .32. Like I previously mentioned, a whore's pistol. I didn't pick it up. Instead, I fished a handkerchief out of my pocket and wet it down with water from Erskine's canteen in the driver's boot of the wagon. That head wound hadn't been caused by a bullet, but a gun barrel. "Hold that against your head," I told him, and walked to the agency road.

Long before I reached the body lying in the center of the road, I had drawn the Smith & Wesson, even though it seemed obvious that this man would never threaten me or anyone else again. Still, I didn't lower the hammer on the .44 and return the revolver to its holster until I had placed my foot underneath the man's stomach, and rolled him onto his back.

Hazel eyes stared straight into the sky, but they would never notice the blueness of the morning.

There had been seven men. Now there were six. No, still seven, now that Bennie was with them.

Bass's slug had hit the man in the road right above his waist, toward the back and left, and blown a hole the size of my fist through his belly just underneath the right-side rib cage. It's a wonder he had stayed in the saddle for as long as he had, and that had only been a few seconds. He had dropped a Colt Peacemaker in the dirt when he had been hit, and I made a mental note to pick up the weapon when I returned to our camp.

I reached into the pockets of his vest, but found nothing that would identify him. No pocket watch, no purse, just a bloody box of matches and a sack of Bull Durham, both of which I left in the vest in case this dead man wanted a smoke in hell.

Hearing hoof beats on the road, I rose and turned, waiting on Bass Reeves, now riding his sorrel, to bring Dutchy to me. After he reined up beside me, I took the reins and asked: "Recognize him?"

Bass's head shook.

"Maybe we'll find his horse a ways up the road."

Again, he shook his head, but this time he spoke. "Like as not, they'll give that mount to Bennie." He looked down the road, and trotted away a few rods, studying the ground. "But," he said, pointing, "you or me did some damage to another one of 'em. Leakin' blood at a pretty good clip."

I wrapped the reins to my bay around a stump, just long enough for me to drag the dead man to the side of the road.

"How's Jones?" Bass asked as he trotted back toward me.

"He'll live." I grabbed Dutchy's reins, and

swung into the saddle.

"We'll see 'bout that."

He kept right on trotting back toward our camp, and I decided it might be better if I didn't bother with the Colt the dead man had dropped. I quickly caught up with Bass Reeves back at camp.

He had wrapped the reins around the wagon's rear wheel, and was pulling the gloves off his hands, staring silently at Erskine Jones, who looked up, holding my now blood-soaked handkerchief against his head, face paling.

After Bass shoved the gloves between his gun belt and trousers, he took a few steps and bent down to pick up the Forehand & Wadsworth. Blowing the dirt off the cylinder, he walked back to Erskine, and knelt in front of him, holding out the .32, which looked like a toy in Bass's giant right hand.

"It's yours, ain't it?"

Erskine just stared.

"I ought to empty it into your head." Instead, Bass tossed the revolver into Erskine's lap and stood, staring down the agency road.

"Bass . . . ," Erskine tried to explain.

"Shut up." Bass stared at the dead mules. "Hell," he said softly, and let out a weary sigh. He reached out, and gripped the

80

smaller front wheel to the wagon. Tense, he was, sweating as the morning warmed. Reminded me of a beaker of nitroglycerin ready to blow itself, and anything around it, into a million pieces.

Erskine had lowered the handkerchief, and was starting to say something, but I swung down from Dutchy and cut him off.

"Damn you, Erskine, you know Marshal Bennett's rules. And our rules. No weapons for the wagon driver. You broke that rule. You could have gotten yourself, Bass, or me killed. Or Bennie."

"He took it. . . ."

"Yeah, he took it from you." In exasperation, I shook my head.

"I'd forgot I had it," Erskine said. "Forgot all about it. He must 'a' seen it, grabbed it, buffaloed me with it. I swear, Adams. Swear to God Almighty, Bass, I'd plumb forgot I had that little popgun. Just brought it along for protection at night. I'd. . . ."

"Man who don't know where his weapon is at all times" — Bass sounded like God speaking to Moses in the desert — "has got no business ownin' a gun." Bass's shadow covered Erskine's face. He just stared, and Erskine's head dropped.

"What do we do?" I asked.

He straightened, Bass did, and his eyes

studied the agency road. "I'm goin' after 'em." He shot Erskine another glance, and, this time, his hand gripped the butt of the Colt he wore high on his hip. I found the Smith & Wesson, worried that I might have to use it to buffalo Bass Reeves if he decided to kill Erskine Jones. "On account of you, you horse's ass . . . ," Bass continued. "I had Bennie. All we had to do was bring him back to Muskogee. Alive. You put his life, and the lives of me and Dave here in jeopardy. It should be you lyin' dead, not them mules. This is all your fault, Jones, and I'm holdin' you accountable."

I wasn't sure how true that was. Yeah, Bennie Reeves had managed to get his hand on that little .32 because of Erskine Jones's carelessness, but Bennie never would have gotten away had those outlaws not come along when they did. It didn't strike me that they had planned on rescuing Bennie all this time. Likely, they didn't even know who Bennie was. Not the way I saw it. They'd just happened along, and maybe they felt the need to follow some code among bandits and thieves that bound them to free a fellow about to be loaded into a tumbleweed wagon. Maybe that's how they recruited their gang members. Maybe.

Well, Bass and I would learn that directly.

"You and Dave get back to Muskogee," Bass said. "Take that dead man in. See if anybody knows who he is, or if anybody wants to claim his body. See if there's any reward the Katy's put on his head."

"How we 'sposed to get there?" Erskine's temperament was returning. "My mules. . . ."

"I don't give a damn how you get there, Jones. Walk, crawl, or ride double. We ain't far from Muskogee."

"But Bennett's orders is that you's got to have a prison wagon!"

"I'll have one." Bass swung into the saddle. "Soon as Grant Johnson and his posse catches up."

I took the reins of my horse, and mounted Dutchy.

Bass stared.

"I'm going with you," I told him.

"I said. . . ."

"I'm going with you," I repeated.

He answered with a curt nod, and eased his horse toward Erskine, looking down at him, then at the dead mules. Maybe pity finally beat back the anger Bass felt, for his voice sounded softer. "Can you get back to town?"

"I reckon."

"You can always walk to Marshall Town.

See if someone'll loan or sell you some horses, or take you to Muskogee."

"Yeah." Erskine spat. "Right."

"Well, someone's bound to come along before too long. When you get to Muskogee, tell Marshal Bennett what happened." Bass waited, chewing over his next words. "You don't have to tell him how Bennie got that pistol. Just tell him that we got ambushed, and my boy rode off with 'em. Tell the marshal that Grant's likely to hook up with me and Dave. That Dave and me set off for the old Creek agency. Tell Bennett that he ought to telegraph Okmulgee that the outlaws was ridin' that way, but I warrant they'll turn north or south long before they get there."

Bass sat ramrod straight in the saddle, gripping the horn.

"You got all that, Erskine?" I asked.

"Yeah."

"If no citizen comes along directly, you can wait on Grant Johnson," I added. "He'll likely send one of his men back to Muskogee with the dead man lying yonder. I doubt if Grant's far behind."

"How come you're so jo-fired positive that Deputy Johnson'll be ridin' this way?" Erskine asked.

"Because," Bass answered, "that was

Cherokee Bob Dozier who pulled Bennie up on the horse behind him." Anger and bile rose in Bass's voice. "That's right, Jones. Thanks to you, my boy's now ridin' with a gang of murderin' train robbers."

Cherokee Bob Doxie who pulled Bonnie
up on the horse behind him. Anger and
hate rose in Hael... ...t "That... right
plans Glenn to pa... ...ng before the middle
of the go... me in...

CHAPTER SEVEN

June 11, 1902
The Creek woman named Ero dropped a
couple of bowls on the table in front of Bass
and me. *"Osafki,"* she announced, and
returned to the kitchen.

I stared into my bowl, and reluctantly
picked up a spoon. Bass, however, didn't
seem to mind the meager and unappetizing
meal. You couldn't find a Creek home in
the Territory where they didn't put *osafki*
on the table, unfortunately for any passing
wayfarer. Creeks turned corn into some
kind of soured gruel, which they cooked
with water and lye. Bass took his first bite
without making a face. I pretended I was
eating grits, and tried washing down the
foul food with strong black chicory, which
didn't taste much better than the gruel.

Alone in the inn, we ate in silence.

Midnight had come and gone since we
had arrived at the old Ebenezer Mission

86

Station. Outside, the moon was just approaching the first quarter, but the night remained cloudless and the stars shone brightly. Now, we could not have found or followed any trail, but enough light remained for us to travel to Tullahassee, or so I thought. Instead, we were supping at what once had been a mission, school, and church.

We'd been there for hours.

The mission had been around since the early 1830s, shortly after the Creeks had been relocated to Indian Territory from the Southern states. The church was the first established in the Nations, founded by black slave Baptists, but others soon came about.

The way I heard it told, why, a Creek Indian could hardly go a couple miles in the area of land between the Arkansas and Verdigris Rivers before he ran across some kind of church, mission, or school — Baptist, Methodist, or Presbyterian — or some two-day revival meeting filled with fire-and-brimstone sermons.

All that had changed, though, over some seventy years. By the time I write about it, the old log buildings at the Ebenezer church had fallen down, and now a Creek family ran a trading post and inn on the old mission grounds.

A map would show that we were only about three miles north of the Arkansas, and some fifteen miles west of old Fort Gibson. That means we hadn't covered a whole lot of territory that day, but Bass Reeves preached and practiced patience, and he had meticulously followed the trail of Cherokee Bob Dozier's gang.

Just biding his time.

Which left me consternated, though I didn't question him.

About two miles from where we had left Erskine Jones, we had found a dead horse. Bass and I hadn't wounded a man, after all, but this blue roan.

"Means two of 'em still have to ride double," Bass had said before he nudged the sorrel into a walk. "At least, till they borrow, steal, or trade for another mount."

That, they had apparently done at a Creek farm east of the old agency. The old farmer had been furious, saying how these men, most of them darkies but at least one Mexican, had ridden up, showed him the business end of their weapons, and taken his good paint horse and a saddle. I wrote down the man's name, a description of his horse, and his brand and the brand's location. Bass had assured the farmer that the law would catch up with the men, and that he would try to return the horse.

We had ridden slowly down the agency road, not talking, Bass on one side of the path and me on the other, looking for any sign that our prey had left the road. Since we were now pursuing Cherokee Bob, we also kept on the look-out for an ambush.

Long before Cherokee Bob and his men, including Bennie, had reached the old Creek agency, they left the road, turning north through the thickets, then forded the Arkansas River between a couple of islands. On the far banks, their tracks told us that they were still pushing those mounts mighty hard.

"They can't keep up that pace," I told Bass. "We might be able to catch up with them."

That's the closest I would come to suggest to Bass Reeves that we stop lollygagging and put our mounts into lopes and catch up with those killers.

Bass's big head slowly shook. "Nah. They'll get fresh mounts at Tullahassee."

So, I figured we'd at least get as far as that colored town, but, instead, we had stopped at Ebenezer Mission Station, arriving there that afternoon. After watering and feeding our mounts, Bass led the horses to a rickety corral, announcing: "We'll spend the night here."

I had frowned, but still gave Bass a nod, and turned toward Ero's cabin, wondering if maybe Erskine Jones had been right, and that Bass Reeves was letting his son get away.

After swallowing the last spoonful of *osafki,* Bass pushed his bowl away, and topped off his cup and mine from the coffee pot Ero had left on a table. We both sat in the corner of the cabin, next to each other, facing the door, away from the windows, and pretty much in the shadows. Our Winchesters lay across the table. So did our revolvers.

Somehow, I managed to finish the gruel, sliding bowl and spoon as far from my sight as possible. I sipped the coffee, which didn't taste quite as horrible or nearly as bitter as it had earlier. Setting the cup by the stock of my Winchester, I slid back from the table, and turned in the seat so that I had a profile view of Bass's face.

"The Katy runs through Tullahassee," I said.

He finished his coffee, placed the cup gently on the table, and pushed back his chair. His massive head turned toward me. Rough fingers reached into his vest pocket and pulled out a cigar, which he offered me. I took it, and Bass fished out a smoke for himself.

I lit my cigar, then held the flaming match toward him. He bent forward, until the end of his long-nine glowed red, and leaned back in the chair, taking a long pull, and blowing a cloud of blue smoke toward the ceiling.

"I know that," he said, watching the smoke.

"I was just thinking," I said. "Bennie could board a train if one came through tonight. Ride out of the Territory, all the way to Saint Louis or south to. . . ." I had to remember how far the Katy line went nowadays. "San Antonio," I said at last.

Bass studied the cigar. He shook his head. "Bennie ain't got money for a ticket, and Cherokee Bob ain't one to loan money for a fare to anywhere, 'ceptin' hell. Besides, Bennie worked on the Katy, so too many people might recognize him. No, he won't take the Katy."

"He could hop a freight."

"No." Bass returned the cigar to his mouth, dragged on it, and exhaled. "Cherokee Bob and his boys robbed that train near Eufaula, and killed one, possibly two men. All of those boys will be wantin' to stay clear of the Katy for a spell. They'll just get fresh horses in Tullahassee, and be on their way."

"But Bennie isn't with Cherokee Bob's gang."

Bass's face hardened. "He is now."

I let that sink in, tried to digest those words.

Bass shrugged. "Bennie didn't ride toward Paris, Texas, where we used to live. Rode north. So I'm thinkin' he wants to get to Fort Smith. That's home to him. Where his ma's buried. And his grandma lives in Van Buren. That's where he'll want to go."

"Bob Dozier won't go anywhere near Fort Smith," I said. "Too many lawmen there. He'll skip that place like the plague. Unless he wants to hang."

"You're right. And Bennie, he won't have the nerve to quit Cherokee Bob. He's lost. Don't know what to do, just wants to run. Run from what he done. We'll just follow those boys."

So why aren't we following them now? I thought, but would never say. Instead, I asked: "You think Bennie told Dozier he's your son?"

His head shook again. "You know as well as I do, Dave, that you don't ask questions about a man in this country. You don't volunteer too much information, either."

92

Conversation played out, we finished our cigars in silence. And just sat there. Neither Bass nor me talked a whole lot, so I was used to the quiet when working with him. Ero came out of the kitchen, collected our dirty dishes, and left without a word. The wind blew, moaning through the log walls.

"Bennie was a good barber."

I looked up, surprised by Bass's voice. Already we had spoken more than we usually spoke in two or three days.

He shook his head, removed his hat, and ran his rough hand over his shaved head. "Not that I had any personal experience with tonsorial artists and the like. Always done my own shavin', but everybody in Muskogee always said Bennie was a mighty fine barber."

I kept quiet.

"He'd treat every customer like he was the mayor visitin' from Guthrie, workin' that crank and leanin' back that chair, givin' 'em a close shave . . . he kept that razor of his so sharp it'd slice through the thickest beard like a Bowie knife goin' through warm butter . . . and workin' 'em scissors and comb like they was musical instruments. Yes, sir. Everybody in Muskogee liked the way he cut hair, the way he made people feel. That's what was great about Bennie.

Makin' his customers feel important, feel like they was somebody special. I heard Roland Bristow say that, the fellow who runs the butcher shop in Colored Town. Just two, three weeks back it was . . . said he had gone into that barbershop, and my Bennie met him at the door, shakin' his hand, askin' 'bout his family. And Bennie, when he asked those kinds of questions, Roland tells me, it's not like he's play-actin' or tryin' to earn a tip. He meant it. He'd listen to what you had to say, Bennie would. Boy was always a good listener."

Laughing, Bass leaned back in his chair, lifted his long legs, and rested the rowels of his spurs on the table. The table was so scarred, I don't think Ero would mind. Bass rocked back in the chair, hands behind his head, smiling.

"I don't know where Bennie picked that up. That gift for gab. Not from me, I guaran-damn-tee you that. And his mama, she wasn't no talker. Talked less than I did. But he picked it up somewhere, somehow. Maybe he was born with it. I don't know. He just seemed to like people, liked makin' 'em feel good. Did the same even when he was working as a porter for the Katy. He'd take those bags and treat everybody with respect, like they was the governor or some senator or Teddy Roosevelt himself, by God. Didn't matter if they was red, white, or black, they was all payin' customers to Bennie, but Bennie, he made 'em feel more than that. Made 'em feel like they was the only customer ridin' the rails."

The front legs of the chair came down hard on the floor, and the smile had vanished from Bass's face.

"Never should have married that girl." His voice cut through the air. "Little hussy. He was smitten, though. And I never said nothin' to him. Let him make his own way, choose his own path. That's how I brung up all my children. She left him, but he went after her, brought her back, quit the Katy, got a job that'd keep him closer to home. Maybe he shouldn't 'a' done that. Maybe should 'a' just kept on porterin' for the Katy."

His eyes closed, and his hands gripped the arms of the chair until I thought he might break the piece of furniture. The arms looked like twigs in his massive hands.

"Robert." Bass's head shook, his eyes still tightly shut. "When Bennie took that job on the Katy, and later when he quit, all I could think of was Robert. Robert wouldn't have gone chasin' after no two-bit harlot, whether they was married or not. If she wanted to run off with some drummer or saddle tramp, he would have said . . . 'Good riddance, hussy. Good riddance, and go to hell.' "

The flickering light from the candle on the table made him look ancient, far older than his sixty-plus years, and those had been hard years, much of them spent wearing a badge in the Indian Territory. I felt fear. For Bass. He had never acted like this, talked like this. Usually having a conversation with him was like pulling teeth. Of course, he had never gone on the scout for a son of his, never had had any child hook up with a black-heart like Cherokee Bob Dozier.

"And Robert," Bass went on, his voice sounding old, reflective, a thousand miles away, "when he taken that job for the Central Arkansas and Houston, he wasn't no porter. No, sir. Robert was his own man. He and his brother Bennie was cut from different pieces of cloth. Robert, now he wasn't one to try to please every *hombre* who asked for help with his luggage. Robert never would treat some bigot like he was the king of Prussia. He done a man's work. Brakeman. Robert. . . ." He stopped talking, eyes open, alert.

At first, I thought he had realized he was rambling like some old hen, and promptly had regained his faculties. Then his right hand reached for the .44-40 Winchester. I heard the noise, too. One of our horses had whinnied in the corral, and the wind carried an answering whicker.

"Ero?" I called out in a hoarse whisper.

No answer. She had probably retired to her quarters.

Bass blew out the candle, and stepped into a corner, thumbing back the hammer on the rifle he always carried with a round in the chamber. I stuck my little carbine in my left hand, drew the Smith & Wesson with my right, and backed into the shadows a few rods away from Bass. I placed myself behind a table, which I could overturn and use for cover. Bass in one corner. Me in the other. The door in front of us, between us.

Silence.

Seconds seemed like minutes, which passed like hours, until the door flew open, slammed against the wall.

Nobody came in, and no one stood in the doorway. We stared — me sighting down a .44 revolver, and Bass holding that big rifle — into the night.

Waiting. . . .

CHAPTER EIGHT

June 11, 1902

"Bass?" a voice called from outside. "That you in there?"

Able to breathe again, I lowered the hammer before holstering my revolver, then fished another lucifer out of a vest pocket to light the candle.

"It's me, Grant," Bass said, relaxing. "Come on in."

The barrels of a Parker twelve-gauge appeared in the door first, then Deputy Marshal Grant Johnson's body. I knew it was Grant because his gold teeth reflected the light from the candle. So did his badge. He tucked the sawed-off double-barrel into the crook of his left arm, and stood in the doorway. After striking a match, and firing up one of his cigars, he called out over his shoulders — "All right, boys!" — and walked inside.

Three long-haired Cherokees, each one

armed with a rifle, followed him in. Two were young men, one of them chewing tobacco. The only one I recognized was the silver-haired Keetowah. The younger men wore white man's clothing, but not old George Littledave. Like most Keetowah, he was a traditionalist, donning a sash turban over his head, a trade shirt secured around the waist by a finger-woven sash, short-fringed buckskin leggings, and moccasins.

One of the younger Cherokees closed the door, and Bass frowned. "Where's Ledbetter and Paden?"

Johnson grinned. "Hell, Bass, I never made it as far as Vinita. Cherokee Bob hit us on the Illinois ferry east of Tahlequah. Last thing I expected him to do."

Maybe that stood to reason. Grant Johnson had proved to be a mighty fine lawman, but he was better suited when chasing horse thieves than train robbers and murderers. Still, I could name only a few men — Bass surely topping that list — that I would rather have standing beside me in a gunfight.

Bass asked: "You find Erskine Jones?"

"I did."

"Recognize the one I killed?"

He nodded. "Not by name, though, but I's seen him shootin' craps in Eufaula."

Grant sank into a chair at the table, and Bass took the seat across from him. I gave the Cherokees a quick nod, and joined the two deputies.

"You done more damage to Cherokee Bob's outfit than we done." Johnson shook his head, and let out a mirthless chuckle. "But that figures."

Bass shook his big head. "Dozier done some damage to us. Killed Jones's two mules, and they taken my boy with 'em. Jones tell you that?"

Grant's nod was barely perceptible. He rolled the cigar in his fingers, staring at the ash on the end, the small trail of smoke. At last, he set the Famous K. of P. smoke on the base of the brass candle holder centering the table. "Sorry to hear that, Bass."

Grant Johnson didn't stand nearly as tall, or look as intimidating, as Bass Reeves. He weighed maybe one hundred and sixty pounds, and that's if you included the two long-barreled Colts he wore on his hips and his shell belt. Quiet to the point of outright shyness, he might have been the last person in the Territory one would have expected to find with a deputy's badge pinned to his vest. He had worn a badge, though, since '87, and had earned a reputation of being a fair man, but hell on outlaws.

100

He had exchanged shots with the badman Jake Stanley. He had wounded and arrested John Tiger, then stopped the citizens of Eufaula from stringing up that no-good drunken Creek. Just a few months earlier, it had been Grant Johnson who had arrested Chitto Harjo, leader of the Crazy Snake Rebellion. He had done that without firing a shot.

In all his years as a lawman, Johnson had never killed anyone till 1901. From the newspaper accounts I read, a colored man named Frank Wilson told Grant that he'd rather die than be arrested, and punctuated his threat with gunshots. He missed. Grant didn't, and Frank Wilson died. Grant never spoke of that. At least, not to me. Yes, Grant Johnson was a good lawman.

I don't know how old he was. Younger than Bass and me, certainly. He might have been born in Texas, though some say he hailed from the Nations. His father had been a Chickasaw freedman, and his mother a Creek freed-woman, and a lot of people in the Territory called him the "Creek Freedman Marshal" — which he was. He could speak the Creek tongue better than some Creeks I had known. Judge Parker called him one of the best lawmen who had ever worked for him, and that was saying something. Like Bass, Grant had first worked out of Fort Smith for Judge Parker, but since around '96, Grant had been based in Eufaula.

As he reached for his cigar, I noticed a bloodstained rag around his wrist.

"What happened to you?" I nodded at the wound.

He looked at it, and shook his head. "Cherokee Bob. When he ambushed us on the ferry. It's just a scratch."

More than that, from the amount of dried blood, but I didn't argue the point. Instead, I tried to figure out what Cherokee Bob Dozier was doing. Perplexing, it was. After robbing the Katy near Eufaula, Cherokee Bob Dozier had ridden north, into Cherokee land. There he had bushwhacked Grant Johnson's posse on the Illinois River ferry. After that, however, he had ridden southwest, better than twenty miles back to the Arkansas River. He had hit our camp, killed Erskine Jones's mules, grabbed Bennie Reeves, and loped west. Only to turn north, cross the river, and head back into the Cherokee Nation.

"He don't like federal lawmen," Bass told Grant.

Grant pulled the cigar from his teeth, blew out smoke, and started to say something, but the old Keetowah, George Littledave, beat him to it.

"He don't like you."

The Cherokee stood over us, all sinew and bones, a nose as crooked as the Verdigris River, and a face as rutted as the country northwest of here.

"Where do you think he'll go?" Bass directed his question to Littledave.

"Where else?" Littledave said with a smile. "Robbers' Roost."

The northeast corner of the Territory. Rough country. The foothills of the Ozarks, full of caves, thick woods, creeks, and a bunch of locals — Miamis, Modocs, and other Indians, who seldom, if ever, helped out any federal lawman. A man could hide out in that country forever.

For that reason alone, I was glad to have George Littledave with us. The Keetowah had been in the Territory longer than any-one. They were the first Cherokees to settle in this part of the country, at least two decades before the Trail of Tears. Ancient as Littledave looked, I would not have been surprised if he had marched over from Georgia or Tennessee back in 1817.

"Cherokee Bob's taking a wide arc to get there," I said.

Littledave shrugged.

Grant puffed on his cigar, and Bass pushed back in his chair again, rocking the legs. About that time Ero returned, grunted something, and told the two younger Cherokees to have a seat, and she'd bring everyone some grub. The young men looked happy. Reckon they hadn't tasted *osafki*.

When she was gone, I explained to Bass, Grant, and Littledave what perplexed me so about Cherokee Bob's get-away ride.

"Cherokee Bob Dozier is not making a lick of sense," I said. "First, he robs the Katy. Fine. Smart man would ride down to the Winding Stair Mountains, hide out there, but he goes north. All right. Let's say he rides that way because he's a Cherokee, likely knows that country better. He ambushes Grant and his posse on the Illinois. That makes sense, too. Yet instead of pushing on north, deeper into the hills, he heads back toward Muskogee. Now that perplexes me. He knows that's where Marshal Bennett's based. He knows that area's chock full of lawmen. And then he bushwhacks us. I don't think he felt that he needed a new gang member. I don't think he had an obligation to save any young boy from the tumbleweed wagon. I don't know rightly what to think, except I've never come across an outlaw like him." I shook my head, longing for a tumbler of Old Crow. "Man acts like he wants to get caught," I added as I found the makings for a smoke.

Bass stopped rocking. "He don't want to get caught. He just wants a certain lawman to come huntin' him."

Our eyes met. "You?"

His head bobbed slightly, and the legs of the chair came down.

"Is that why he rescued Bennie?" I asked.

"Nah. Like I've said before, I don't think he even knowed Bennie's my boy. Hope to God Bennie don't tell him. No tellin' what that *hombre* might do."

"Why does he want you?" one of the younger Cherokees asked.

"Personal." Bass let it go at that.

I started to say something, but Ero returned with a platter of her foul gruel, corn pone, and a fresh pot of coffee. Still, I might have pressed Bass, but the front door opened.

Erskine Jones walked inside. "I grained and watered the damned horses, Johnson. Put 'em up in . . . ," he said, and stopped, his voice trailing off.

Bass rose slowly, eyes boring through Erskine Jones, but directing his question to Grant Johnson. "What the hell's he doin' here?"

"You know Marshal Bennett's rules, Bass," Johnson said. "Gots to have a tumbleweed wagon."

"I figured we'd take yours," Bass said, his eyes never leaving Erskine Jones. "With your driver."

Grant shook his head, suddenly looking older than dirt. "Be hard to do, Bass. My wagon's at the bottom of the Illinois River. And my driver, Gringo Gomez, he be buried on the banks."

Bass sank back into his chair. Erskine Jones just stood there, not daring to move a muscle. "That must have been some ambush," Bass said.

Grant shrugged.

"Good fight," George Littledave said with a smile. "Waited till we were midway across the river. Then they cut the ferry's ropes and opened up on us."

"Sharps Big Fifty," one of the young Cherokees said.

"Nah. Winchester Centennial," the other one corrected.

They returned to their *osafki* and coffee.

"Horses started rearin'," Grant said. "Ferryman, he leaped overboard. Saddle mounts started jumpin' into the river. Bullets splinterin' that little boat we be on, and that boat just rockin' up an' down like it was the biggest gale ever blowed up in them parts. Tumbleweed wagon went over the front. That dipped the boat. Then we was all. . . ." He sighed.

"Can you swim?" I asked Grant.

His head shook. "Gringo Gomez couldn't, neither."

"But I can," George Littledave said.

"We made it back to the banks," Grant said. "Well, all of us but Gringo Gomez. Littledave here, he pulled me to shore. Don't know how he done it, but he saved my bacon. Took cover in the woods. They killed one of the horses, but Wes yonder" — he nodded at one of the hungry young Cherokees — "he come out, got the rest of our mounts into the woods. They kept shootin' a couple minutes. Then they taken off. When they was gone, Wes rode downstream, found Gomez's body hung up on some driftwood. Told the ferryman to bury him, then we borrowed a horse from the ferryman, swum our mounts cross the Illinois. . . ."

"Which is what we should have done in the first place," George Littledave said.

Grant ignored him. "I was like Adams, there." He tilted his head toward me. "Thought those boys would ride north, toward the Ozarks. But a few miles upstream, they crossed the Illinois again. Turned south and east. Found Erskine Jones while he was barterin' with a Choctaw for the loan of a couple draft horses. You know the rest of the story, pret' much."

"What did you do with the body of the man Bass killed?" I asked.

"There was another deputy with us. White man named Scott. Rides with me every now and then down McAlester way. I sent him back to Muskogee with the dead man and to inform Marshal Bennett what happened to me, and what happened to y'all."

"Scott coming back?" I asked.

Grant sniggered. "I thinks, after that little ruction on the ferry, he's done found religion. Won't be ridin' in no posses any more."

"So," I began, "unless Doc Bennett sends us some more marshals. . . ."

"We don't need no more lawmen!" Bass roared. He slammed his fist on the table, and rose. He frowned harder, and looked across the room toward Erskine Jones. "Might as well eat, Erskine," he said at last, his voice milder, calmer. "I reckon you're with us. But you foul up one more time and you'll rue the day you was born. I ain't forgettin' how you acted when we was after that boy's daddy."

"Go to hell," Erskine snapped.

I had heard enough. "All of you shut up," I snapped. "Let's start acting like we're professionals, damn it."

To my surprise, everyone seemed to listen to me.

CHAPTER NINE

June 11, 1902

Like they were watching a circus come to town, colored men, women, and children lined the warped plank boardwalks as we rode into town late that morning. Only this circus frightened them.

I guess we looked something fearful, already sweating from the morning heat, with dust caked to our clothes and mounts; a white man, me, riding in the center, flanked by a giant man of color, Bass, and a smaller Negro, Grant. All three of us carried rifles across our saddles. Then came that wretched Erskine Jones in the tumbleweed wagon pulled by a couple of fine Cleveland bays. Behind the wagon rode three Cherokees, two young men — named Wes and Usdi, I had learned — and old George Littledave.

At last, a man in black broadcloth, holding a wide-brimmed gray hat at his side,

110

stepped out of a single-story brick building, and walked down the center of the street, toward us. He was smiling, nodding pleasantly. He wore no gun.

We had arrived in Tullahassee.

In the Creek lingo — *tulwa* meaning town and *ahassee* being something old — it meant old town, and I reckon it was old at that.

Back in 1850, a Creek mission had been built alongside the Texas Road. At first, the Creeks hadn't been pleased with missionaries and the schools they kept building, but they had grown to like the Koweta Mission, so they made an arrangement with the Presbyterians to build another mission. The Creeks even put up one-fifth of the money needed to build it. Not too long after, a Presbyterian minister bought seventy acres, a brick building went up, and eighty Creeks started learning to travel the white man's, and God's, road.

More Creeks started coming to the area, bringing their slaves with them. That school must have been something. It kept right on till a big fire there in 1880 or '81 destroyed the mission school. After that, the Creeks sent their students to another mission, and they deeded the remnants of the school, and the land, to the freedmen. Thus Tullahassee became a colored town, and a right prosperous one at that.

This wasn't some woolly burg like Marshall Town, full of desperadoes, whiskey peddlers, concubines, and the like. Tullahassee had a post office, a general store, a wagon yard, a blacksmith's shop, livery stable, a cotton gin, two barbershops, the Katy railway, several churches but not one dram shop, and the Tullahassee Town Site Company to entice new residents from all across the South.

We reined up in the center of the street, and let the man walk to us. He settled that big hat on his head, and gave me a smile, especially after, sensing no danger, I slid my Winchester into the scabbard. Bass and Grant did the same.

"Howdy, brothers," the man said, nodding at us, but keeping his eyes trained on me. A slight Negro with broad shoulders, maybe in his forties, wearing bifocal spectacles. "I'm A.J. Mason." He hooked a thumb toward the brick building. "Run that store with my brothers, and I'm president of Tullahassee Town Site Company. What brings y'all to our fair city on this beautiful June morn?"

I hooked my thumb toward Bass. "He's in charge."

112

Mr. A.J. Mason blinked. Guess he had not considered the fact that a black man could be leading a posse.

"Bass is the oldest." Grant Johnson grinned.

The look on A.J. Mason's face prompted me to clarify. "We're not here to arrest anyone in your town."

Suddenly A.J. Mason was practically dancing in the street. He whipped off his hat, slapped it across his thigh, and approached Bass. "Bass. . . . That means you'd be Bass Reeves. By jingo, this is an honor, sir. Deputy Marshal Bass Reeves. The Iron Marshal. Marshal, this town is yours. Anything you want, yes, sir." He extended his right hand proudly.

It hovered there for the longest time.

The leather of Bass's saddle squeaked, and he slowly shook his head. "Sorry, Mister Mason," he said. "I don't shake nobody's hand."

Kicking his horse into a walk, Bass headed for the livery.

Grant followed, and I heard Erskine Jones cursing at his Cleveland bays. A.J. Mason stood in the center of the street, thunderstruck, staring at his hand as if it were some foreign instrument, then lowering it, and stepping out of the path of the tumbleweed wagon. I eased my horse toward the board-walk, and swung down. I offered my hand to Mr. Mason, and he slowly took it, as though he was struck dumb.

"Don't mind Bass," I said, turning my head to see the big deputy dismount at the livery and walk to a black-bearded Negro in overalls and mule-ear boots. "He didn't mean any disrespect."

Mason stared at me blankly.

It wasn't my place to let Mason know what Bass had once revealed to me: that during the late War Between the States, George Reeves, his master who Bass had assumed was also his friend, had extended a hand, then belted Bass's jaw.

"Bass is a lawman," I said. "Been shot at too many times. It pays, in our profession, to keep our hands free."

Of course, I had shaken the merchant's hand.

"I see," Mr. Mason said.

He didn't. Hell, I didn't. I tilted my head toward his brick store. "We need some provisions. I can pay you in vouchers while Bass talks to the liveryman."

His head bobbed, and he seemed to stand erect again. As he walked down the street, I pulled my horse behind me, asking: "Some riders come through town yesterday? Seven men or thereabouts? On horses worn to a frazzle."

"Yes, Marshal. They did not stay long."

"Traded horses, I reckon."

He shrugged. "I could not say. Not for certain, though I warrant your suspicion is correct. Still, you'd have to ask Saul Washington."

Which was what Bass Reeves would be doing right then.

"But one of them came into your mercantile." I didn't ask that. Just stated it as a fact, even though I wasn't sure.

"Two of them," he corrected.

"Buying supplies?"

He wet his lips. "Ammunition. Bought every last box I had of Forty-Five-Seventies. For Winchester repeaters."

Usdi had been right. When Cherokee Bob had ambushed Grant's posse on the Illinois ferry, they had been shooting Winchester Centennials, and not Sharps rifles.

"That all?"

We had reached the general store. I wrapped the reins around the hitching rail, listening as Mr. Mason answered.

"No, sir. Some Forty-Fours, centerfire. Shotgun shells. Buckshot. Twelve gauge. Three boxes of Forty-Fives. Powder, lead, and an old bullet mold for a Thirty-Six."

I joined him on the boardwalk, as he opened the door. "That must be some hunting trip they've got planned."

"Indeed," he said, and we went inside.

"Any grub?" I asked as we walked across the well-swept hardwood floor, my spurs jingling as we moved through stacks of cotton and fancy dresses for the women of town.

"Not here. A few of them went to Del's, I'm told. Ate there."

At the counter, I helped myself to a dill pickle, and asked for two boxes for my .25-35, a couple of boxes for Bass's .44-40, and a box for my Smith & Wesson.

"You must be going hunting, too," Mr. Mason said.

"Seems like Bass and I are always hunting," I said.

"Yes. What a shame. Will there be anything else, Marshal?"

"The man who bought all of that ammunition," I said. "What did he look like?"

Being a former newspaper editor, Doc Bennett had once said I had a gift of interviewing, that I could fish out information easily. I didn't intimidate folks, just acted like we were carrying on a pleasant conversation. The marshal said I would make a crackerjack newspaper reporter. Newspaper reporters didn't get shot at, either.

"A man of color," Mr. Mason said. "Mustache and goatee. Some beard growth covering the rest of his face, but I dare say only because he had not had time for a shave. High cheek bones. Fancy boots with fine spurs. A beaded buckskin jacket. Two Remington revolvers, butts forward. He filled up the empty loops on his shell belt while I filled his order. He spoke as if he had education. He paid in cash money."

Likely stolen from the Katy north of Eufaula.

Mason looked at me. "It was Cherokee Bob. But you knew that already."

I nodded at the shelves behind him. In Muskogee, we had outfitted for three men, yet now there were seven of us. I asked for flour, beans, salt pork, coffee, potatoes, beef jerky, and airtights of peaches and tomatoes. As Mr. Mason began collecting the food, I asked about the other man who had come into the store.

"Young man," he said, grabbing two cans of peaches. "Colored, but more mulatto. Floppy hat with a high crown. Quiet. Didn't say a word, just stood at the door. Kept his hands in his pockets the whole time."

He turned back to the shelves, picked up a can of tomatoes, and I could see he was studying on something as he put the airtight on the counter. A.J. Mason looked at me. "He wasn't as big as that marshal out there. Didn't have facial hair, not even a day's growth of beard. Face was smooth as a baby's bottom, but . . . I don't know. The eyes maybe." He laughed. "Well, it's nothing."

"I don't know about that, Mister Mason," I said, wiping the briny juice from the pickle on my chaps. "If most witnesses I interviewed had a memory like yours, well, I'd be in hog heaven."

He nodded at the compliment, but turned again, this time yelling across the store to a young colored man in an apron and sleeve garters. "Felix! Grab a side of salt pork, will you!"

"You were saying about the younger man?" I prompted.

"Wasn't saying a thing." Mason shook his head. "Just that, well, he looked a bit like Marshal Reeves."

Felix laid the salt pork beside my plunder. I reached for the vouchers I carried in my vest pocket.

"Was this young man heeled?"

Now it was A.J. Mason who laughed. "I was distracted," he said. "Cherokee Bob was standing two feet in front of me, spinning

118

the cylinder of one of his Remingtons. I was wondering if he might be about to rob my store. Or kill me."

I grinned back at him. "But you noticed enough about Ben— about the young man to see he kept his hands in his pockets."

Hands in his pockets. That meant the outlaws had gotten those handcuffs off Bennie's wrists.

Mr. Mason's eyes cocked as if in thought, and his head bobbed slightly. "Yeah. You're right, Marshal. I remember looking at him before Cherokee Bob started loading his revolvers. First I thought he might have a hideaway pistol." He shrugged. "Maybe he did. Those hands never came out of the pockets. But he wasn't wearing a belted gun, I'm pretty sure of that. Cherokee Bob put all the bullets and stuff in a grain sack. Carried them out with him. The boy walked out ahead of him. And that was it. They were gone."

"I could use a grain sack myself," I said.

"Felix!" Mr. Mason called.

As the clerk loaded my supplies in a sack, I handed a voucher to the store owner.

"So you know Cherokee Bob," I said.

He tucked the paper into his cash register. "Only by sight. It's not like we're both deacons in the same church." He grinned at his joke. "He has been through here a time or two before." His Adam's apple went up and down. "It's not that I want to do business with a ruffian, Marshal, but, well, Cherokee Bob isn't the type of man you don't do business with. If you want to stay in business."

I offered Mr. Mason my hand again. We shook before I gathered the food and ammunition, and walked out of the general store.

No one had seen which direction Cherokee Bob and his men rode when they left Tullahassee. No one admitted so, anyway.

Instead of fording the Verdigris, we followed the winding trail that ran along the river's west banks. We pushed our horses hard, moving north toward Vinita, and did not stop for a noon meal. The jerky I bought from A.J. Mason, therefore, came in handy.

The heat turned oppressive, trapped among the thick forests and the heavy clouds. My shirt stuck to my skin, and sweat streamed down my face. Bass Reeves had been moseying along since we had left Muskogee. Now he kept at a hard trot, like he was one of those long-distance endurance riders I had read about in the *National Police Gazette*. I spurred Dutchy, and caught up with Bass at the point.

"Horses are about done in," I told him as I bounced in the saddle.

Bass looked straight ahead, eyes moving across the road, Winchester cradled in big hands that loosely held the reins to the sorrel.

"Mine ain't," he said. The sorrel never broke its stride.

Jerky and hot water from my canteen sloshed in my stomach. A hard trot wasn't much fun for two minutes. We'd been at our latest for nigh twenty.

"Maybe we don't have horses as strong as that sorrel, Bass," I said. "And those Cleveland bays pulling that tumbleweed wagon surely can't keep up this pace."

They were big, strong horses, each better than sixteen hands, but they had been laboring for breath, their bodies caked with a sweaty foam.

On rode Bass Reeves.

"You keep this up," I said, "and we'll be walking to Robbers' Roost." This time, I reined Dutchy to a stop. Turning in the saddle, I pointed to a little clearing at the edge of the road.

"Hold up there," I told Erskine, and the crazy Choctaw turned the wagon. The three Cherokees quickly followed into the shade,

121

and slid from their mounts, loosening the cinches, reaching for canteens.

I removed my hat, mopped the sweat from my brow, and swung down to the ground. After patting the bay's neck, I heard hoof beats, and a shadow crossed my face.

"Reckon you're right, Dave," Bass Reeves said.

The Winchester, I noticed, had been shoved back into the scabbard.

After dismounting, he fumbled for his canteen. That hard pace had caught up with him, and I saw him leaning against the horse, his face glistening with sweat. His gun belt hung loosely. Too loose. I would have bet that Bass — hell, all of us — had sweated off five pounds at the least. Yet he took only a small sip from the canteen, then removed his hat and filled it with water. He brought the offering to the sorrel, and let the big horse drink.

From the camp Erskine and the Cherokees were making, I heard Erskine yell out: "Robbers' Roost! What a stupid name for a hide-out. And you lawdogs can't find a bunch of bushwhackers dumb enough to choose as their hide-out a place called Robbers' Roost." He cackled, and lowered his voice. "Where you think that gang of train robbers be hidin' out, Matilda?" Raising his voice: "Oh, I don't know. Robbers' Roost, you reckon?"

Even Bass smiled. Shaking his head, he put his dripping hat back on his head, and yelled toward the camp: "Shut up and cook up some chow, Jones. And it'd better be good."

"Or what, you damned big oaf?" Erskine fired back. "What you gonna do? Kill me like you done your last cook?"

Bass went rigid, like a ramrod. His hands turned into balled fists, clenched so tightly that they shook.

All of that heat left me in a second. A chill raced up my backbone, and my face turned pale. Not from heatstroke, but from the look on Bass Reeves's face.

"Choctaw," George Littledave told Erskine Jones, "you are a fool." The grizzled Keetowah was looking over toward Bass and me. "Maybe a dead fool."

CHAPTER TEN

1884–1886

If you believe the legend, it happened like this.

In the early spring of '84, Bass Reeves was bringing in five prisoners from the Chickasaw Nation to Fort Smith. He had hired William Leach, a cantankerous Negro, as cook, and, since he had no deputies and five prisoners, Bass went against Judge Parker's orders and let Leach carry a revolver.

Some folks say that Leach should have been inside that tumbleweed wagon with the rest of the ruffians. Others would argue that it was Bass Reeves who belonged shackled by iron.

They made camp near Cherokee Town. Bass got the prisoners out, let them answer Nature's call, then chained them in front of the campfire while Leach prepared supper. Bass sat away from the wagon, Winchester in his lap, and began playing with a dog he had brought along on the trip.

Bass sure loved that little dog. More mutt than anything, too small to be much of a watchdog — the little cur seldom even barked — but Bass loved him. He had trained it so that it would stand on its hind legs and beg for food, and that made Bass laugh every time the dog did it. William Leach, however, found no humor in the mutt's antics.

Leach didn't care much for Bass, either.

Why Leach got crossways with Bass no one ever really knew, but Leach began taking out his resentment on the dog. That night outside of Cherokee Town, a few days from Fort Smith, Bass told the foul cook to lay off that dog. The dog was standing on its hind legs, right at Leach's feet as he tried to cook supper. Finally, with an angry curse, Leach kicked the dog, sending it rolling over.

"That dog ain't doin' nothin' it ain't been doin' since we crossed the Arkansas three weeks ago!" Bass snapped. "Give him some food, and he'll leave you alone."

Sure enough, the dog — not harboring any grudge, and too gentle to understand the cook's cussedness — came right back to Leach, jumping up and down on its hind legs, begging again for food. Fool animal didn't know any better.

"I'll feed him," Leach said, and lifted a skillet from the fire. Smiling, he tilted the skillet, and fiery grease poured down the dog's throat.

The dog screamed. Bass shot to his feet, bringing up the Winchester. William Leach had already dropped the skillet, stepped around the fire, and grabbed the old Navy .36 in his waistband.

Five prisoners stared in disbelief.

The cook fired, thumbed back the hammer, cursing.

Bass's rifle spoke, and the slug caught the cook in his throat. The cap-and-ball relic flew from Leach's right hand, clanging against the metal bars of the tumbleweed wagon. Both hands gripped his throat, as blood gushed between his fingers. Eyes wide, William Leach fell to his knees, then pitched headfirst into the fire.

Bass jacked another round into his rifle, swept the Winchester toward the prisoners. "Stay put!" he barked, and used the toe of his boot to push Leach out of the fire. He didn't bother checking on the cook, but instead turned his attention to the dog, lying on its side, whimpering.

He leaned the Winchester against a rock,

and scooped the dog into his hands, holding it in his lap, stroking it with his big hands, tears streaming down his face as he watched that little dog die.

With a sigh, he tucked the dead animal underneath his arm, grabbed his rifle, picked up the old Colt revolver by the tumbleweed wagon, and walked out of camp to bury the dog with his own hands. When he returned to camp, he went straight to William Leach's body, and rolled it over with his boot.

Sightless eyes stared out of a scalded face.

"You son-of-a-bitch," Bass told the corpse, and rolled William Leach back into the fire.

The prisoners said nothing that night, or anything over the next few days as Bass Reeves brought them to Fort Smith's hell on the border.

Bass never spoke of what had happened, but the story got out, and Bass let it spread. Not a bad idea, considering a story like that would put even more fear into the outlaws Bass had to track down.

Anyway, that's how the story goes. . . .

If you believe the legend.

It didn't happen that way, of course. What really happened would be brought out in a Fort Smith courtroom. It went something like this.

■ ■ ■ ■

Methodically Bass signed his name on the receipt, and stepped back as the guards led the last of his prisoners into the Fort Smith jail. Sniffling, Bass returned the pen, and wiped his nose with thumb and forefinger.

"Judge Parker wants to see you," the jailer said, and Bass looked up. He picked up the rifle he had laid on the counter, and stuck it under his shoulder, just to do something. Steam rose from his mouth on that frigid, windy morning. His lips were chapped, eyes bloodshot, bones and muscles aching from better than two weeks in the Territory. What he wanted was a bath and a shave, to feel Jennie in his arms, to hear his children laughing, to pull off those boots, burn the remnants of his socks, and prop his feet up on the ottoman by the stove in his living room.

"Judge Parker?" Bass spoke uneasily.

"You best go," the white deputy said. "Before he leaves his chambers for dinner."

He felt the stares, and turned. A trusty dropped his eyes, began vigorously pushing a broom. Another federal lawman busied himself rolling a cigarette.

Bass ran his tongue over his dried, peeling

lips, and thanked the deputy, and climbed up the steps, turned left, and walked across the sleet-carpeted dead grass to the main entrance into the former military barracks that had been transformed into a federal courthouse.

Ten years on the Fort Smith bench had aged him considerably, but Isaac C. Parker — six feet tall, two hundred pounds or better, and with penetrating blue eyes that could stare down the most vigilant lawyer or hardened criminal — still filled a room, commanding attention, demanding respect. Stroking his graying goatee with long fingers, Judge Parker motioned toward a chair.

"Jubal," he called before his secretary closed the door, "tell Deputy Marshal Fair to join us!"

"Yes, Your Honor."

The door shut. It sounded like a cell door closing.

"Bass," Judge Parker said as he sat in his thick-cushioned leather chair, "you have performed you duties better than most deputies I have had the honor to know during my tenure here."

Good God, Bass thought, *the judge is leavin' us.*

Parker grinned. "How is your wife, sir?

Your family?"

Oh, hell. He ain't leavin'. He's about to fire me.

"Fit," Bass said. "Leastwise they was before I left for the Nations. I was hopin' to get home directly and see 'em."

Parker slumped in his chair, sighing heavily. A light tapping sounded on the door, then it cracked open, and Jacob Winslow's head reappeared as he announced: "Marshal Fair, sir."

The judge nodded, the door opened wider, and Deputy U.S. Marshal S.J.B. Fair, a slim but powerful man in an ill-fitting plaid sack suit and bowler, entered the room, corncob pipe clenched in his mouth.

"Marshal Reeves," Parker said, rising, "please stand. No, sir. Leave your rifle on the table. And I must ask you, sir, to unbuckle your gun belt."

What the hell is goin' on?

Bass felt as if he were shaking too much to follow Judge Parker's instructions. The heavy Colt dropped onto the cushioned chair, and he turned, heart pounding, vision blurring, as Deputy Fair reached inside his coat, and withdrew a paper, unfolding it carefully, handing it over to Bass.

It was a paper Bass Reeves had seen many times over the past decade.

He looked down, and read, Judge Parker's words sounding like his own inner voice, or God: "I've said countless times during my tenure here to so many grand juries . . . 'Permit no innocent man to be punished, but let no guilty man escape.' "

United States of America
Western District of Arkansas
I do solemnly swear and believe from reliable information in my possession that Bass Reeves did in the Indian Country, within the Western District of Arkansas, on or about the 10th day of April 1884 feloniously, willfully, premeditatedly, and of his malice aforethought kill and murder William Leach, a Negro and not an Indian.
Against the peace and dignity of the United States, and I pray a writ:
S.J.B. Fair
Subscribed and sworn to before me this 18th day of January 1886.
Stephen Wheeler
United States Commissioner

He lowered the warrant to his side, and brought his left hand up to rub his face. A million thoughts swam through his head. He felt dizzy, dropping his left hand, shaking his head, trying to understand what was happening.

The floorboards squeaked as Deputy Fair approached him, and Bass straightened, tense, taut. Anger flashed through him as he saw the manacles in the lawman's hands. Fair stopped, swallowed.

Looking at Judge Parker, Bass said: "That was an accident . . . what happened to Leach."

Parker's head bobbed.

"Ain't like I hid it from nobody. I told you, told everyone what happened as soon as I got back here."

The judge nodded again. "I know, Bass."

His head shook. "That was almost two years ago, Your Honor. Why they bringin' this up now, after all this time?"

Parker swallowed, but didn't answer. Maybe he didn't have to. Bass Reeves could figure things out for himself.

John Carroll had been appointed marshal back in October. Carroll wasn't only a Democrat, he had served as a colonel for some Confederate regiment during the late war. He was the first former Reb to serve as a marshal under Parker. Bass didn't know the new marshal well, but he could tell from their few meetings that John Carroll did not care for Bass Reeves. Yet the marshal had wed a quadroon. No, that didn't make sense. Was it Fair? Did Deputy Fair despise him enough to get a warrant issued for his arrest. Hell, he had never done Fair any wrong. What the hell was going on?

He glanced at the warrant again. Premeditated murder. He wadded the paper into a ball, and tossed it on the floor in front of the judge's desk. Murder. Not manslaughter. Not negligent homicide.

"It was an accident," Bass said. "Not like all 'em stories that. . . ." He sighed again.

"Bass," Parker said, "there will be a preliminary hearing. Perhaps this should have been handled back in April of 'Eighty-Four, and everything could have been cleared up then. Be that as it may, we have laws and those laws apply to all men, white men, red men, men of color. And lawmen as well as outlaws."

The manacles clinked, but Parker stopped Deputy Fair with a sharp word.

"Marshal Fair," Judge Parker said, his voice calmer but still resonating, "I see no reason to serve that warrant at this moment, sir. I think it would be better if you would serve it in Van Buren. After Marshal Reeves has time to visit his family, make some arrangements. Say two hours from now."

Fair stared hard at the judge. "Begging Your Honor's pardon . . . ," he began, but stopped when Parker waved his hand.

"Mister Fair, if Bass Reeves has not fled this jurisdiction during the course of the past twenty months, I do not believe he poses a flight risk, sir."

"No, sir." Fair lowered his gaze, and the handcuffs.

"Two hours," Parker told Bass. "I'm sure this matter will be resolved in the preliminary hearing. I dare say it will never come to trial."

"Thank you, sir." Bass knelt, picked up the warrant, opened it, tried to smooth out the crumpled paper, and tentatively offered it to Deputy Fair.

The lawman returned the warrant to the inside pocket of his coat.

"I'll meet you out front of my house," Bass said. "Don't want my children seein' this."

Fair nodded.

"And don't bring those." He tilted his chin toward the handcuffs in Fair's hand.

He stepped toward the door, but Parker stopped him.

"I am sorry, Deputy Reeves," the judge said, "but, before you leave, I must request that you turn in your badge."

CHAPTER ELEVEN

1886–1887

"You get used to the smell," Bass had once told a green deputy marshal who had stepped into Fort Smith's basement jail for the first time.

He had been wrong. Nobody could ever get used to the stench. Maybe if you were a lawman, depositing prisoners, staying in the jail for ten or twenty minutes, an hour at the most. Perhaps then you might make yourself believe that you couldn't smell the sickness, the vomit, the piss, shit, and other filth. Trusties tried cleaning the place, whitewashing the stone walls, scouring the flagstone floors with lime, but none of it did any good.

A preliminary hearing, Judge Parker had said back in January. That's all it would be. Yet the grand jury had brought in an indictment for first-degree murder, and Bass Reeves had been in jail since. No one had come to visit him, except his lawyers. Oh, Jennie had cried, said she would visit him every day, bring the children if Bass wanted, but Bass didn't want that. Not at all. No child of his, no wife would ever see him like this. Rotting in jail. Living with animals. Living like some damned animal.

For three months, he had been locked inside, freezing night and day, breathing foul air, watching where he stepped. He never relaxed, and rarely slept. They hadn't given him trusty status, but instead kept him locked up with the general population. White prisoners, blacks, and Indians, murderers and rapists, robbers and whiskey runners, men he had arrested himself. Now they laughed at him, threatened to kill him, or both.

That morning, the marshals had come for James Wasson and Joseph Jackson.

He didn't know Wasson, who had killed two men. The first victim had been back in 1872, but no one in the Nations or Fort Smith circuit seemed to care about the late Henry Martin. When Wasson had coldbloodedly murdered Almarine Watkins in '84, however, the Watkins family had posted a big reward on Wasson's head, and the arm of the law had finally caught up with the murderer.

On this day, April 23, 1886, he would share the gallows with Joseph Jackson.

Bass sat on the cold flagstone, his back against the rugged wall, watching. By now, his pants had become filthy rags, stained with tobacco juice and who-knows-what, his Mackinaw ripped and filthy, barely keeping him warm. Spring had come, but in name only. Down in this jail, winter held an icy grip, late for Arkansas. He heard a deputy marshal say it was snowing, but no one in the hell on the border could know for certain. Not in this dark, dismal dungeon.

Two basement rooms, with fifty to one hundred prisoners in each, sometimes a whole lot more. One wash basin per room, with the water changed twice a day. One urinal tub per cell, the contents emptied, also, twice a day. Supposed to, anyway.

Bass had dumped prisoners into these cells as healthy men, and watched them come to trial two months later (if they were lucky) broken, wretched creatures, hardly human. And for those who had to stay incarcerated four months, six months, eight . . . well. . . . Bass shook his head. More than a few had been carried out of jail before their day in court, to be buried in the pauper's cemetery.

They were constructing a new jail, a three-story brick building, to help ease the overcrowding, but it wasn't scheduled to be completed for another three years. Bass wondered if he'd still be locked up in this pit when the new hell on the border opened for business.

"Give me a minute, you stinkin' laws," Joseph Jackson barked.

"Come on, boy," a deputy said. "Don't keep Maledon waitin'."

George Maledon. The Prince of Hangmen. A German, now in his fifties, who seemed a little slow but was incredibly thorough. Once, Maledon had operated a sawmill in the Nations before taking a job — finding his calling, he often said — as prison guard and executioner back in '71. He had been sending prisoners to hell since the days of the corrupt Marshal Logan Roots, but Judge Parker had kept him on. The man knew his job, and he had had plenty of practice.

"Shut up, you damned law." Shuffling his feet, the iron clanging, Jackson turned to stare at Bass. "Hey, nigger."

Bass looked up, not speaking. Jackson was a big, burly black man, hands that made Bass's look tiny by comparison. Those hands were manacled, with another heavy chain dropping from those cuffs to leg irons. He wore a new suit. Owing to his Presbyterian roots, Judge Parker never sent a man to the gallows wearing filth.

"How's it feel?"

When Bass said nothing, Jackson laughed so hard, he spit saliva. "Come on out, nigger. Come on and see what it looks like to see a nigger hang."

"I've seen men hang," Bass said.

Jackson laughed, the way he had laughed during his trial. He had killed his wife just more than a year earlier in Oak Lodge in the Choctaw Nation. Killed her with those rugged, brutal hands, beating her so badly, few people would have recognized the corpse.

"Yeah, and pretty soon, you's gonna get an even closer look. You son-of-a-bitch. You miserable. . . ."

The deputy slammed a club into the small of Joseph Jackson's back, and the behemoth grunted, stumbled.

"Move, damn you!"

Another lawman jerked Jackson to his feet, and shoved him down the hallway. Above the eerie sound of chains rattling, Bass heard Joseph Jackson's laughter, and a chilling cry: "I'll see you in hell, Bass Reeves! I'll see you there real soon!"

■ ■ ■ ■

The *Arkansas Gazette* and Van Buren *Press* had all but convicted Bass in their newspaper accounts of his arrest and hearing. He wasn't just a murderer, but he had extorted money from the prisoners he brought to Fort Smith, he had made indecent proposals to white women, he had murdered several people, yet it took the courage of the new marshal to bring this rogue felon to justice.

He found himself listening, wondering if he could hear the trap door spring, wondering if the sound of Joseph Jackson's and James Wasson's necks snapping would carry to the basement. The din from the crowd gathering outside for the double hanging did manage to carry through the jail's thick rock walls, or was that his imagination?

Although Bass kept his eyes open, he could picture what was happening outside.

The gallows were new, a little larger than the previous scaffold, built of oak with room to hang a dozen criminals at once. By now, the two prisoners were climbing the twelve steps, to be placed over the trap door, to have black hoods pulled over their faces. George Maledon would place a noose over each man's head, ropes eight inches in diameter, oiled and stretched, stretched and oiled, stretched and stretched until the hangman knew they would not botch the job. The guards, usually deputies but sometimes soldiers from the fort, would wear their uniforms.

The pay for working an execution was pretty good. Some extra money, and smart clothes to wear, per Judge Parker's orders. Bass, however, had never wanted that job.

A parson would pray, maybe lead the spectators in song, and there would be plenty of people, coming all the way from Tahlequah and Dardanelle to see the show. Talk was that these public executions would soon be banned, and that a fence would be erected around the gallows, so today's hanging would bring in even more people, some from as far east as Little Rock. This might be the last hanging they'd ever get to see.

The death warrant would be read, and that would seemingly last forever. Bass had always wondered how a condemned man could stand through all that speechifying. Sometimes they didn't. Some would faint. Others might lean against the doomed man next to him. The marshal would nod at Maledon, who would pull the lever.

Bass listened . . . but he couldn't hear the

crowd any more. He heard only the wind's moans.

The sun blinded him when he stepped out of the damp, humid jail on June 19th. Not free. Not yet, by a damned sight. He had posted a bond co-signed by Deputy Marshal James Mershon and his three attorneys. As his eyes adjusted to the intense light, he inhaled deeply, the first air he had breathed that didn't reek of excrement, of human sweat.

"Bass."

He looked at the well-dressed attorney standing beside him.

"Yes, sir, Mister Clayton."

"Go home. Be careful. Don't talk to any newspaper reporters. And no whiskey. Don't pull a cork until after the trial." The attorney grinned. "After your acquittal, I'll buy you a bottle of the best rye in Fort Smith." He nodded. "I'll be in touch."

"Yes, sir." He turned before William Clayton offered his hand.

Under the conditions of his bond, he couldn't leave Van Buren or Fort Smith, so he hoed weeds in the garden, went to church with Jennie and the children, and met with William H.H. Clayton and his co-

counsels, Thomas Marcum and William Cravens, lawyers recommended to him by Judge Parker. The best defense attorneys in the Western District of Arkansas. Lawyers who did not work for free. He had his attorneys make out applications for witnesses, request continuances for his trial, and they met every Monday and went over and over and over exactly how he had shot and killed his cook on that spring evening in 1884.

He broke horses for Jim Head. Shod the mounts of Mershon and a few deputy marshals. Swamped Elijah Goldstein's mercantile. And visited his mother in Van Buren when he couldn't handle his children asking him: "When you goin' after some more bad guys, Daddy?" Or their mother: "How come Daddy's spendin' so much time with us now, Mommie?" His mother never said a word about his trial, about William Leach. He wondered if she knew what was happening to him.

August found him walking absently down the cobblestone streets of Fort Worth, lugging a forty-pound saddle from Jim Head's stables. Sweating profusely, he dropped the saddle at his feet and looked through the window of the City Hotel, watching the beer-jerker fill mugs with draught beer. Damn, but he had acquired a powerful thirst. Clayton had told him to lay off whiskey, but the lawyer hadn't said a word about beer.

Still. . . .

Someone tapped his shoulder, and he whirled around, reaching for a revolver that wasn't there.

"I scare you, Bass?" The man before him was white, his vest unbuttoned, cravat loosened, eyes bloodshot. His breath smelled of forty-rod. He twirled a walking cane in one hand — that's what he had used to tap Bass's shoulder — then, grinning, leaned against the brick wall and twisted one end of his mustache with his free hand.

"Do I know you?"

"You should. Name's A.J. Boyd."

The name meant as much to him as the white man's face.

"I'm on the jury panel for this term of court." He moved his greasy fingers to the other end of his mustache. "I was hoping you might tell me about how you killed that darky cook."

"If you're on the jury panel, you ought to know better than to be jawin' at me, mister."

The man moved his cane from one hand to the other. "If you want to save your damned neck, you'd better talk to me."

"You're drunk."

"You damned son-of-a-bitch." He raised the cane as if to strike, but Bass never flinched. "Damn you, I'll break your neck with a hangman's rope just as sure as I've got this stick in my hand. And I ain't the only one. Me and three others are going to make sure you swing, you uppity nigger."

"Well," Bass said, "that's all right."

Picking up the saddle, he turned and walked away.

William Clayton said it was mighty damned funny, that they were in Judge Parker's court in September, testifying in a contempt-of-court case against A.J. Boyd long before Bass's own trial.

Bass didn't find anything amusing. That was just more to the bill he'd get stuck with when all of this bullshit was over.

The jury found Boyd guilty. Bass wondered how long a weasel like A.J. Boyd would last in hell on the border.

October 1887.

He sat at the table beside his lawyers, watching Judge Parker, listening to the prosecuting attorney question the first witness.

"Missus Grayson," M.H. Sandels, the prosecutor, asked, "you were at the defendant's camp at Cherokee Town on that April evening, were you not?"

"Yeah," answered big-boned Mary Grayson, her hair pinned up in a bun, a shawl draped over the shoulders of an ill-fitting calico dress. "I mean, yes, sir. I sure was."

"The defendant had invited you there, correct?"

"Yeah. He had a sick prisoner he wanted me to tend to."

"And there was a dog in camp. A dog, I should say, other than the defendant."

Parker's gavel sounded like a howitzer before William Clayton could rise to object. "Mister Sandels," the judge said to the prosecutor, "one more remark such as that and you, sir, will rue your poor attempt at humor in our jail, sir, for as long as I deem fit."

The prosecutor paled. "There was a dog in camp, Missus Grayson?"

"Yeah. Yes, sir. Reeves yonder told that black cook to drive that dog away, to get him the hell out of the camp. Leach, he didn't do nothin', and Reeves got up. That's when Leach told the dog to get out of there before the marshal shot him. The dog bolted under the horses. And Reeves grabbed his rifle and shot Leach dead. Killed him. Deader than dirt."

146

"What did Leach do?"

"Leach. He didn't do nothin'. Just fell dead."

The courtroom exploded in laughter until Judge Parker's gavel silenced the outburst.

"I meant . . . oh, never mind. Do you recall why the defendant wanted the late Mister Leach to drive the dog away?"

"No. Can't say I do."

Bass pushed back from the table, shaking his head, as prosecutor M.H. Sandels returned to his chair. So this was how his trial would go. He looked down, saw he was gripping the arms of the chair, might break the piece of furniture if he didn't control that rage.

"Missus Grayson." Co-counsel William Cravens had risen, but did not bother to approach the witness. "You say Deputy Marshal Reeves had asked you to his camp?"

"That's right."

"To treat a sick prisoner?"

"That's what I said."

"Who was this prisoner?"

Mary Grayson hesitated, and that was all William Cravens wanted. "He was your husband, was he not, ma'am?"

"Yeah. Jim had taken sick."

"Jim was a prisoner, wasn't he?"

147

She nodded. Judge Parker told her she had to answer verbally. "Yeah." Barely audible.

"There were other prisoners, too, weren't there?"

"Oh, 'bout four others, I recollect."

Cravens glanced at the notebook beside his fingers. "Yes. Toby Hill, Big Wiley, Little Charly, and Lewis Tiger. Four Creek Indians. Your husband . . . oh, never mind about him. I'll get the honor to cross-examine him when he testifies. You say William Leach fell dead after Deputy Marshal Reeves's rifle discharged."

"He discharged it."

"What was Marshal Reeves doing before the fatal shot?"

"Sittin'. Just sittin'. Cussin' that dog."

"Were you surprised when you heard the gunshot?"

"Yes. I reckon I was."

"You didn't expect it?"

"No."

"Where was William Leach struck?"

She pointed to her neck. "Right about here."

"Did the bullet lodge in his neck?"

"I don't know."

"You don't know? Didn't Marshal Reeves bring you into his camp to tend to your sick husband? Aren't you a trained doctor?"

"No. I ain't no doctor." She practically cackled.

"No, you're not. Your husband was sick, and Marshal Reeves brought you to camp because he feared Jim Grayson might be dying."

"Jim ain't dead."

"Most certainly. He's sitting there in the back row, between two federal deputy marshals."

Judge Parker sustained the prosecutor's objection.

"William Leach did not die immediately. Isn't that true, Missus Grayson?" Cravens said, nonplussed by the objection and the judge's rebuke. "In fact, after Leach was wounded, Marshal Reeves sent for a doctor. A real doctor. Isn't that so?"

"I reckon. Been a long while back. Can't remember ever'thing."

"Mayhap you recall this, ma'am? Didn't Marshal Reeves tell William Leach he was sorry for what happened?"

"I didn't hear nothin' like that."

Jim Grayson told pretty much the same story as his wife had to the prosecutor. William Clayton handled the cross-examination.

"This isn't your first time appearing in

Judge Parker's court, is it, sir?"

"No. I been here three, four times, I reckon."

"Indeed. For larceny the first time. For selling whiskey the second time, not to mention theft of a yearling. You got ninety days, for that one. And let's see, please tell the court why Marshal Reeves was bringing you in in the spring of 'Eighty-Four."

"There was a misunderstandin'."

"Yes. That led to a warrant for your arrest for assault and attempted murder. Where do you live, Grayson?"

"Creek. . . ."

"No, where are you now, sir?"

"The Detroit House of Corrections."

"Thank you, sir. You are serving fifteen months after being arrested by Deputy Marshal Bass Reeves. My God. The wife of a convicted felon and the convicted felon himself. And the solicitor brings in these scoundrels to slander the reputation of a peace officer who has spent better than a decade bringing law and order. . . ."

The gavel cut him off. "Save that for your closing argument, sir," Judge Parker said.

He had testified more times than he could count. He couldn't even remember the last time he had appeared before Judge Parker

— not counting the case against the drunken juror, A.J. Boyd. Yet he couldn't remember ever being this damned nervous.

Of course, his life hadn't been on the line in all those other cases.

"Deputy Reeves," William Clayton said, "what happened on the evening William Leach was shot and killed?"

"I was workin' on my Winchester, tryin' to get a cartridge out of it."

"Could you explain that, sir?"

"Yes, sir. I'd accidentally put in a Forty-Five shell. I carry a Forty-Five Colt revolver. Put one of my revolver shells in my rifle. Too big for my Forty-Four Winchester. I had the rifle on my lap, tryin' to pry out that Forty-Five. I was reachin', and, well, sir, I just don't know. Either my knife or my hand struck the trigger, and the rifle went off, and the next thing I hear is someone screamin' . . . 'Lordy, you have hit Leach.'"

"What did you do then?"

"I threw down the rifle, and I ordered one of my prisoners to help me tend to Leach. I took out my handkerchief, soused it in a water bucket, put it on Leach's neck."

"Did you intend to shoot him?"

"No, sir." Bass's voice cracked. He felt tears in his eyes. Not for himself. But for William Leach. For years, he had tried to

151

block that image from his mind. Tried. But he couldn't forget. He'd never forget that night.

"Leach was the only help I had on that trip. I had five prisoners, and, in that country, you can't hardly trust yourself. So I definitely didn't shoot Leach on purpose."

"We've heard testimony about a dog," Clayton said softly.

"It was just some Indian dog, runnin' around. I told Leach . . . 'You'd better kill that dog.' I just said it."

"Did you speak to Leach after you had accidentally shot him?"

"Yes, sir." Tears ran down his cheeks. "I told him I was sorry. Said the rifle had just gone off accidentally."

"What did Leach say?"

"He says . . . 'I know, Bass. I know.' "

The Regulator clock chimed seven times that evening as Judge Parker asked the jury if a verdict had been reached.

"We have, Your Honor."

"What say you?"

The foreman, Edward Hunt, took a deep breath, and slowly exhaled. Bass Reeves held his breath.

"We the jury find the defendant not guilty as charged in the written indictment."

152

Someone slapped his back. Bass turned, still stunned, could hardly see. Not a damned thing. Tears practically blinded him. Cheers. Boos. Judge Parker's gavel. His heart slamming against his ribs. His ragged breath.

"Marshal Reeves! Marshal Reeves!"

He turned, made out Judge Parker standing. The judge might have been smiling. "Sir," Parker said over the din. "Before you leave this courthouse, please see me in my chambers. I have something of yours to return to you, sir. Your badge, Marshal. Your badge."

Chapter Twelve

June 12, 1902

"Folks still think that you shot it out with that cook over a dog," I told Bass as we rode toward Vinita. "And not just anybody. Chris Madsen was telling a bunch of lawmen the story, like it was gospel, last time I saw him over in Guthrie."

Madsen had fought in Cuba during the late Spanish-American War, a short, stocky Dane, and maybe one of the best federal peace officers working the Oklahoma Territory. If he believed the legend, well, I guess Bass put it best when he told me: "Can't help what folks believe. They believe what they wants to. Newspapers back then believed me guilty. Hell, so did Fair, the commissioner, Marshal Carroll, that idiot juryman, just about everybody in Fort Smith, Van Buren, and the Territory."

"But not Judge Parker," I said.

A slight smile creased his face, but

just briefly.

"No," he said, "not Judge Parker. And a few marshals. No more than a few. They knowed the truth, stuck by my side, more or less. Well, anyhow, they didn't seem to hold nothin' against me when I started ridin' for the court again."

I nodded. "I'm glad you told me what happened. The truth. And everything worked out for you. At least you were free."

He let out a mirthless chuckle. "Free? I don't know how free I was, Dave. Six months locked up in that dungeon with men I'd arrested, men who'd sworn to kill me. Then more'n a year waitin' for my day in court, my chance to clear my name." Bass turned, looked at me with cold eyes. "You're a white man, Dave. You think a judge and grand jury would have believed a lie told by a man I had arrested, a no-account who'd been convicted at least twice before, and his hard-rock wife? You think they'd have believed 'em enough to have arrested *you,* and locked you up in that hell on the border?"

I didn't answer, and Bass looked away. I didn't have to answer. We both knew the truth.

Bass grunted. "Didn't mean to take it out

155

on you, Dave. You're a man to ride the river with."

"So are you, Bass."

Silence. Then, after about three or four minutes, Bass spoke again. "My lawyers wasn't doin' their work *gratis*. That's why I pushed myself so hard, always ridin' out on a scout for outlaws."

No surprise there. While he was working out of Fort Smith, he had made probably more arrests than any other marshal. Back then, a deputy would draw about $500 a year in salary, but he'd get other money, too — expenses and rewards — although the U.S. marshal took a quarter of any deputy's earnings. Bass hadn't slowed down one whit after he was transferred to the court in Paris, Texas. Even in Muskogee, after he was into his sixties, he still rode hard, and often.

"Had to sell our home," Bass said. "Any money I had managed to save went to Mister Clayton and them other lawyers. Moved in with Mama for a couple of years, then somehow managed to buy a little home on Twelfth Street. Wasn't much of a home. . . ." His voice trailed off, and he stared down the trail for the longest time.

The hoofs of our horses clopped. A blue jay cried.

Finally Bass spoke again, but I'm not altogether sure he was talking to me.

"Reckon I never made it much of a home, gone like I was."

Bass hadn't killed Erskine Jones the previous night like George Littledave had suggested he might. Fact was, he didn't even say a word to the cook, just tended to his horse, and spent the night without talking much. By the following morning, he seemed to be his old self again; no longer rushing toward Vinita, but working as he usually did, methodically, cautious but determined.

By midmorning, however, as we rode along, he brought up William Leach, and told me the story as I have just related.

"Bass."

We both turned in our saddles to look back at Grant Johnson, riding a few rods behind us alongside George Littledave. Behind them came Erskine Jones in the tumbleweed wagon, with the two other Cherokee posse men bringing up the rear.

Johnson pointed off toward the northeast, and we followed his gaze, reining up at the sight.

Buzzards circled above the tree line.

"How far you make them?" I asked.

Grant eased his horse alongside ours,

while George Littledave stayed behind, and the others stopped just behind him.

"Right close," Bass said. "Couple of miles." He looked to his left, and got a nod of confirmation from Grant Johnson.

"Likely just a dead skunk or cow," I ventured.

Bass nodded. "Likely."

Saddle leather squeaked. "Y'all stay put," he told George Littledave. "Rest your horses for twenty minutes or so, then come and find us." He gestured at the buzzards.

"If we hear shootin'," Erskine Jones said, "we'll come a lot quicker."

Bass shot the Choctaw a withering glare, like he was remembering something from away back when. His face changed, and he said softly, more to the rest of us than to Erskine Jones: "You won't hear no shootin'." Bass kicked his horse into a plodding walk.

A mile up, the trail forked, and we veered to the right onto a woods road. Hemmed in by the forests, we rode in single file, keeping a good distance between us. I had unsheathed the Winchester, and, when I heard a horse whinny, I reined up. Bass, riding point, did the same, and eased from the saddle, thumbing back the hammer on his big rifle.

We walked our horses about a hundred

yards before Bass motioned Grant and me to hurry up toward him. When we stood together, Bass handed me the reins to his sorrel.

"You stay here, Dave," he said. "Me and Grant'll mosey up yonder, see what's goin' on."

Didn't like the notion of playing horse-tender, but my head bobbed in consent, and I took the reins to Grant Johnson's mount, too, watching the two black lawmen hustle down the trail in a crouch, then leap into the darkening woods.

I listened for the sound of twigs snapping, but heard only the breathing of the three horses I held, the swishing of their tails.

Sweat dripped over the bridge of my nose, soaked my shirt, and there was no breeze in that humid perdition. After what seemed like an hour, but in reality had been only ten minutes, a voice called: "Dave, come ahead!"

I swung onto Dutchy and, pulling the two mounts behind me, loped down the path.

In a clearing off to the left, I found Grant and Bass, and what had attracted those carrion flying overhead. To my surprise, I also discovered Paden Tolbert and Uncle Bud Ledbetter. That wasn't overly shocking, I suppose, for where you found Ledbetter, you often found Tolbert.

They had served as federal lawmen. Tolbert still wore a deputy marshal's badge, based in Vinita, and Ledbetter had also until he had been hired as Vinita's city marshal.

Tolbert was a young man, probably still in his thirties, whose Georgia roots were easily detected once he opened his mouth. His drawl might have been as thick as his gut, but he had an education. I had heard that before pinning on a badge, he had taught school after his family had settled in Arkansas. He was stout, with a round face and dark mustache. With a cough like a lunger and having to stop often to catch his breath, he sure didn't look like a Indian Territory lawman. That said, he was one of the bravest men who rode for Doc Bennett.

Paden Tolbert had led the posse, along with Cap White, that finally had tracked down and killed Ned Christie back in '92. Tolbert had ridden up to Kansas, and brought back the Army cannon the posse had used to try to blast Christie out of his cabin in the Going Snake District. When that had failed, Tolbert had dynamited Christie's Rabbit Trap fortress himself. It had been Deputy Marshal Tolbert — and not the Pinkerton detectives as the railroad claimed — who had thwarted Texas Jack

Reed's attempted robbery of an American Express Company car, and it had been Paden Tolbert who had captured the Jennings gang in the summer of '97.

Bud Ledbetter had been with him on all three of those deals.

Everybody called him Uncle Bud, but I doubt if James Franklin Ledbetter was older than either Bass or me. Maybe fifty, he was Arkansas-born and had first come to the Territory when he was just eighteen, working as a Wells, Fargo guard for a couple of years. After that, he got hitched, tried farming, but he just wasn't cut out to work a plow. Eventually he had been appointed marshal of Coal Hill, Arkansas, then took a job as a sheriff's deputy.

Around 1894, he had moved his family back to Indian Territory, and was hired by the American Railway Express to guard the Katy's run to Checotah. That's what he was doing when the Cook boys tried to rob the Flyer near Muskogee. There was only one guard — Uncle Bud — and I don't know how many bandits, although there were definitely fewer members of the Cook gang when those outlaws skedaddled.

Within a year, he was working as a deputy U.S. marshal, first out of the Fort Smith court, and later out of Paris, Texas, and finally Muskogee. Often, he would ride with Paden Tolbert.

I liked Bud Ledbetter great deal. Enjoyed his company, whether we were on a posse together or just grabbing a cup of coffee and some hot cakes at some Indian Territory café. I can't say the same, however, about Paden Tolbert. Oh, Tolbert was nice enough around me, distant maybe, but a good man to have with you in a fight. Yet I was a white man. Bass Reeves and Grant Johnson were black, and I had always sensed a great deal of friction between Tolbert and Doc Bennett's colored marshals.

"Hello, Dave," Uncle Bud greeted, taking the reins to Grant's and Bass's horses.

I slid the Winchester into the scabbard, and dismounted, taking in the scene before me.

The blackened remnants of a covered wagon stood at the edge of the woods, the bark on the closest trees scorched by flames. Leaves had been turned brown from the heat of the fire, like some blight had stricken this part of an otherwise verdant forest. Flour carpeted much of the terrain like snow, although by now the white meal had been scattered by boots and hoofs, the wind, and wild animals.

After hobbling my horse, I knelt beside a

three-bushel barrel on its side, and looked inside. Roughly half of the flour remained, and I reached inside, digging deeper through the rough meal.

"There's no whiskey left, Dave," Uncle Bud told me. "Whoever did this knew what they were after."

I rose, fished a handkerchief from my pocket, and wiped the flour off my hands.

Whiskey runners often hid their contraband in flour barrels. Sometimes the barrel would have a false bottom, the top half loaded with wheat or rye flour or cornmeal, and the bottom full of Taos Lightning. Other times, the runners would simply put a few bottles or kegs in the barrels, hiding the whiskey underneath all that meal, which would also serve as a cushion on the territory's rough roads.

I found another busted barrel a few rods away, piles of flour spilling from the broken ribs. Bits of glass lay beside a rock, and I walked over and placed a finger on the largest shard, but found it dry. The whiskey had evaporated. Figures. When I touched the charred tongue, it wasn't even warm.

"How long ago?" I asked.

Uncle Bud shrugged. "A day or so."

"No other wagon tracks," I noted. There was no telling how much whiskey these runners had been packing, but I didn't think this crew had been ambushed by some rivals, nor by any well-meaning temperance leaders in the Cherokee Nation.

I found only the tracks of shod and unshod horses, and my gut told me that Cherokee Bob Dozier had done this. He had waylaid the runners, stolen their whiskey — at least enough of it to get him and his men roostered — and had taken the team of mules or horses or whatever had been hitched to the wagon. He was responsible for something else, too.

"Dave," Uncle Bud said, "you mind looking at the bodies? Just on the off chance you might be able to identify them, though, well . . . hell. . . ."

I had glanced at Paden Tolbert and Bass when I had first ridden into the clearing, but hadn't paid much attention to either, my mind preoccupied on the burned wagon and busted flour barrels. Now I looked across the camp, and found Deputy Marshal Tolbert pushing a shovel deep into the earth, heard him grunt, saw him work the tool free, and toss a load of dirt onto a small pile.

A few yards away, Bass Reeves stood, staring at something on top of the blackened earth, wringing a hat in both hands. It wasn't Bass's hat. His wide-brimmed black Stetson still topped his head. It was a gray slouch hat, one of those cheap numbers you could buy for 50¢ out of a Sears, Roebuck, and Company catalog.

The same kind of hat Bennie Reeves had last been seen wearing.

CHAPTER THIRTEEN

June 12–14, 1902

"It ain't Bennie," Bass said softly.

No, it wasn't. Neither of them was.

"But he was here." Those words came out of Bass's mouth like a weary sigh.

Bile rising in my throat, I stared at the charred corpses, their hands and feet staked to the ground, as I stood beside Bass. You have to understand that I'd been working as a federal lawman in Indian Territory for thirteen years, and I'd seen a lot.

A lot I'd care to forget, but never could.

Murdered men and women, shot, stabbed, pummeled with fists, two even beheaded with an axe. Men who had been hit by a shotgun blast at close range. A cowhand who had been roped, then dragged to death over rough country a good two miles. I had fished bloated corpses out of rivers, ponds, and cisterns, and had buried the victims of trains that had been derailed on purpose.

166

Anything a person could somehow do to his fellow man, I had seen it all. At least, I thought I had.

"Lord preserve us." Kneeling, I brought out my handkerchief again, placing it over my mouth and nose, savoring that scent of dirt and flour, somehow managing to swallow down the gall, the disgust.

Cherokee Bob Dozier hadn't used that whiskey to get drunk. At least not the bulk of it. Next to the corpses, a mound of broken glass lay beside a chunk of granite. The fiend who had done this must have poured the rotgut over the bodies, then smashed the empty bottles against the rock. From the amount of glass, the clothes of the two men had to have been thoroughly soaked with liquor.

I pictured Cherokee Bob standing where I knelt, laughing, a whiskey bottle in his left hand. Imagined him taking a swig or two, then splashing the last of the lightning on one or both of the bodies. Busting the glass against the rock. Striking a match against the butt of one of his revolvers. Taking a step back, then flicking the match toward the staked men. I could see, and feel, the roar of the flames. The ground had been wet from recent rains, or else this entire forest could have been left in ash.

167

A blue jay cried out from the forest, but, to me, it sounded like Cherokee Bob Dozier's maniacal cackles.

I fetched my notebook out of my pocket, began jotting descriptions of the two dead men, the scene, things like that.

"This one . . ." — I pointed my pencil at the man on the right — "he was likely dead before they set his body afire."

"Uhn-huh." Bass spit. "But the other one wasn't."

"No," I said, and forced myself to examine the other body. His burned skin peeled back to show that open mouth, his teeth locked in some horrible scream.

Somehow he had managed to free one of his arms from the stake. His body was twisted, a burned arm across his chest. Probably he had been trying to beat out the flames on his face and chest when he had died.

What had Bennie Reeves been thinking as he watched this carnage unfold? Had he been scared? Appalled? Or had he taken a part in such a heinous crime?

Behind me, Uncle Bud Ledbetter cleared his throat. "I been a lawman too damned long," he said.

Uncle Bud's voice brought my focus back to the bodies. So had I.

"What do you think, Dave?"

I looked at the faces. Shaking my head, I returned pencil and pad to my pocket. "I can't say I know them," I said. "But I can't say I don't, either. Nothing about them, though, brings anyone to mind." I raised my eyes. "You find anything in the wagon?"

"Nothin'."

Paden Tolbert came to us, dragging the shovel. "I'm a lawman," he said. "Not a damned gravedigger. That's slave's work."

Silently I sucked in a lungful of air, watching Bass, who pretended he hadn't heard.

"Well," Tolbert said impatiently, "let's get them bodies planted, and then get after the vermin who did this."

Bass tossed the hat he was holding into the woods behind him, and we carried the deceased to the shallow grave they would share for eternity. Or until, on the off chance, someone would claim the bodies, and have them re-interred in some family plot. As Uncle Bud quoted a little Scripture, we bowed our heads, hats in hands.

"How'd you come find the bodies?" Bass asked.

"Fella deliverin' supplies to that oil well in Chelsea found 'em," Paden Tolbert answered. "He made a beeline to Vinita."

Uncle Bud tossed dirt over the grave, and

handed me the shovel. "Paden came by my office, deputized me, and we lit a shuck down here."

"Those murders are in my district, Bass," Tolbert said.

I stopped shoveling.

"You want to lead this posse, Tolbert," Bass said, "that's fine with me."

"Actually," Uncle Bud put in, "Bass here is senior to all of us. He should. . . ."

"I don't mind," Bass interrupted. "Let Tolbert run this deal."

Sweat trickled down my neck. Of course, I had been sweating most of the day, but only now did I really feel it. Tension hung in the clearing like the thick, humid air.

Tolbert coughed, sucked up mucous from his throat, and spat into the grave.

"We're after Cherokee Bob, Tolbert," Grant Johnson said. "Likely we'll need every gun amongst us."

"And we got the tumbleweed wagon and three Cherokees in our posse," I said. "Don't know what's keeping them, but they should be here directly."

Tolbert kept his eyes on Bass. "You said Dozier robbed the Katy?"

Bass nodded. "Just north of Eufaula."

"That's Johnson's territory."

Now, I understood. Tolbert was fishing.

170

Trying to figure out why two top peace officers had taken the trail of a train robber. Cherokee Bob Dozier certainly didn't have enough of a reputation to warrant that much firepower. I guess that's how Paden Tolbert saw it. Dozier wasn't Ned Christie, Texas Jack Reed, or the Jennings gang.

"I tol' Marshal Bennett that I'd try to fetch you," Grant Johnson told Tolbert, without explaining the presence of Bass and me. "Said I'd do just that if I didn't catch up to Cherokee Bob before I reached Vinita." He gave Uncle Bud a friendly smile. "Tol' the marshal that we'd even deputize you if your duties as town marshal wasn't too pressin'."

"They weren't," Uncle Bud said easily. Then, his tone hardening, to Tolbert: "Come on, Paden. Like you said, those killers got enough of a head start as it stands already. No sense squabbling over picayune matters about who's leading who!"

Tolbert wasn't budging, though. "Did the Katy put up a reward for Cherokee Bob?"

Bass shook his head in disgust at Paden Tolbert's mercenary streak. "I reckon. Don't know how much. Grant and me didn't wait to find out."

"Listen, Tolbert." Grant's voice rose in anger, a tone I rarely heard from him.

"Cherokee Bob killed one, maybe two, men on the Katy. Then he bushwhacked my posse on the Illinois River ferry. He give me this." He lifted his arm to show him the bandage wrapped around his wrist. "And he killed the driver of my prison wagon, Gringo Gomez. Uncle Bud's right. We need to finish this buryin' and start ridin'."

"Gomez knew the chance he was takin'," Tolbert said. "He ain't the first posse man killed in the Territory. Same with them men workin' for the Katy. But these two men here . . ." — he gestured at the grave — "these was citizens in my district, and he had no call to do what he done."

No one saw my eyes roll. Citizens? They had been running whiskey.

"I want the reward for Dozier," Tolbert announced.

There. It was finally out.

"Take it," Bass said. No argument from him. I hadn't expected one. Bass wasn't hunting Cherokee Bob Dozier.

A wry smile creased Tolbert's face. His head bobbed, and he stepped toward Bass, offering his hand. "Shake on it?" he asked.

I gripped the shovel, brought it up, thinking that I might have to slam the spade into the back of Paden Tolbert's head. Bass stared at that gloved hand like it was the

172

most offensive thing he'd ever seen. Tolbert's malicious offer repulsed me, because he knew Bass's policy. Every lawman working for Doc Bennett knew that Bass never took anyone's hand.

"I told you." Frost tinted Bass's words.

"His word's good enough for me," said Uncle Bud, ever the peacemaker. "Let's finish this burying, and get after Cherokee Bob."

Yet Tolbert wasn't finished.

"I've offered my hand," he said. "And if he's so damned uppity. . . ."

"Paden," Uncle Bud said, "you know Bass don't shake nobody's hand. Not even Judge Parker's or Doc Bennett's. Not even a preacher's."

"That's because he arrested his own preacher," Grant Johnson said.

I laughed. Just like that, the tension seemed removed, and Uncle Bud slapped his knee. Slowly Paden Tolbert lowered his hand, and hooked his thumbs in his gun belt.

"Grant ain't fooling," Uncle Bud said. "Bass did arrest his preacher. I heard tell of it."

The story was gospel. Back in November, Bass had arrested a colored preacher named Wilson Hobson, who was charged with selling liquor. In fact, the Reverend Hobson was selling intoxicating spirits to members of his congregation to raise money to help pay off a church debt. Members of the church didn't see anything wrong with that. Bass, however, did. Selling whiskey was against the law, so he went to the church, and brought the minister out in handcuffs. The good reverend was placed under a $500 bond. What made the story even more incredible was the fact that it had been the Reverend Wilson Hobson who had baptized Bass Reeves about three years earlier.

Trace chains jingled down the trail. George Littledave and the rest of our posse had arrived.

We finished covering the bodies with sod, and followed the woods road.

A series of thunderstorms hit over the next couple of days, harsh, violent affairs that slowed our progress, and often stopped us altogether. Lightning streaked across the skies that darkened noon into midnight, and often those bolts struck downward, too close for comfort. A few times, we would relieve our bodies of anything metal — revolvers, Winchesters, shell belts, spurs, even our badges — loading them in the back of Erskine Jones's wagon.

"Fine, fine," the Choctaw would grumble. "If all this hardware don't attract a bolt that'll turn ol' Erskine Jones into fried chicken, I'll charge ever' damned one of you a toll for haulin' your things."

We donned our fish skins, buttoning the red wool collar in a vain attempt to stay reasonably dry. The buttons on those camel-colored slickers, of course, were metal. I wondered if it would be my luck that the button on my fish skin would attract the lightning bolt that turned me, and not Erskine Jones, into fried chicken.

God smiled on us, though. Lightning struck trees and the granite boulders around us, but never even singed us, although it played hell on our nerves. Most of our nerves, I should correct myself.

Bass Reeves rode ahead, oblivious to the torrent around us.

Pushing northwest, we found the country growing tougher, the forests thicker, the granite hills steeper. Rain turned the roads into quagmire. At least three times, we had to stop to fell trees and corduroy the path in order to get the tumbleweed wagon across.

Luckily we had crossed the Verdigris before the clouds burst, fording the river a few miles below Vinita. We had ridden east a spell, then turned north, east of the Grand River.

Paden Tolbert led the posse, but only in theory. Rain had washed out any trail, but all of us knew where we were going: Robbers' Roost.

On the evening of the Fourteenth, the storms seemed to be moving past us and on to the southeast. A steady, cold drizzle fell, but the wind had stopped roaring, and the skies were beginning to lighten. I could even spot rays of the setting sun breaking free of the clouds. We had made camp near a natural amphitheater that provided some shelter, enough, at least, for Erskine Jones to heat up some of his bitter chicory and warm up beans. We filed past the cook fire like soaked, worn-out waddies on a cattle drive, with Erskine Jones filling our mugs with steaming black goo, and ladling beans on our plates.

"You expectin' an ambush here, Bass?" Paden Tolbert asked with a sardonic snicker.

I had just taken my supper, and turned. Paden Tolbert stood behind Bass, watching the big Negro marshal collect his chow. He had a plate of beans in his left hand, and cup of coffee in his right. His hands were full, but his slicker, now unbuttoned, had been pushed behind the butt of his holstered Colt.

Ignoring the comment, Bass walked toward me.

"I guess your hands are too full to shake my hand now, eh, Bass?" Tolbert shook his head, and held the empty plate for Erskine Jones to fill.

"Why don't you lay off?" Uncle Bud spoke sharply.

"You mind your own affair, Ledbetter. I don't care who Bass Reeves thinks he is, he don't have to act like he's better than me, better than you, better than the late Judge Parker. I killed Ned Christie, by God. Who the hell did Bass Reeves ever kill? Nothin' but niggers and Indians." He came to us, standing. Bass had slid down the rocky wall beside me, and was sipping his coffee with his left hand, his plate on his lap.

"Tell me, Bass." Paden Tolbert was like a festering sore. "You never faced anyone like Ned Christie. Ain't that right?"

Without looking up, Bass said, "Hell, Tolbert, Ned Christie killed me."

With a grin, I remembered. Back in '91, the Van Buren *Press* had reported that Bass Reeves had been killed by Ned Christie in the Flint District. Reports of Bass's death at the hands of the Cherokee outlaw were published as far away as Dallas.

Tolbert started to say something else, but George Littledave spoke up.

"I would not be proud of having killed Ned Christie. Killing him was a shameful, disgraceful act."

Tolbert whirled. "What the hell do you know about it?"

"Enough. He was Keetoowah. A true Cherokee. The Creator gave our people the name Kituwah. It is the rightful name of the Cherokee. Ned Christie fought against the railroads. He was no outlaw. He was a hero to many of us."

Seeing Tolbert's neck and ears turning crimson, I set my plate and coffee aside, wishing I had a spade handy. It looked like I'd have to stop another fight.

"And how many deputies did it take for you to kill Ned Christie, Marshal Tolbert?" Littledave went on. "Using a cannon from Coffeyville? And dynamite? Against one man? How many?"

"Sixteen," Uncle Bud answered. "Too damned many."

Tolbert's wrath turned on the white lawman. "You weren't so damned offended by what we was doin' back then."

"Just doing my job, Paden. Sometimes my job stinks. Like you do now."

Paden's plate and cup fell to the mud. He

reached for a revolver.

"Leave it be, Tolbert," Bass said to the lawman's back. I was stepping up, my hand on the butt of the revolver. "And you sit down, Dave."

I obeyed.

"Littledave, I don't know if Christie was a good man or a bad one, and it don't rightly matter," Bass said. "He's dead, but killed a lot of good lawmen before he was planted, and 'em lawmen was just doin' their job. What I do know is this . . . iffen we start fightin' amongst ourselves like we been doin', we won't need to worry none 'bout Cherokee Bob. So let's just shut up. We ain't far from his country. And it'll be just as hard catchin' Cherokee Bob as it was killin' Ned Christie. You want a go at fisticuffs, Tolbert, that's fine. I'll accommodate you. But after we bring in Ben . . . bring in Dozier."

It was the most I'd ever heard Bass Reeves say in one sitting to a group of lawmen.

Announcing that he would check on the horses, Tolbert stormed into the brush. George Littledave muttered something in Cherokee, and returned to his place beside Wes and Usdi. I picked up my coffee cup, just to do something to keep my hands from trembling so.

Bass shook his head, and muttered an

oath. "Maybe I should have shaken that bastard's hand. But he was proddin' me."

"Hell, Bass," I said, not really thinking, "we've never even shook hands."

He looked at me, but I couldn't tell what he was thinking. Bass didn't offer to shake my hand. I hadn't expected him to.

Lifting his fork, he resumed eating. Not speaking much. Eventually he finished his supper, and took his and my dishes to Erskine Jones's wreck pan. When he returned, he sat back down beside me, drew his Colt, emptied the shells, and began cleaning and oiling the piece. Then he worked on his rifle. At some point, he glanced up, not at me, but staring into the fire.

"I shaken one man's hand," he said softly. "Since I pinned on this badge."

CHAPTER FOURTEEN

1883

He went by the name Jim Webb, and most people said he hailed from Texas. Some claimed he had Mexican blood. Everybody who had ever met him knew they never wanted to tangle with him.

Sometime around 1882, Jim Webb drifted into the Chickasaw Nation. Tough country, and Jim Webb was as hard a rock as they made. Six-foot-one, two hundred pounds of muscle and scars, and those clear blue eyes of a Texas man-killer. Nobody had ever whipped him in a fistfight, and those who had tried to shoot him had been buried. Fast, deadly, with no room for compromise, and the fists to back up any argument. He knew cattle, too.

In short, Billy Washington couldn't have found a better man to ramrod his spread — and that was saying something because bull-headed Colonel William Edward "Billy"

Washington could outfight just about anyone in the Territory.

Washington had arrived in the Nations around 1880, and, along with his brother, Jerry, partnered with Dick McLish to claim a huge ranch that stretched from the Red River to the Arbuckle Mountains. McLish and Jerry Washington may have been partners, but Billy ran the show. He had a commissary on his ranch, even printed script that the local banks would take as sure as they'd accept gold. The outfit ran between ten thousand and twelve thousand cattle, and any cowhand hired to ride for the I.S.-Reverse brand had to know how to use a gun, and not be afraid to use it. In later years, Uncle Billy fled the Nations for New Mexico Territory, I hear, after killing a fellow in a gunfight. But in 1883, he had Jim Webb do any killing that was needed.

So it was with the Reverend William Steward. When he wasn't riding the circuit and preaching the coming of the Lord, Steward ran a ranch himself, one that bordered the Washington-McLish empire.

In early spring of 1883, the Reverend Steward started a small grass fire. Steward didn't just read the Scripture, he was well-versed in all sorts of theories on improving grazing pastures. He didn't call himself a rancher, but a range manager. He didn't stock his ranch with longhorns, but Herefords. Webb and Washington were old school, raising Texas longhorns and doing it the way men had been ranching out West for generations. Steward also believed that if you burned your grass in the early spring, it would grow stronger, with more nutrients. You'd get a better return when you brought your cattle to market. Yet spring in the Nations can be unpredictable. After a warm winter, the spring stayed dry. The winds kicked up, as they are prone to do, and that little fire suddenly ballooned into a raging inferno.

The fire spread to the Washington-McLish range.

That's all it took.

Jim Webb, face blackened with soot, his hair singed from fighting the flames with his cowhands, galloped over to the Steward Ranch, where he found the preacher and his cowhands beating back the fire with wet grain sacks. Maybe Webb didn't ride over there to kill him, but the two men soon began arguing, the reverend raising his fist, telling Webb to get off his property, that if Billy Washington wanted to hold him accountable, fine.

"Don't get bricketty with me, Webb. You

send Uncle Billy over here, and we'll talk," Steward snapped. "But after . . . *after* . . . we get this fire under control! I don't have the time or inclination right now to be bandying words with a butt-ender like you."

I probably should mention that the Reverend William Steward was a man of color. Hailing from Texas, Jim Webb wasn't one to take such talk from a Negro. He pulled his revolver, and put two bullets into Steward's chest, and left him lying on the smoking, blackened prairie.

About a half dozen of Steward's waddies had witnessed the murder, and roughly half of the men who rode for the I.S.-Reverse were colored. They weren't ones to stand by and let a black man of God be murdered and see his white killer ride off as if he had just killed a coyote. Word reached Fort Smith, and the U.S. commissioner issued a writ for Jim Webb's arrest.

"I hope Judge Parker sends the best man he's got," Webb said over a whiskey when he learned of the warrant. "Because I ain't never gonna spend a day in that Arkansas shit hole."

Bass Reeves took the warrant, and lit out from Fort Smith with a white deputy named Floyd Wilson. No tumbleweed wagon on this trip. Bass knew that bringing in Webb would be a ticklish affair. His horse and saddle would pass. A cowboy appreciated a good mount, and wanted to see a fine, clean saddle. Bass changed his boots for scuffed brown ones, and donned a pair of big-rowel spurs, threw on a pair of battered, grease-stained leggings, and traded his big black Stetson for a wide-brimmed slouch hat with a few holes for ventilation and a rip in the brim so that the front blew flat against the crown whenever he faced the wind. His badge he slipped inside his vest pocket, tied a threadbare silk bandana around his neck, and ripped the pocket off the front of his boiled shirt. He looked like any black cowhand riding the Nations. Floyd Wilson dressed like an itinerant waddie, too.

Around 8:00 A.M., they rode into the Washington-McLish headquarters. Most of the cowhands would have ridden out at first light, and the place looked deserted. A horse snorted in the corral, a dog barked, and a door squeaked as it opened.

For a ranch of its size, the buildings were humble. A dogtrot cabin served as bunk-house and chuck house, connected by the breezeway, and spurs sang out a tune as a white man stepped out of the chuck house and onto the warped porch. The man stuck a cigarette in his mouth, lighted it, then shook out the match and tossed it to the ground. When the smoke was in his lips, he calmly drew his revolver, leaving the long-barreled Colt hanging at his side. Cocked.

He was a big man, dark-haired, sporting a handlebar mustache and two or three days of thick beard stubble. Duck trousers were tucked inside his black boots, which featured white stars inlaid in the tops. A wide-brimmed, high-crowned hat, beaten beyond recognition, topped his head.

"That's him," Floyd Wilson whispered.

"I'd like to take him alive," Bass said. "Let's just do it the way we planned. Iffen we can."

Another man stepped over the threshold, and moved to Webb's side, cursing at the dog to shut up as he pulled a Schofield from his holster, keeping the revolver at his side, but ready.

Bass and Floyd reined up in front of the chuck house.

"What do you want?" Webb spoke with the cigarette hanging on his lips.

"Lookin' for work," Bass said easily.

Webb's cold eyes locked on his. "We're full up."

Bass sighed, but grinned. "Then I reckon we's ridin' the grubline." He had thickened his accent. "Reckon your cook could fix us some breakfast?"

Neither man looked away from the two riders, but Webb removed the smoke with his left hand, and hollered into the open door: "Hey, Monty! Got a couple of grubline riders here. Feel like feedin' 'em?"

An unintelligible reply came from somewhere inside.

Webb nodded at the door. "Step in, gents." The two men waited, still holding their guns, while Bass and Wilson dismounted, wrapped their reins around the hitching rail, and stepped into the chuck house.

The cook, wearing a filthy apron and a pepperbox pistol in a shoulder holster, dropped an armful of firewood in a box near a stove. "There's coffee," he said with a nod. "Help yourselves. I'll fix some bacon and warm up the biscuits."

"Mighty fine, sir," Bass said eagerly, his head bobbing like a man who hadn't eaten in a week. "Sounds mighty fine."

Webb pointed the Colt's long barrel at a bench. "Have a seat."

Bass removed his hat, tossed it on the table, and turned toward his hosts. "Iffen it's all right with you, sir, I's likes to tend to our hosses first. And I'd be plumb happy to chops any wood or do anything you needs

done 'round here . . . to pays for our breakfast."

"No need for that," Webb said. "But you
can feed and water your horses."

With a friendly nod, Bass stepped outside.
Wilson moved to the coffee pot. The man
with the Schofield stayed inside, but Jim
Webb followed Bass onto the porch. He
flicked his cigarette onto the planks, ground
it out with the toe of his boot. His cold eyes
never left Bass. His right hand never relaxed
on that Colt.

After loosening the saddle girths, Bass led
both horses to a pump, and worked the
handle to fill a tub with water. While the
horses slaked their thirst, he scooped grain
out of one of the saddlebags and into two
nose bags. When the horses had finished
drinking, he fed them.

Next, he easily drew the Winchester from
its scabbard, watching Webb raise his own
pistol, tense. The man didn't lower his
weapon until Bass nonchalantly leaned the
rifle against a corn crib, and headed back
toward to the cabin.

"Come and get this slop!" the cook yelled,
and Bass widened his grin, and hurried onto
the porch. Webb stepped away, out of Bass's
reach. Playing it safe.

Bass found his place beside Wilson, and

lifted a mug of coffee. Webb and his partner hung by the open door. The cook was nowhere to be found.

"What do you think?" Wilson whispered.

"They suspicion us," Bass said over the steaming cup. "That's certain sure." He spread bacon grease over the biscuit.

"When you boys got your bellies full," Webb said, "step outside for a moment. Have a seat. Smith and me'd like a word with you two. Might have a job for y'all after all."

Both lawmen turned, nodding at the cowhands.

"That'd be mighty fine, sir," Bass said, smiling. "Mighty fine." He turned back to the table and bit into a biscuit.

"They'll kill us," Wilson said, picking up a piece of bacon, staring ahead. "They know we're the law."

"Just wait for my signal," Bass whispered.

The food tasted mighty good.

Breakfast finished, they stepped outside. Smith, the one still holding the Schofield, led the way — then Bass — then Wilson. Jim Webb followed last, closing the door behind him. He pointed to a bench leaning against the chuck house, and Bass sat down, stretching out his legs. Webb stepped in front of him, putting his left hand against a wooden column. Smith steered Wilson to another bench in front of the bunkhouse, and the deputy took this seat.

"Judge Parker send you?" Webb asked.

Bass laughed, and slapped his thigh. "That's a good one, boss. No, sir. I ain't never mets the Hangin' Judge. Mighty glad of that."

"You know who I am, don't you, boy?"

"No, sir. Floyd and me, sir, we was just tol' that Uncle Billy runs a good operation, always needin' cowhands."

"You're a deputy marshal, ain't you, boy?"

Bass shook his head, still grinning. "Nah. You's joshin' me, boss. I ain't never heards of no colored lawdog."

"I have. Named Bass Reeves."

The smile faded, but Bass shook his head. "Don't knows him, but Floyd and me's new to this country. You ain't funnin' me, boss? You mean to tell me they's a nigger lawman ridin' for that Hangin' Judge over in Fort Smith?"

"That's the name I'll carve on your tombstone, boy."

A violent oath exploded from inside the chuck house, and the door flung open. "You damned grubliners!" The cook appeared, roaring with anger. "You sons-of-bitches don't leave your dirty dishes for me . . . !"

Webb had stepped back, turned, staring at the cook. The killer's attention had lapsed for only a second, but that's all Bass Reeves needed. He vaulted from the bench, drawing the Colt with his right hand in one swift, deft motion, latching his left around Jim Webb's throat. Webb tried to bring up his Colt, but Bass slammed the barrel under the foreman's nose.

"Drop it!" he snapped.

Somehow, Webb managed to say — "I . . . give . . . up. . . ." — although his words came out more as a gurgle. His revolver clattered on the porch.

The dog barked, but stayed near the corral. The cook stepped back inside the cabin, cursing in astonishment, but not reaching for the pepperbox pistol. Bass had moved so quickly, striking like a rattler but without warning, that even Floyd Wilson looked too stunned to react.

Smith, on the other hand, turned, raising his pistol, snapping a quick shot. The bullet slammed into the column, barely missing Webb's head. Webb's cry came out as a strangle. Smith thumbed back the hammer, fired again. That bullet buzzed past Bass's ear. Without releasing his hold on Webb, Bass whirled, aimed — taking his time whereas Smith had rushed his shots. The cowhand had thumbed back the Schofield's hammer again when Bass Reeves fired.

"God!" Smith groaned. "I am killed." Gripping his stomach with both hands, he dropped to his knees, the Schofield tumbling onto the dirt.

Now running back and forth, the dog kept barking.

The cook's head reappeared, his face paling as he looked at the blood streaming out of Smith's gut.

Floyd Wilson recovered his senses, and shot out of the bench, side-stepping around the wounded Smith, drawing his revolver, and pointing it at the cook. "Drop that pistol, mister!" he barked.

The cook didn't seem to hear. He lifted his apron, looked at his britches. "Damnation," he muttered, "I've soilt me britches."

"Drop that pistol!" Wilson didn't wait. With his left hand, he snatched the pepperbox from the shoulder holster and sent it spinning toward the corral.

"Fetch my handcuffs, Floyd," Bass said, still holding Jim Webb's throat. He didn't release his grip until Floyd had locked the iron bracelets, securing Jim Webb to the chuck house's wooden column.

Methodically Bass ejected the empty casings and thumbed in another round before holstering his Colt. He stepped back, avoiding the pool of urine flowing toward a crack in the porch, and pulled the six-point badge from his vest pocket. Once he had pinned on the badge, he stared at Jim Webb.

The killer had slid to his knees on the dirt, sucking in deep breaths of air, his cuffed hands around the column reaching up as if begging for mercy.

"Jim Webb," Bass said.

Webb looked up.

"I arrest you for the murder of the Reverend William Steward," Bass announced, and pulled the writ from his rear trousers pocket, tossing it at the foreman's face. "I'm Bass Reeves."

Then he went to check on the man named Smith.

CHAPTER FIFTEEN

1884

Hat in hand, Bass entered the office of U.S. Marshal Thomas Boles, surprised to find Judge Parker sitting in the chair across from Boles's desk. Both men rose, and the marshal motioned Bass to the empty chair on Parker's left.

Bass liked Boles, an Arkansas native in his late forties and former Union cavalry officer who had been appointed marshal back in February of 1882. He had served a couple of terms in Congress, and rumors around Fort Smith and Van Buren said Boles would likely run for governor. Yet Boles had no airs about him. He had spent only one year in school; everything else, he had learned on his own.

After everyone was seated, Boles twisted one end of his mustache, and slid a warrant across his cluttered desk top. As Bass reached for the writ, Judge Parker spoke.

"Jim Webb's trial was to begin this morning. Only Mister Webb did not grace our court with his appearance."

After glancing at the warrant, Bass slipped the paper into his coat pocket.

More than a year had passed since Bass had brought Webb into custody. Frank Smith, the cowhand Bass had gut-shot, had died before they had reached Toshomingo, and he had been buried in a cemetery in the Chickasaw capital. Deputy Floyd Wilson and Bass had delivered Webb to the Fort Smith jail, where he had been bound over for a murder trial after a preliminary hearing before the U.S. commissioner. The man who had vowed he would not spend one day in that "shit hole" had, in fact, spent better than a year in Fort Smith's hell on the border before a couple of friends had posted a $17,000 bond. Webb had walked out of the dungeon, crossed the Arkansas River by ferry, and disappeared into the Nations.

"You brought him in the first time," Marshal Boles said. "Figured you'd like to bring him in again."

Bass ran his tongue over his lips. "What was the names of 'em pals of his who made his bail?"

Boles shook his head, but Judge Parker

answered: "Jim Bywater and some man named Smith, Chris Smith." The chair squeaked as Parker leaned forward, announcing firmly: "They won't get that money back."

"No, Your Honor. I don't reckon they will."

He didn't know any Chris Smith, but he had met the other. Jim Bywater ran a store near a spring on the Whiskey Trail in the southern Arbuckles — a good week's or ten days' ride from Fort Smith, and not far from the Texas border. If Webb had disappeared into Texas, he would be out of Bass's jurisdiction. Yet Jim Webb didn't strike Bass as the kind of man who'd run. Of course, after killing a preacher, he wouldn't show up for a murder trial to face George Maledon's noose. Nor, however, would he leave the Chickasaw Nation. He'd be in the Arbuckles — waiting.

"I have told Gringo Gomez to be ready with the prison wagon," Parker said, "and you can deputize as many men as you feel necessary. This man Webb foully murdered a Negro preacher, and, if convicted, he must pay for his crime."

Bass rose. "Just the same with you, Your Honor, I druther ride out without Gomez. And reckon I'd need just one man."

196

Parker considered this, but did not commit.

"We go ridin' down yonder with an army, Webb's pards will warn him, and we'll never flush him out," Bass explained. "That's mighty rough territory. Me and one deputy, that's all we need."

"You going undercover, Bass?" Marshal Boles asked.

He shook his head. "Not this time. Webb knows me. Ain't likely to forget." He was thinking: *And he ain't likely to let me bring him in alive . . . not this time.*

Parker gave a reluctant nod, and Boles said: "All right, Bass. But I'm sending Deputy Mershon to the Chickasaw Nation with a big posse, a prison wagon, and a passel of warrants. You and your man ride out with Mershon at first light. When you get near Toshomingo, you can go your own way, do the job as you figure best. But bring in Webb. Dead or alive."

John Cantrell, always willing to ride for any Fort Smith marshal, led the way on a dun mustang. Bass followed, Winchester across the pommel, the horses splashing through Honey Creek as they picked their way through oaks and red cedars. The summer air lay heavily in the forested hills. They followed no path, and leaned back in their saddles as they eased their horses down the slick limestone as the clear water cascaded better than seventy feet into a pool of water below.

"That's right pretty," Cantrell said.

Bass grunted something, paying scant attention to a rare waterfall.

As mountains, the Arbuckles didn't amount to much, rising maybe five hundred feet above the rolling plains. They were, however, quite formidable. Thick forests, rolling hills and deep arroyos, with occasional sandstone or granite formations, and enough caverns so that Jim Webb could hide out forever in these hills. Eventually, however, a man on the run — a man like Jim Webb — would need whiskey, and the only place to get that would be Jim Bywater's store.

For three days, they camped in the edge of the Arbuckles, spying on Bywater's cabin through a brass telescope Bass had purchased from a retired Army officer in Van Buren.

On the afternoon of the third day, Cantrell lowered the telescope. "Bass," he said, "a rider just came out of the hills west of us. Heading to the store."

Bass shoved two more cartridges into his

Winchester, and crept underneath the oak Cantrell was using as a backrest. He laid the rifle on the ground, and took the telescope. The horseman sat deeply in the saddle, his back to Bass and Cantrell. Long, greasy hair touched his collar. He wore a shell belt, and carried a repeater in his right hand. Jim Bywater came out of the store, waving slightly. The rider eased from his mount, and an Indian boy collected the reins, and led the weary horse to the corral, about a hundred yards from the store. Bywater shook the man's hand, and the two disappeared inside the log cabin.

"What do you think?" Cantrell asked.

"Big fella. Armed to his eyeteeth." Bass snapped the telescope shut. "Could be our man."

"How should we play our hand?"

Bass picked up his Winchester. "Webb knows me. So does Bywater. But they ain't never seen you before. You ride down yonder." Cantrell started to unpin his badge. "Uhn-uh. Keep that tin star on. Sun's likely to reflect off it. And if that's Webb, once he sees that badge, he'll start footin' it for his horse."

"If he don't shoot me out of the saddle."

Bass didn't respond. A man who pinned on a badge ought to expect to get shot at from time to time. Still, he didn't think Webb would risk a shot without knowing how many posse men might be with the deputy. Most likely Webb would make a dash for his horse. Had Bass ridden down there, it would have been a different story altogether.

They tightened their cinches, mounted, and rode until the trees ended. Rolling prairie, dotted by occasional scrub and rutted with arroyos, stretched out toward Bywater's place. Bass hung back in the thicket of the foothills on a big gray Andalusian stallion, watching John Cantrell ride his dun casually toward the cabin.

He didn't see Cantrell turn in the saddle, didn't see the deputy waving his hat over his head, signaling Bass to hurry. He didn't have to. Bass had spotted Jim Webb leap through an open window, rifle in his right hand, revolver in his left, and dash toward the corral.

The powerful-legged stallion exploded as Bass raked his spurs. Cantrell was yelling something, drawing his revolver, turning his horse after Webb.

Webb snapped a revolver shot.

Cantrell dropped his pistol, and grabbed the saddle horn, pulling leather as the dun bucked and spun.

Bass brought the reins to his mouth, clamped his teeth on the leather, lifted the Winchester, fired. Dust flew up a good ten yards in front of the running Webb. Bass jacked the lever.

As fast as his stallion galloped, Webb would never make it to the corral and mount his horse, not before Bass got there. Webb must have known that, too, because before Bass could fire again, Webb had angled off, away from the horse, heading for some brush.

Bass took the reins in his left hand, spat out the taste of dusty leather, brought the rifle to his shoulder with one hand. "Surrender, Webb!" he bellowed.

Webb slid to a stop, twisted around, dropped to his knee.

The Winchester barked. Still holding the reins, Bass levered another round into the rifle. About three hundred yards in front of him, Webb cut loose with a fusillade, firing as quickly as he could work the lever and squeeze the trigger. The first bullet tore off a chunk of Bass's saddle horn.

"Throw down your weapons!" Bass roared. Two hundred fifty yards now between them. Webb's shot clipped a button from his coat. Two hundred yards. "Give up, damn you!" One hundred fifty. A bullet cut both reins.

Dropping the dangling ends of the reins from his hand, Bass pulled the trigger, knowing he had missed, and dived from the saddle. He landed hard, rolled over, tasted blood in his mouth. Two fingers on his left hand felt jammed, maybe busted. His eyes stung from dirt. He coughed, pushed himself to his knees. The air smelled of cordite.

Through the dust, another shot roared. That bullet clipped the brim of Bass's hat. He thought: *How the hell did my hat stay on after that wreck?* "Don't make me kill you, Webb!" he shouted.

"You ain't takin' me in, Reeves!" Webb screamed. "I ain't goin' back to that hell hole!"

The cloud of dust had blown away. Bass could see Jim Webb standing, walking, coming at him, less than a hundred yards distant, shouting: "I ain't gonna hang, Reeves!" Smoke erupted from Webb's rifle. The bullet whined off a rock just a few feet in front of Bass. "Hangin' ain't no fittin' way to die!" He had stuck the Colt in his waistband. He levered another round into his rifle. "I'm gonna kill you, Reeves!"

Bass pulled the trigger, hoping his rifle hadn't jammed from the fall. Worked the lever. Fired again. Standing, he moved to his right, cocking the Winchester, and stopped.

Jim Webb lay spread-eagled on the ground.

Something sounded behind him, and Bass whirled, raising the .44-40, then lowering it. Bywater and a hatless Cantrell sprinted toward him, Cantrell's horse still bucking its way back toward the Arbuckles.

Bass spit out blood. His lips were busted.

A voice called out weakly: "Bass . . . Bass Reeves."

He walked toward Jim Webb.

Webb's Henry rifle lay in the brush, but Webb's .45 Colt had fallen out of his trousers and lay, cocked, at his side. Blood spilled from both corners of his mouth, and from two holes in his chest. A crimson stream flowed toward a prickly pear a few feet away.

"Bass . . . ," Webb groaned. "Bass Reeves."

Aiming the rifle at the prone man, Bass moved cautiously till he stood over the dying killer.

"Give me your hand, Bass," Webb said. He lifted his own toward Bass. How Webb summoned enough strength to do that, Bass could only marvel.

"You're a brave man . . . Bass . . . Reeves."

Cantrell and Bywater, lungs laboring for

breath, had arrived, but stood back a few feet.

"I. . . ." Webb coughed, spit out bloody phlegm. "You take my guns, Bass. My Colt. My rifle. . . ." Another coughing spell. "I want you to take my . . . scabbard, too. . . . Take 'em. You killed me. You . . . deserve . . . 'em." His eyes moved to his hand. He flexed his fingers. "Take . . . my hand . . . Bass Reeves."

Bass shifted the rifle to his left hand, and gripped Webb's with his right. Even dying, Jim Webb possessed a powerful grip.

"I killed . . . eleven men with . . . 'em . . . guns." More coughing. "Four here . . . in . . . the Nations." Webb smiled. "Figured to make you the twelfth." The hand relaxed, and Webb closed his eyes.

Bass knelt, and laid the arm across the dead man's chest.

CHAPTER SIXTEEN

June 15, 1902

"I always thought Jim Mershon killed Jim Webb," I said.

Bass's lips creased into a little grin as he shook his head. "Jim Webb was a white man. Oh, I reckon he might've had some Mexican blood, but he worked for a big white outfit. Marshal Boles and Judge Parker talked things over, and they agreed that most white folks wouldn't tolerate a black lawman killin' a white gunhand. So the ink-slingers was all told Mershon killed Webb." He glanced over at me. "I didn't mind none. Jim was a good lawman, and a good friend. He helped go my bail after I got arrested for shootin' down William Leach. It was policy is all." He shrugged.

We were riding again, the air humid but the rain gone.

Let me take a moment to point out that Bass Reeves did not tell me everything that

I have just recorded about his pursuit of Jim Webb. Far from it. That evening at camp, and the following morning he had given me the bare facts. The rest I had to put together from research, including Mershon's and Bass's files at the Fort Smith court, and correspondence with Jim Bywater and former Marshal Boles. By the way, Boles did run for governor in 1884, but lost to a Democrat. He eventually became a judge before his death in 1905.

Before I could ask Bass another question about Mershon, Grant Johnson appeared at the crest of a hill, waving his hat over his head. Grant had been scouting ahead of us, so Bass and I immediately spurred our horses and galloped to the deputy. Once we reined up, Grant twisted in the saddle and pointed to a clearing down the hill.

"Camp," he said.

Smoke drifted from the ashes of a campfire. Even up on the hill, I could see where the horses had been grazing, the mounds of manure, a whitened log that had been dragged from the roadside in front of the campfire, and a trail leading through the high grass back to the road.

"It couldn't be Dozier's," I said. Still, I pulled the Winchester from the scabbard, earing back the hammer.

"I haven't cut any sign that anyone on this road was between Cherokee Bob's gang and us," Grant said as he put his hat back on his head. "And we ain't seen nobody ridin' toward us."

A heavy metallic click sounded like a rifle shot as Bass cocked his big Winchester. He dismounted, and knelt, ground-reining his horse, cradling the rifle as he scanned the country below. About that time, Uncle Bud, Paden Tolbert, and George Littledave joined us, and I could hear the jingling of trace chains and Erskine Jones's curses as the tumbleweed wagon climbed the hill, followed by the two Cherokees.

"I don't see anybody down there," I said.

"Me, neither." Bass rose, focusing still on the camp and woods below. "But I don't like it."

Nor did I. Cherokee Bob Dozier and his group had at least a half-day's jump on us, yet the smoking remains of that campfire — if it indeed had been Bob Dozier's camp — told us we had cut that distance considerably.

Maybe, I thought, Dozier, Bennie Reeves, and those outlaws had spent too much time here drinking the remains of the whiskey they had stolen from those runners they had murdered. That theory I certainly found plausible, for I had lost count of the number of men I had arrested because they had gotten drunk and passed out. Something like that would make sense, but not when Cherokee Bob was leading the gang.

"Hell's fire," Paden Tolbert said, "we should put these mounts of ours into a lope. Close as we're to them now, we could catch up with those boys before sundown." His horse seemed to sense Tolbert's enthusiasm, champing at the bit, hoofs digging up the ground, ready to run.

"I'm a cautious man, Tolbert," Bass said.

"Cautious my arse, Reeves. You're either a damned fool or a damned coward. Quit dragging your heels!" He spurred the horse, and loped down the trail.

Uncle Bud Ledbetter spat, and wiped his mouth with his sleeve. "Nobody would blame you, Bass, if you was to shoot that loud-mouthed son-of-a-bitch."

Bass had gathered the reins to his horse, and was swinging into the saddle, offering another rare smile, but the grin disappeared as a rifle shot barked down below.

Paden Tolbert's horse went down, throwing him over its head. The deputy crashed into the dirt. Another bullet kicked up dust in front of him.

"Where are those shots comin' from?"

Grant yelled, trying to steady his prancing horse.

That was the problem with smokeless powder. Back in the days when everyone shot black powder, it was easy to locate whoever was trying to put a bullet in your person. Since 1894, those times were rapidly coming to a close.

Raking spurs across his horse, Bass raced down the hill, and I galloped right behind him.

Ahead of us, across from the camp, Tolbert staggered from his dead horse, fell back on the road, tried to pull one of his revolvers from his holster. Something kicked him like a mule, and the pistol dropped as he went flying backward, landing against the neck of his dead mount.

I put the reins in my mouth, aimed, fired into the woods, levering the rifle and pumping lead as fast as I could cock the .25-35 and pull the trigger. Not sure I could hit anything, I could only guess where that assassin was hiding. It must have been a good guess, though, because nobody returned fire.

Bass's sorrel could run like the wind, and they had pulled ahead of me and Dutchy. When he reached Tolbert's horse, Bass leaped out of the saddle, letting the big sorrel lope past the bend in the road, out of sight, out of harm. I grabbed my own reins, jacked the rifle, stopped Dutchy, and sent another shot into the woods. Bass scooped Paden Tolbert into his arms, lifting him as if the wounded lawman weighed nothing more than a rag doll. He threw Tolbert over his left shoulder, and ran toward the old camp. I slid out of the saddle, slapped Dutchy's rump with the hot barrel of my Winchester, and watched him raise dust down the trail, chasing Bass's horse.

A bullet nicked my cheek, and I dropped to a knee, sent another bullet into the woods. Now I knew where our shooter was. I cocked, fired, and took off after Bass. Gunfire erupted from behind me, up on the hilltop. I chanced another shot. Looked ahead. A bullet plowed a furrow just behind Bass. Uncle Bud's guns spoke. From the corner of my eye, I spotted him running toward us.

Bass pitched his Winchester forward, and dived behind the old log near the smoking remains of the campfire. A bullet thudded into the ancient piece of oak. I dropped behind the cover, too, helped Bass roll Paden Tolbert close to the dead tree. Ducked. Began feeding bullets into the rifle.

Someone dived to my left. A bullet whined

off a rock. I ran my tongue over chapped lips, and saw Uncle Bud Ledbetter drag himself closer to the cover. "Hope nobody else comes here," I said. "This tree isn't big enough for anybody else."

Another bullet splintered the top of the log between Bass and me.

I leaned a bit lower.

Uncle Bud swore, examining one of his revolvers. Dirt, mud, and grass remnants clogged the barrel, and he pitched it aside, found his other revolver, and plunged the empty shells from the cylinder.

I chanced a glance up the hill. The Cherokees were holding the horses behind the tumbleweed wagon. Grant Johnson and George Littledave squatted near the wagon, rifles in hand. Kneeling in the boot, Erskine Jones pointed a finger toward the woods.

"Bass!"

Turning, I found Bud Ledbetter pointing his empty pistol toward the woods. I rolled around, levered the Winchester, watched a man on a black horse racing down the edge of the woods. From the hilltop, a rifle — either Grant's or Littledave's — roared, but that was a tough shot from that distance. The rider leaned low in the saddle. The black horse exploded like the fastest Quarter horse I'd ever seen.

"Kill that bastard!" Uncle Bud yelled.

I squeezed the trigger. Missed. Leaped to my feet, jacking the lever.

"I'll break his neck," Bass said calmly, and his Winchester boomed as the horse turned onto the road.

The horse kept running. The rider pitched over the black's neck, landing face down, spread-eagled onto the road.

A groan cut through the ringing in my ears, and I looked down as Uncle Bud rolled Paden Tolbert on his back. The lawman's face had turned ashen, blood soaked his shirt front and bubbled between his lips. As my hearing returned, I could make out the sucking sound every time Tolbert tried to draw a breath.

"Lung shot," Uncle Bud said as he unfastened his bandanna, rolled it into a ball, and pressed it against the wicked hole in Tolbert's chest.

I studied the woods, but there had only been one gunman, and he lay on the road. Bass was already walking toward him, and Uncle Bud motioned me to follow.

"I'll tend to Paden," Uncle Bud said, adding softly: "May be a horse's ass at times, but he's my pard."

Behind us, the rest of our posse came down the hill as I caught up with Bass. He worked his Winchester's lever, aiming the barrel in the general direction of the fallen assassin. No need to do that. Before we were twenty yards from the road, I could tell this man was deader than the fellow Bass had nailed on the agency road.

Bass realized that, too, because he lowered the hammer on his .44-40, and let out a little breath. He reached the dead man, put his boot under the man's belly, and rolled him over.

"Recognize him?" Bass asked.

I hadn't looked at the corpse's face. I was studying where that bullet had struck, leaving a gaping hole the size of my fist when it tore out of his throat, and the odd angle the dead man's head had in relation to the rest of his body.

"You broke his damned neck," I said.

"That's where I was aimin'." Bass spit.

I looked back at the campsite. Had to be a good six hundred yards. After whistling and shaking my head, I muttered: "I missed, and I was aiming at the horse."

Bass said: "I like horses."

The woods had been too thick for him to maneuver through, so our ambusher had attempted to make his escape riding along the tree line. A few more yards, and he would have made it.

The dead man's flat-crowned hat, crushed from his weight, now lay on his chest, secured by a horsehair stampede string. He sported a neatly trimmed mustache and a dark under-lip beard. Sightless black eyes stared out of a rich bronzed face. His black satin shirt front was embroidered with red and yellow roses and decorated with shiny buttons that I assumed were mother of pearl, and he wore fancy woolen pants, with wide stripes of deep blue and rich green, the open-sided, concho-adorned *calzoneras* favored by *vaqueros* south of the border. A yellow sash had been knotted around his waist, an old model Remington revolver stuck in his stomach, which Bass grabbed and stuck in his own waistband.

The dead Mexican's boots were shiny black, his spurs had large rowels, and the straps were elaborately tooled. A crucifix hung from his neck, soaking in the blood. He'd need that little hunk of jewelry where he was going.

Yeah, I recognized him, even though I had only gotten a glimpse of him when he and Cherokee Bob Dozier had ambushed us between Muskogee and Marshall Town, had snatched Bennie Reeves from us. I could hear his voice: *"¡Muy pronto, hijo!"* Snapping shots from that Remington at Bass and me.

"He should have waited," I said. "Let all of us get into that camp, then cut loose. Likely would have done a lot more damage."

Bass's head shook. "Couldn't. Not with Tolbert ridin' like hell down the road. Couldn't let Tolbert get out of sight."

"Dozier sacrificed him," I suggested, and shook my head. "One man against a posse. Damn' fool."

"Nah. Dozier didn't know we'd have Tolbert and Uncle Bud ridin' with us. Way I figure it, this Mexican was left here to start a little ruction, try to lead us into an ambush up the road." He nodded in approval. "Old Injun trick. Might have worked, too, were I not such a damn' fool and damn' coward." Surprisingly there was no bitterness in the last words Bass said.

"If you ask me," I said, "it was still a fool thing for one man to try."

Bass shrugged. "It's a hard game." He shifted the rifle to his other hand. "Come on, Dave," he said. "Let's drag this carcass off the road. Then we'll need to bury Tolbert."

215

CHAPTER SEVENTEEN

June 15, 1902

Turned out, Paden Tolbert wasn't dead.

Uncle Bud had fastened some kind of bandage, tightening the compress he had made against the wound in Tolbert's chest, and the big exit wound in Tolbert's back. By the time Bass and I had walked back to the old campsite, Uncle Bud was trying to put a Bible he had fetched from his war bag into Tolbert's hands, but Tolbert wouldn't take the Good Book.

"Paden," Uncle Bud kept pleading, "that slug tore through your lung, son. You're spitting up blood. It's a mortal wound, Paden. You need to get right with God."

Somehow, Paden managed to lift his head, his face tight with grit, and, after he spit out bloody phlegm, he said in a forceful tone: "I refuse to accept your diagnosis, Doctor Ledbetter!" The effort exhausted him, for his head fell back on the saddle blanket Grant

Johnson had rolled up as a pillow.

Sighing and shaking his head, Uncle Bud looked up at Bass and me. "That gunman dead?"

Bass nodded.

"Bass . . . B-Bass Reeves. . . ."

We looked down to find Paden Tolbert pushing himself up into a seated position, although the two young Cherokees, squatting behind him, had to support him, and Uncle Bud pressed his arm on the man's shoulder, urging him to lay back down.

Stubbornly Paden Tolbert shook his head. "Bass. . . ." Blood dribbled from his trembling lips.

Bass squatted, and took the deputy's outstretched hand.

"You. . . ." He shook his head, trembled, and I thought Tolbert would pass out, or die, then and there. "You . . . saved my . . . life."

I wet my lips, and hung my head. Saved his life? Not for long. Might have been better had Bass left Tolbert out on the road, let that Mexican put a bullet in his head. Would have ended his suffering.

"Best lie back down, Paden," Bass said.

Tolbert's head shook. "Not till . . . I had my . . . say." Somehow, he suppressed a cough. "You . . . you're a good . . . law-

217

man . . . Bass Reeves. Didn't mean . . . nothin' . . . ridin' you so." He couldn't hold back the need to cough any more, and a savage coughing spell almost doubled him over, drooling, and left his chin stained with blood. He straightened, squeezed Bass's hand hard, and shook his head. "Best . . . lawman . . . in the ter— ter'tory."

"I been telling you that for years, Paden," Uncle Bud said softly, and he and the Cherokees eased Tolbert back down.

Paden Tolbert's eyes burned with an intensity I'd never seen in a wounded man. "Get those . . . bastards," he said.

He closed his eyes — I expected for the last time — but his chest kept moving up and down. That ugly sucking sound made my skin crawl every time he managed a breath.

"Wes," Bass said, and one of the young Cherokees rose. "Mount up," Bass told him. "Ride down the road, fetch my sorrel and Dave's horse. Bring 'em back fast as you can." The Cherokee nodded gravely, and started to make a beeline for his horse. Bass kept talking. "With luck, the black that gunman was ridin' will have stopped near our horses. If you can herd that one back, too, that'd be a mighty fine thing. But if that black ain't there, don't go lookin' for him none. You get our hosses back here. *Pronto.*"

"Yes, sir." Wes had already mounted. He kicked his horse into a lope.

"Jones," Bass said.

The Choctaw grunted.

"We'll put Tolbert in the back of the tumbleweed wagon. You get him to the doctor in Vinita."

"I ain't doin' no such thing. He don't need a doctor. He needs a buryin'."

"You'll do it, damn your hide, or I'll bury you." Bass turned, nodded at me, and I motioned to Usdi, the other Cherokee. I grabbed Tolbert's boots, the young Cherokee took his shoulders, and we carried the injured deputy to the prison wagon. Uncle Bud opened the back door, Grant Johnson gathered the blankets and such, and we made Tolbert as comfortable as possible on the wagon's floor bed.

By the time I stepped out of the wagon, Wes was herding three horses toward our camp. The black hadn't kept running.

Bass nodded in approval, a plan formulating in his head. "Littledave," he said, "you know this country better'n anyone. If you was to plan an ambush, where'd you set it up? Near here. Real close."

The ancient Keetowah stroked his chin.

"Tie 'em horses to the wheels yonder,

Wes," Bass ordered. "Everybody, grab the reins to your hosses. Hold 'em tight. Jones, make sure that team don't bolt." Moments later, he pulled his pistol, and fired three rounds in the air. Then he drew the Remington he had taken off the dead Mexican, and squeezed the trigger. Waited ten seconds. Fired twice more. He looked at Littledave.

The old Indian nodded. "There is a good place. Two miles, perhaps three. No more."

Holding the Remington in his left hand, Bass fired again. Then pulled the trigger on the Colt he held in his right. "Wes . . . ," Bass said, started to add something, but paused, trying to size up the Cherokee. Finally he let out a breath, and asked: "Wes, you willin' to try somethin' that might be . . . well . . . ticklish?"

"Yes." Blunt and to the point. You couldn't knock the Indian's bravery.

"I don't think . . . well . . . don't matter, it could get you killed."

"I go."

Bass nodded. "All right, run yonder to that dead Mexican. I want you to put on his shirt, his hat, his sash, and 'em fancy britches. Quick, boy. Time's a-wastin'." He punctuated his orders by firing rounds from the two pistols he held, then dropped the empty Remington to the grass, and began spilling the empties from his Colt into the grass at his feet.

"The road turns, cuts through steep ridges on both sides," George Littledave said. "Black granite. Maybe fifty yards long, and the road is very narrow. Beyond that, men could hide their horses in the trees, climb up on both sides. For anyone riding through the pass, there would be little place to hide."

I understood what was going on, and fired my Winchester steadily till it was empty. Cherokee Bob was waiting down the road with his men — and Bennie Reeves — planning an ambush. Sound carried far in this country, so shooting our weapons would make that train robber think his Mexican was still in a set-to with our posse.

"There a place right before that turn, where we could climb up that ridge?" Bass asked. "Without bein' seen or heard by Cherokee Bob?"

The Keetowah's head bobbed again. "Yes, but it will be difficult to climb. Rains will have made that granite slick. And the woods are thick. But it can be done."

Bass reloaded his Colt, holstered it, shoved his rifle in the scabbard, and mounted the big sorrel. "Everybody mount," he said. "Jones, you get Paden to a doctor. Now!"

Taking the reins to the black, Bass loped across the grass to where Wes was pulling on the dead Mexican's garb.

I caught up with Bass at the edge of the road.

"You gotta keep ridin' hard," Bass was telling the Cherokee, bobbing his head nervously as he tucked his long black hair under the crown of his hat. "Tighten that stampede string, keep that hat on your head. Pull it down some. That's good. Now, get on this horse." He handed the reins of the dead man's horse to Wes. "Stay low in the saddle," Bass instructed him as Wes mounted. "Once you get to that narrow pass, put the spurs to him, kinda lean over that black's neck, just keep ridin', and don't stop ridin' till you're a good mile past that bend in the road. Then pull into the woods. And wait. Wait for us."

Could a young Cherokee pass for that Mexican? I wasn't sure, but Bass had forgotten more about disguises that I'd ever know. Cherokee Bob would notice the hat, the shirt, the pants, and especially the horse. What would he think when Wes kept riding? I had to believe that the Mexican would be expected to stop once the shooting started, and join the fracas.

Well, by then, the ball would have started.

But . . . had Bass Reeves figured Cherokee Bob's intent correctly, that the Mexican had been left behind to shoot at us, then lead us into an ambush? Dozier could have kept riding. The Mexican might have had something else in mind. And what if George Littledave was wrong? What if those outlaws had set up an ambush somewhere else, maybe just farther down the road? We would be climbing that granite ridge, fighting through brambles and rocks, and Bass might be riding to his death, for we would be unable to help him if the ambush had been planned somewhere else. That's the problem when you think too much. Therefore, I kept telling myself that Bass knew Cherokee Bob Dozier down to a T.

The others rode up behind us.

Bass turned in the saddle. "Damn your Choctaw soul to hell, Erskine Jones, you've tried my patience . . . !"

I whirled, found Erskine Jones mounted on Usdi's horse.

"Shut your trap, Bass Reeves," Jones fired back. "I tol' that Cherokee to fetch Tolbert to a doc in Vinita. Hell's fire, man, he knows this damned country better'n me, knows where the doctor is. Undertaker, too."

The prison wagon, driven by Usdi, was making its way up the hill. We didn't have time to stop it.

"I'm gonna prove to you, Reeves, that I ain't no coward," Jones said. "This ain't gonna be like that time in 'Ninety-Two."

Bass jerked the Winchester from the scabbard, jacked a shell into the breech, shook his head, but he did not shoot Erskine Jones out of the saddle. "Wes rides through," Bass said. "I'll ride after him, pretendin' to be pursuin' him. The rest of you'll stop, climb up 'em rocks."

"One of us ought to ride with you, Bass," I argued. "Make it look better."

Bass's head shook. "It's me Cherokee Bob wants. No . . . I'll go it alone. Y'all . . . shit! Hell, Jones, you can't climb them rocks, not if they's as slick as Littledave says they'll be. That's why I didn't want you. . . ." He furiously muttered an oath.

"I'll ride with you, you black bastard," Jones said, smirking. "Like Adams just said, make it look better. More authentic-like."

Bass didn't like it one bit. Can't say I did, either. But we had no time to spare.

"All right, Wes," Bass said. "You ride. Not too fast. Dave, you and the others ride ahead of him. You'll have only a couple of minutes, if that long, to climb up those rocks before we come ridin' into that ambush." He pulled his hat down low, finally stopped for a breath. Then drew his pistol, fired twice into the air.

Uncle Bud spurred his horse, and Littledave followed. I gave a nod to Bass, and followed them, galloping alongside Grant Johnson. I looked back, thinking how this might be the last time I saw Bass Reeves alive, but instead my eyes were drawn to the prison wagon being driven by Usdi as it disappeared over the hilltop. That, I thought, would be the last time I ever saw Paden Tolbert alive. Thought I might be seeing him in the hereafter pretty soon.

God rode with me, though, on this day.

God also rode close to Paden Tolbert.

Even shot through one lung, that lawman showed his toughness. The Mexican's bullet wouldn't kill him. In fact, Paden Tolbert would live almost two more years before those bad lungs called him to Glory.

Yes, God would protect the two of us. But not everyone in our posse.

CHAPTER EIGHTEEN

June 15, 1902

Following is, in my opinion, the most accurate reconstruction of what the *Cherokee Advocate* of Tahlequah headlined *Bloody Massacre, Blazing Gun Battle at U-lo-gi-dv Pass Leave Several Dead* — but where newspaper reporter Se-la-gwo-ya Johnston relied mostly on hearsay and outright lies, I have based this account on interviews with survivors, and my own personal recollections. Besides, I was there; Se-la-gwo-ya Johnston wasn't, and he never talked to Bass Reeves or me about what happened.

With maybe a fifty-yard lead on Wes, we reined up just before the pass. No time to tether our horses. Instead, we led the mounts into the thickets, and dropped the reins. I pulled the lariat from the saddle horn, hurried just ahead of George Little-dave to the rock-face wall. On the other side of the road, Grant Johnson and Uncle Bud

226

Ledbetter had already begun their ascent.

George Littledave had been right. Those rocks felt as slippery as greased ice. Shaking out a loop, I tossed up the hemp rope and managed to snag a stump. I pulled the lariat tight, started climbing while holding onto the Winchester rifle with my left hand. George Littledave was already working his way up the slick granite, finding finger- and toe-holds.

The black horse galloped past with Wes leaning low in the saddle. Just a few rods behind him came Erskine Jones and Bass.

A gunshot roared, its echo bouncing throughout the woods, off the granite walls. The black stallion screamed. More shots followed, sounding, with all those echoes, like a Gatling gun.

To quote Se-la-gwo-ya Johnston: *Vinita City Marshal J.F. Ledbetter sacrificed Wes Bushyhead, a brave, young Cherokee whose only flaw was his willingness to obey the white man's law unconditionally, sending him into the pits of Hades to learn the location of the alleged Cherokee bandits.*

That's hogwash. Bass Reeves, and not Uncle Bud, had asked Wes if he'd make that ride, had warned him, too. However, Se-la-gwo-ya Johnston was right on one account, Wes Bushyhead was as brave as any Cherokee ever born.

The first rifle shot killed the horse, and sent Wes flying over the black's head. Eight bullets ripped through young Bushyhead's back and head, but the outlaws could have saved their powder and lead. The fall had broken Wes's neck.

I don't know why they killed Wes. Maybe those man-killers realized that it wasn't their Mexican ally galloping past them. Maybe we had underestimated Cherokee Bob Dozier. Perhaps one of the gunmen got excited, accidentally fired the first shot, and the rest of the gang opened up. It could be that Cherokee Bob even planned on killing his accomplice. It doesn't really matter. Wes Bushyhead was dead, and the ball had started.

"Shit!" The eruption of gunfire startled me so that the Winchester slipped from my hands, clattered on the rocks below. Yet I was too far up the ridge to go back down for it. Erskine Jones and Bass Reeves had ridden into the pass, and more gunfire bellowed.

All together, Cherokee Bob had four men and Bass's son with him. Dozier, another Cherokee, and a Negro outlaw named Cutter Beckham hid on the south-side wall, the one Uncle Bud and Grant Johnson were climbing. On the northern ridge top waited a Creek outlaw named Cauley and an Osage half-breed called Big Thom. And Bennie Reeves.

Bass went down, flying from the saddle with a bullet in his thigh. A bullet ripped off Erskine Jones's hat. Another nicked his earlobe. Two more brought down the horse he was riding. He hit the ground, rolled over, came up. A bullet shattered his left elbow. Erskine Jones ran. Above the roar of gunfire, I heard his screams. Three buckshot pierced his thigh, and another round tore off two fingers on his left hand. Yet somehow, despite a bum leg and multiple gunshot wounds, he managed to dive, hit the ground, then slither, bullets kicking up dirt and whining off rocks all around him, till he lunged into the thicket at the entrance of the pass.

Another voice rose over the gunfire. "Let that son-of-a-bitch go! Kill the big nigger! Kill him!"

While the gunmen concentrated on Erskine Jones, Bass had managed to crawl to the dead horse. He practically buried himself under the black's stomach. Bullets from the southern walls ripped into the animal's flesh, but Bass worked his Winchester and fired, forcing the assassins on the northern side to keep their heads down.

I'd made it to the top by grabbing a branch, then saw a gnarled copper hand reach for me. How George Littledave had managed to scale that cliff and reach the top before I had — well, he was something else. I took his hand, and he helped pull me up. Then took off running. I scrambled to my feet, jerked my double-action .44 from the holster, and followed.

Brambles, vines, low branches slapped my face, knocked off my hat. To my left, about ten yards ahead of me, sprinted Littledave. I gained on him, and, when we burst through the clearing, we were dead even.

Cauley, the Creek, whirled. He was in the process of reloading an 1897 model Winchester, but had to pitch the pump shotgun, and stand, trying to jerk a short-barreled Colt from a holster. It was the last mistake he ever made, because, when he stood, Bass Reeves, thirty-five feet down below, put a bullet through the back of his head.

Unaware that Bass had just killed him, I sent a bullet in Cauley's stomach as he began falling, then I turned, snapped a shot at Big Thom, who ducked behind a boulder. That's when I saw Bennie Reeves, spinning, sweating, bringing up a pistol. I dived. A bullet cut bark off the tree behind me.

Another clipped a branch.

My cheek was still bleeding from the bullet wound — and eventual scar — the Mexican had left me. Other scratches about my forehead and neck, and one over the bridge of my nose that stung like a bastard, seeped blood. I scurried on my hands and knees a few feet, came up, fired, ducked.

Across the pass, Grant Johnson and Uncle Bud had scaled the walls, and they cut loose.

A Cherokee outlaw, who was never identified and his body never claimed, had moved to the edge of the pass, leaning against a tree, practically leaning over the side, desperately trying to draw a bead on Bass Reeves below.

"Hands up!" Uncle Bud yelled, but Ledbetter and Grant Johnson had been wearing a badge far too long in Indian Territory. Rarely did bandits give up; they died game.

The long-haired Cherokee, spun, firing from the hip, and Grant put two bullets in his stomach. Ledbetter sent another through his groin. The Cherokee's Marlin rifle cartwheeled into the air, and he dropped like a sack of potatoes to the road below.

Cutter Beckham sent two loads of buckshot over Grant's head. Then the lanky Negro dropped the shotgun, and started running.

"Damn!" Cherokee Bob Dozier fired his rifle from his hip, backing into the dense brush. Ledbetter shot twice. Had to reload. Grant leaped over a fallen log, emptied one pistol, then performed the old border shift, tossing the empty to his left hand, while drawing his other Colt with his right. A bullet from Cherokee Bob's rifle tore through Grant Johnson's upper left arm, missing the bone. Grant acted as if the bullet had been a feather. Ignoring the pain, he thumbed back the hammer, pulled the trigger.

Cutter Beckham screamed, fell, clutching his left arm, scrambled to his feet, kept on running.

It was a scratch shot. Grant Johnson knew that. But he would take it. He kept firing till his pistol was empty, but had no more luck.

Beckham and Cherokee Bob slid down the natural granite ramp to the bottom. Their horses were tethered to a tree.

"My arm's broke!" Beckham wailed. "That son-of-a-bitch broke my arm."

Ignoring him, Bob Dozier mounted his horse.

"Help me into the saddle," Beckham said. "I can't get on."

"Get on yourself," Dozier said, "or get killed."

Spurring his horse out of the woods, Dozier hung over the paint horse's neck, Indian-style, and raced down the road.

Bass rose to his knees, took careful aim, let out a breath as he pulled the trigger. The hammer landed with a loud click.

Empty.

Cherokee Bob had escaped.

At that moment, Bennie Reeves came darting across the road from the other side. His eyes locked on his father's, but he never raised the smoking pistol he held in his right hand. A bullet, fired by Uncle Bud, whined off the rock behind him. Bennie disappeared in the woods.

"Help me, boy," Cutter Beckham said, and Bennie hooked his fingers together, knelt at the side of Beckham's horse. The Negro put his boot in Bennie's hands, and Bennie boosted him into the saddle.

Beckham didn't bother offering any thanks. He grabbed the reins, kicked his horse, and chased after Cherokee Bob. Bennie leaped onto a blue roan, exploded out of the woods, took off after the others.

By then, Bass Reeves had reloaded the big Winchester. He was standing, though far from steady with his thigh stained with blood. He quickly brought the rifle's stock to his shoulder, thumbed up the rear sight, aimed.

A bullet scorched his side. He spun, tripping over the dead horse. Another bullet thudded into the horse's belly. Bass rolled over, came up, saw Big Thom racing across the road toward the horses. I saw him, too.

That was their mistake. They should have tethered their horses on both sides of the road, not just the north side.

With my Winchester down below, I had picked up a Spencer one of the outlaws had left behind. I squeezed off a round, worked the lever, led Big Thom a bit more, and fired another shot. The Osage went down, a bullet in the small of his back. He came up, grabbed the pistol he had dropped. My third shot tore off his hat. He sat up, looked at me, then at Bass. Uncle Bud fired once, but Big Thom was out of pistol range, especially from that far up the hillside.

Bass pulled the trigger, and the .44-40 slug hit the Osage plumb center. He dropped, still trying to thumb back the hammer on his Schofield, but never managed to cock that big .45 before he bled out.

I could breathe again. Smoke, sweat, blood stung my eyes. The air smelled of saltpeter. Like hell.

Below, Bass Reeves slumped back against the dead black, unknotted his bandanna, and wrapped it over the bullet wound in his leg. Across the road, high on the ridge, Uncle Bud Ledbetter and Grant Johnson waved their hats over their heads, letting me know they were all right. I reached for my hat, realized it wasn't there, then remembered a branch knocking it off back in the woods. Instead, I lifted the Spencer — felt as if it weighed a ton — and gave a little nod.

"George?" I called out.

No answer, and I spun, mouth turning dry.

Gunsmoke hung about the lower limbs of trees like fog. I looked around, scanned the small clearing littered with brass casings and shotgun shells, a canteen, a couple empty whiskey bottles, and Cauley, lying face down, dead in a mound of rotting leaves.

"George Littledave!" I shouted. From behind a granite boulder, a hand appeared, fingers flexing, then dropped out of sight. Laying down the rifle, empty by now, I hurried, ducked underneath a branch, saw the outstretched legs.

The silver-headed Keetowah sat, leaning back against the large chunk of granite, tightening both hands just above the sash wrapped around his waist. Blood pulsed between the fingers. Littledave craned his neck, managed to offer me a weak smile.

His turban lay askew, and he leaned forward suddenly, groaning, then straightened again. Slowly he started rocking slightly.

I put my hand on his shoulder, choked down the bile, bit my lower lip.

"George."

He shook his head. He whispered something, too softly for me to hear. I leaned forward, put my ear to his lips. He spoke in Cherokee, but I couldn't understand the words.

His hands slipped, revealing the widening crimson pool on his shirt front. The hands dropped by his side. His head leaned back against the rock. Blood poured from both corners of his mouth. He shook his head again, swallowed the blood in his mouth, and spoke again, this time in English, this time loud enough for me to understand.

"It was him. . . . It was him. . . ."

His head fell forward, the turban came off, and he slumped against me. After easing him onto the ground, I closed his eyes.

Cauley was deader than he'd ever be, so I returned to the woods, found and donned my hat, just to do something to clear my mind, to stop shaking. Once back in camp, I lifted George Littledave's body over my shoulder. Natural stairs, though often wide, deep, even unsteady, made a path down the northeastern side of the ridge, leading me back to the road, where I laid Littledave's body in the shade, and made my way to Bass Reeves.

He was using his Winchester as a crutch, staring at the body of the Cherokee Uncle Bud and Grant Marshal had sent over the ridge. The outlaw was still alive, but just laid there, staring up with malevolent eyes, blackguarding us with the foulest curses in Cherokee and English. But only for a few minutes. Then he joined Wes Bushyhead, George Littledave, and the outlaw's companions in death.

Bass limped away from the dead man, and I followed him. I fought the urge to put my arm around Bass's waist, to help him, but knew he'd hold no truck with anything like that. We made it to where Uncle Bud was dressing Erskine Jones's wounds. Grant Johnson made his way around the carnage, checking on the other bodies.

Jones cursed. Tears ran down his face and into his filthy beard. "You don't reckon they'll saw off my arm, do you, Uncle Bud?" Ledbetter didn't answer, and eased the Choctaw's bandaged hand and arm into a sling. Jones wailed in agony. His eyes found Bass. "Damn it, Reeves, this is all your fault! If I only got a stump. . . ."

"Shut up." Surprised, I realized those words came from me.

Even more shocking, Erskine Jones stopped his rant, even stopped sobbing. He bit his lip, and rocked with pain.

"Littledave?" Uncle Bud asked.

I shook my head.

"That's too bad." Uncle Bud sighed.

"All he said was . . . 'It was him. It was him,' " I said as I reloaded my revolver, reminding myself to pick up the Winchester I had dropped climbing the ridge.

"You get any of 'em on your side?" Bass asked me.

I nodded, and told him of the dead Creek, whose body would be identified by his wife at the funeral parlor in Vinita.

"Three of 'em got away," Grant Johnson said as he made his way to us. His left shirt sleeve was slick with blood, but he seemed to be in no pain. Maybe it was shock. Perhaps it was pure gumption. "That's Big Thom over there with his guts shot out." He stared at the dead Cherokee. "Don't recognize this bird." When he looked up, he said softly: "Wes Bushyhead's dead. Neck's broke. Shot to pieces, too."

"George Littledave got gut-shot," I said. "He's dead."

Johnson bowed his head, and swore.

"Looked like Cherokee Bob got out without a scratch," Uncle Bud said. "One of them . . . a big colored boy . . . was favoring his arm. I don't know about the other kid."

"That other kid," Bass said, "is my son."

CHAPTER NINETEEN

June 15–16, 1902

No denying it, we were in a bad fix. Two
members of our posse dead, two marshals
with flesh wounds, Erskine Jones grievously
injured. Three outlaws dead. Three more
hightailing it toward the Missouri or Kansas
border, or, more than likely, Robbers' Roost.

Uncle Bud took charge. "We'll get the
dead strapped on the horses. Bass, you and
Grant will have to take the bodies, and Jones
here, back to Vinita. Me and Dave will keep
after Cherokee Bob."

"No." Bass was reloading his revolver, having finished pushing cartridges into the Winchester.

"Look at that leg of yours, Bass," Uncle
Bud said. "You got a ounce of lead in there,
and it needs to come out."

"I'm ridin' on. This is my concern. It's
my. . . ." He slid the Colt into its holster.
"My son."

240

"And it's Cherokee Bob," Uncle Bud argued, "who has killed one . . . probably two . . . employees of the Katy, butchered a couple of whiskey runners, wounded two federal peace officers, wounded a deputy, and killed two other members of a duly appointed posse."

"Three," Grant Johnson corrected, remembering Gringo Gomez and the ambush on the Illinois River ferry.

"Four." Erskine Jones had found his voice. "Gotta expect that damned Tolbert's barkin' at the devil by now."

"I'm goin'," Bass announced. "Goin' alone." He limped down the road. I didn't know how far his sorrel had run, and Bass didn't, either. He found one of the horses the outlaws had been forced to abandon in the brush, somehow pulled himself into the saddle, and took off, first at a walk, then at a trot, finally disappearing around the bend.

"Man's head's thicker than a mule's," Uncle Bud said, sighing, and turned to his medical duties to Grant Johnson's arm.

No one tried to stop Bass Reeves, for our parents had not raised fools. I fed the last bullet into the .44, and stepped closer to Johnson and Uncle Bud.

"You all right, Grant?" I asked.

"I'll live."

"If you don't bleed to death," Uncle Bud muttered through clenched teeth.

"Can you get everyone back to Vinita?" I didn't have to add — without me?

Uncle Bud turned away from his task, and wiped his bloody fingers on the front of his vest. His lips tightened, but he nodded ever so slightly. "Might have to leave the bandits to rot, but I'll make sure Littledave and Wes get back to Vinita. Grant and Jones, too." He went back to dressing Grant Johnson's arm.

I walked back down the road, to the brush, grabbed the reins to Dutchy, and swung into the saddle. I spurred the bay into a fast lope.

Ten minutes later, I had caught up with Bass Reeves. He didn't say anything, barely even looked at me. He was riding his sorrel by that time, pulling the outlaws' piebald mare behind him. We kept our horses at a lope for a few minutes, then slowed them to a walk. His thigh was soaked with blood by then, but we kept riding.

In retrospect, Se-la-gwo-ya Johnston did get one thing right about that ambush in his article for the *Cherokee Advocate*. He attributed a quote to Marshal J.F. Ledbetter, though Uncle Bud always denied — and I believe him — that he ever spoke to the reporter. Yet the quote rang true: *Cherokee Bob and his gang surprised us. But I reckon we surprised them a little bit more.*

"You ready?" I asked.

Bass took a final long pull from the flask of rotgut whiskey we had found in the saddlebags on the piebald. "Ain't drunk," he said, "but reckon I'm numb enough." He offered me the whiskey, and I took a swallow — burned my throat like hell's fires — and splashed the end of the stick I had whittled into a sharp point.

We were camping in the woods, heavy with tall oaks and pines, the tops rustling in the wind so much that it sounded like rainfall. Bass had pulled down his britches to his knees, and I'd sliced into his long-handle underwear. After tossing the empty flask aside, I stoked up the fire so I could see better. Next, I cut into Bass's flesh, pushed back the skin, and laid the knife on a rock by the fire.

Bass stiffened, cursed, and I pushed the stick into the hole in his thigh.

"You got the touch . . . ," he said through clenched teeth, stopping to suck in a lungful of air, "of a two-bit whore."

"I wouldn't know," I said, and pushed the stick deeper. Blood poured over his leg, but that seemed to be a good thing. It would clean out the wound, some. Beads of sweat popped out on my forehead, and I longed for another full flask of whiskey. I wet my lips with my tongue, probed and pried, and, slowly exhaling, I drew the stick from the wound. "I can't get that bullet out," I said. "Think it flattened against the bone."

"Didn't bust the bone, though," Bass said, and sat up. He breathed heavily, and looked at his bleeding leg.

"No, I didn't see any bone slivers."

"Need to stop the bleedin'."

"You need a doctor," I said.

"Don't start preachin', Dave. Just patch me up as best you can."

I had found some pitch pine to start the fire, so I walked back to the stump, broke off some more chunks that smelled like coal oil, and returned to the fire. I shaved off the bark, dumping everything in the coffee pot I had filled with water. Once the pot went on the fire, I waited until the water started bubbling. It seemed to take a lifetime.

"You ready?" I asked at last.

Bass took the stick I had used as a probe, and put it in his mouth, biting down as he nodded. I pulled on my gloves, picked up the burning hot pot, and slowly poured the boiling pitch onto the bloody bullet hole in

Bass's thigh.

The stick in his mouth broke, and Bass spit it out and let out a howl, then cussed me, Cherokee Bob Dozier, his son, Sheriff George Reeves and the entire Reeves family, and anyone else whose name he could recall.

When he was finished, I wrapped torn strips of shirt around his thigh, and Bass pulled up his britches. The bleeding had stopped. Bass mopped his sweat-soaked face with a handkerchief, and I tossed the ruined coffee pot away. My coffee was bad enough without tasting like coal oil. I found a broken branch of an oak tree that would suffice for a cane, and handed it to Bass, who nodded his thanks and took a long pull from his canteen.

I fished out some hardtack and jerky, passed some to Bass, and squatted by the fire, warming myself even though I wasn't cold.

"Man wants to leave behind a legacy," he said softly.

I shot him an odd glance. That whiskey had finally taken hold. Or the shock from the bullet wound, and my so-called surgery. Or the loss of blood. Or a combination of everything, including the past hard week.

"Wants his kids to be better'n he was.

Wants 'em to amount to somethin'."

"You've done all right," I said.

His head shook. "This is all my damned fault."

"Wes Bushyhead knew the chance he was taking," I reminded him. "So did Tolbert, Grant, Jones, and George Littledave."

"That ain't what I mean, Dave." He grimaced, straightened his leg, stared into the fire. "Few days back. . . ." He shook his head, slowly sighed. "Bennie was over at my house, and we was drinkin' some hooch after supper. Sittin' out back, just sippin' whiskey and smokin' cigars. He told me how his wife was actin', told me about him suspectin' her of callin' on John Wadly. Asked me what I'd do iffen it was my wife cheatin' on me."

I moved away from the fire, biting my lip, staring at Bass. He sat there for the longest while, eyes not blinking, chest barely rising and falling. He just stared into those flames, and I lacked the nerve to speak.

"So I tells him. . . ." His voice broke the silence. "I tells him." His head shook. "I says . . . 'I'd shoot the hell out of the man and whip the livin' God out of her.' "

The words caught in his throat, and he buried his face into his huge hands. "God," he cried. "Lord God, Lord God, Lord

246

God. . . . Why, oh, why, did I tell Bennie that?"

The treetops rustled. A horse snorted, stamped its hoofs, and, off in the distance, a coyote yipped, joined in by a chorus of others.

"Bass," I said when the coyotes had finished their howls, "you can't blame yourself for what Bennie did." He kept shaking his head in his hands. "Bennie didn't whip her. He shot her down. He never even laid a hand on Wadly."

"No. . . ." He looked up, tears in his eyes reflecting the flickering flames from the fire, streaming down his dirty face. "You don't understand, Dave."

"It's not your fault," I said.

"It is." He took a deep breath, and lifted his head, staring at the night sky. "I never treated Bennie right. Never give him the respect he deserved. Always compared him to his older brother. Always tossed whatever Robert had done in the boy's face. He wasn't as good as Robert, not to hear me talk. Wasn't as strong as Robert. Wasn't as smart as Robert. Wasn't killed . . . like Robert." He sniffed, shook his head, and cursed himself. "Robert died couplin' cars. I reckon when he died, a bit of me died, too. Bennie tried to fill in, but . . . hell, I wasn't no good

247

as a daddy. Wasn't good at nothin', no time in my life. Nothin' except workin' with hosses. And lawin'. Left the raisin' of the children to Jennie. And after she died, I left it all to Winnie. Never told Bennie I was proud of him. Bennie was a good barber, good porter before that, and he'd made a good husband if he had married a fit gal. He was tryin' to make his mark in the world. But . . . I just never told Bennie nothin', except to kill his wife."

"You didn't tell him to kill his wife, Bass," I said forcefully.

"Sure I did." He wiped his eyes. "Maybe not in so many words. Maybe it was the whiskey talkin'. But I told him. It's my damned fault. I've gotten him killed."

"He's not dead."

"He will be. By a lawman's bullet or a hangman's rope. Or by Cherokee Bob. No." He sighed again. "I'm to blame for all this mess." He laid down, putting his forearm over his head, not speaking.

I sat there, not speaking, trying to comprehend all he had told me, until the fire died out. Bass was asleep by then, snoring slightly. I didn't sleep that night.

That next morning, neither Bass nor I brought up our conversation about Bennie.

Some things you just let lie.

Bass moved stiffly, relying on the make-shift oak crutch I'd given him, but when I put on fresh bandages, the wound looked better. No sign of infection, anyway. I saddled our horses, and we rode out without breakfast. We'd be running a cold camp for the rest of our trip. After all, we no longer had a coffee pot since I'd ruined ours by boiling that pitch pine.

That was all right, however. I didn't think we had much longer to go.

"They've turned south."

Making use of the oak limb, Bass pushed himself to his feet, then tipped back his hat, staring down the trail that ran through the woods along the east banks of the Grand River.

It was late afternoon, June 16th.

"Robbers' Roost is north of here," I said.

Putting his hands on the saddle horn, Bass stared up at me with one of those I-know-that-you-damned-fool looks, and I grinned at my stupidity. Grunting, he pulled himself into the saddle, and tucked the limb inside his saddlebag, then withdrew his Winchester from the scabbard.

"They're still together," Bass said as he

nudged the sorrel into a walk. "Three of 'em."

I tugged the lead rope to the piebald, and kicked Dutchy, taking time to draw my Winchester, and lay it across my lap.

"How far ahead are they?" I asked.

A shrug was his answer.

"We're spitting distance from the Missouri state line," I said.

"Yeah."

"Where's this road lead?"

"Grove," he said.

I knew a little about Grove — Monroe Grove, Tablor's Grove, Round Grove, Grove Springs, or whatever name it happened to be called on any given day. Once a resting spot on the Texas Road because of a freshwater spring, a town had finally sprung up in the late 1880s, though the city wouldn't be officially laid out until around 1901. These days, Grove had a newspaper, a livery, a few restaurants, one or two hotels, Aunt Jane Longmire's Boarding House and, with luck, a doctor. That might be a good thing, considering Bass's leg.

"We should get a doctor in town to treat your leg," I suggested ever so cautiously.

"I'd rather just grab a bite to eat at Little George Thomas's Chili Joint," Bass said, yet he nodded. "That's probably one reason

Cherokee Bob turned south. I warrant that Negro who caught a bullet in his arm . . . imagine that arm's started festerin' him."

"You don't let a doctor fix your leg, you'll be in the same boat he's in." My tone wasn't quite as cautious now.

Bass smiled, and shoved his big rifle in the scabbard. "Grove," he said at last. "Hell, I've been such a dunderhead. Had this all wrong. This was Cherokee Bob's intent all this time. He never planned on headin' to Robbers' Roost. He ain't goin' to see no doctor." His head bobbed. "Yep, makes sense."

"What makes sense?" Maybe Bass's head was festering.

"Grove," he answered. "Around here's where I killed that boy's papa."

CHAPTER TWENTY

1890–1892

It started with the theft of a horse.

In the summer of 1890, Bob Dozier stole a horse from Sam Stratton in the Seminole Nation. It wasn't just some Indian pony or cow horse, but a fine racer with thorough-bred blood, valued at $100. It was a horse owned by a white man. Bob Dozier was a black freedman farming in the Cherokee Nation.

"I haven't heard of this man Dozier," the U.S. commissioner said as he dipped his pen in the ink. "You say he's a farmer?"

"Yes, sir, that's right," Bass replied. "A good farmer from what I hear."

As the commissioner signed the writ, he asked: "Why did he steal this man's horse?"

"I'll ask him, sir," Bass replied. "Once I catch him."

Grinning, the commissioner looked up. "You do that, Deputy Reeves." He handed him the warrant.

A good farmer, a good horse thief. That was just the beginning.

Bob Dozier was good at everything he ever tried, Jacob Yoes wrote me in 1904. *People talk about Ned Christie, but Bob Dozier had him beat. He was a burr under the saddle of my deputies for two years, and an itch on my neck that I could not scratch.*

Appointed U.S. marshal of the Western District of Arkansas in 1889, Jacob "Blake Jake" Yoes would become one of Judge Parker's most famous chief marshals. A big man in his early fifties, Yoes walked with a limp after taking two bullets in both hips and another slug in his left leg during the War of the Rebellion. Although he hailed from Arkansas, he had served with a Union regiment. Limp, yes, but those wounds didn't slow Yoes down. He had been a merchant with several business interests, had served in the state legislature, and had been elected Washington County sheriff before his appointment as federal marshal. Like Doc Bennett, Yoes didn't while away the hours pushing papers, sharpening pencils, and sending his deputies out to risk their lives. Often, he rode with them.

Often, between 1890 and 1892, Yoes rode after Bob Dozier.

Stealing one man's horse just started Dozier's career. He rustled cattle. He robbed stores. He held up banks, stagecoaches, but never a train — perhaps that was why his son, wanting to best his father's reputation, robbed the Katy near Eufaula in 1902. He ambushed cattle buyers on the Texas Road, relieving them of their wallets filled with cash. Once, he even unexpectedly joined a high-stakes poker game at the Hotel Hazel, on the corner of Second and Hazel in Grove. He stuck around for only one hand, robbing the six stud players of their cash, watches, and pride. Years later, the Grove *Sun* reported: *Bob Dozier showed that his one ace (a nickel-plated .45 Colt) trumped J.C. Chandler's jacks and tens and Darius Robson's three nines. That winning hand netted him a pot totaling more than $2,359, plus Dr. Jasper Madden's 18-karat gold repeater watch.*

"Why you keep botherin' me and my family? What you want to pester my husband so?"

The plump woman in calico and a dirty apron stood on the porch of their cabin, two young daughters clutching their mother at the waist, while a ten-year-old boy stood at the door, shaking with rage.

"Because, ma'am," Marshal Yoes replied, "your husband kills people."

Not that anyone ever put an exact total on the number of men Bob Dozier had killed. Cattle buyers, drummers, and drifters found dead on the trails throughout Indian Territory. No witnesses. No money. Maybe Dozier had killed them, or maybe someone else had committed the crime and let the law lay the blame on Dozier. He had yet to kill a federal marshal, but he had left notes tacked to trees and fence posts, warning anyone with a badge that he wouldn't hesitate to pull a trigger if they got too close.

He had, however, killed Creek Jimmy down in the Sansbois Mountains. Most people, of course, wouldn't shed tears over the passing of a whiskey seller and horse thief like Creek Jimmy. Dozier had been selling some of his stolen horses to Creek Jimmy, but that $750 reward for Dozier proved too tempting, especially since the U.S. commissioner had said he would not prosecute Creek Jimmy if he helped bring Bob Dozier to justice. All Creek Jimmy had to do was let the law know when Dozier would be in the Sansbois trying to unload stolen horses, lure Dozier back to his trading post, and let the marshals kill or capture the outlaw.

Cherokees, Creeks, Seminoles, and Choctaws alike all said Bob Dozier was loyal to his friends, but if you crossed him, you would pay. Creek Jimmy paid. His daughter found him in the barn, strung up with baling wire.

"Bosh." The Cherokee woman spit brown juice into a snuff can on the porch. "My Bob ain't never kilt no *man*."

"Excuse me." Bass put his hand on the boy's shoulder. Dozier's young son tensed, turned, and jumped aside, glaring at Bass as he stepped out of the cabin, shaking his head at Marshal Yoes.

"Keep your filthy hands off me," the boy said to Bass's back.

Ignoring the boy, Bass tipped his hat at Dozier's wife, and stepped off the porch.

Grant Johnson was coming out of the barn, shaking his head, too.

"What you wanna be chasin' after my man, nigger?" the woman asked Bass as he walked away. She wiped brown juice off her lips with the sleeve of her tobacco-stained dress. "My man's same color as you is. What you want to go rilin' my man? What you want to be lawin' for them white men?"

Bass didn't turn to face Mrs. Dozier. He let his long legs carry him to the horse whose reins a white deputy marshal was holding, yet he heard the woman's curses, directed at him, at Grant Johnson, at the other twelve members of the posse. He pulled himself into the saddle, and followed Marshal Yoes as he led the men out of the farm, and toward the Illinois River.

"I don't understand these people," Yoes said. "They protect this murderous thief and assassin. Even the high price on Dozier's head has yielded us nothing."

Back in Fort Smith, they sat in Yoes's office, the marshal filling a tumbler with brandy, Bass Reeves trying to get his cigar to draw.

"Bob Dozier ain't done 'em no wrong," Grant Johnson tried to explain. "At least, that's how they see things. It ain't personal, Marshal. It's just that they don't see no reason they should get involved, as long as Dozier ain't hurtin' 'em."

Jim Mershon sent a river of tobacco juice into the spittoon beside his chair. "After what happened to Creek Jimmy, it's gonna be damned harder to find somebody willing to help the law. They know. You turn on Bob Dozier, you'll pay. Pay dearly."

"Oh, mark my words, gentlemen, it will be Bob Dozier who pays," Yoes said, and paused just long enough to sip the brandy.

"For nigh two years, Bob Dozier has made a mockery of this court, of the marshal's office. Well, I intend to flush him out of the Nations. If a dozen lawmen can't do it, I'll send forty after him." Another drink. This time, he emptied the tumbler and slammed the glass on his desk. "By jacks, I have two hundred deputies at my disposal, and I'll send an army of lawmen after that scoundrel. And once they've delivered Dozier to justice, we'll flush out Ned Christie. As God is my witness, I don't know which of those vermin is worse. Yet we must stop Ned Christie and Bob Dozier. If it takes an army!"

Bass gave up on the cigar, and set it in the ashtray. He spit into the cuspidor, and cleared his throat. "With all due respect, Marshal Yoes, I don't reckon an army of lawmen is the best way to catch this *hombre*."

Yoes glared. "You haven't had any luck bringing this man in, Reeves. I seem to recall that it was you who had that first arrest warrant, yet I don't remember you ever bringing Bob Dozier to our fair jail." The anger passed, and Yoes dropped into his leather seat, splashing two more fingers into the glass. "I am sorry, Bass. There was no call for such a rebuke. You've done more than anyone in trying to bring Bob Dozier to justice."

Bass shrugged. "I ain't done much, Marshal. Bob Dozier's still out in the Nations, still committin' crimes. Maybe I've gotten close a time or two. Reckon I at least got us some descriptions that we could put on them wanted dodgers. But I ain't catched him. That's certain sure. And, like you said, it's been close to two years. But. . . ." He sucked in a deep breath.

"Let's hear your idea, Reeves," Marshal Yoes said. "At this point in time, I am all ears to any plan."

Bass leaned forward in the chair. "Dozier knows the Territory better'n anybody, I warrant. He's got people sendin' him word whenever a posse's around. Posses got too many people. No, sir. I reckon this is a job for one man, two at the most. One man. He could flush out Dozier."

Tobacco juice rang against the brass cuspidor, and Jim Mershon wiped his mouth. "You that one man, Bass?" Mershon smiled.

"Well, I think I've learnt a passel about Dozier since the summer of 'Ninety. I know what he looks like, where he lives, how he operates. A big posse . . . that'll scare him into the hills, and you ain't never gonna flush him out. But me and another fellow . . . an Indian, I'd suggest, or part-Indian, a man who knows the Nations as good as Dozier . . . yes, sir. I'd say the two of us might just be able to do the job."

Silence.

"I got some experience in these kinds of things," Bass said. "Back in the 'Eighties, I operated like this when I was chasin' Jim Webb."

"Yes," Marshal Yoes said, "but Jim Mershon killed Jim Webb, if I recall correctly."

Mershon laughed, and Bass smiled.

"I like Bass's plan," Mershon said at last. "And Bass is right. He can do the job. I'd bet a year's salary on that."

Grant Johnson picked his fingernails, and Marshal Yoes rubbed his face with the back of his hand.

"All right, Bass," Yoes said at last. "You take your one man, and you go after Bob Dozier. I'll send my army after Ned Christie."

He slapped a $5 gold coin on the counter, and the clerk took it, turning around to reach for the sack of Arbuckles' coffee. When he faced Bass again, the pockmarked clerk said: "You're Bass Reeves, ain't you?"

Bass nodded.

"Got a message for you, Marshal." The clerk's Adam's apple bobbed. "From Bob Dozier."

"Let's hear it."

"Dozier says that, if you don't stop hounding him so, you're a dead man."

Bass put the coffee in the bag with the rest of his purchases. Laughing, he told the clerk: "Well, next time you see Bob Dozier, you tell him this. Tell him that Bass Reeves says that he'd have to stop runnin' to kill me." He touched the brim of his hat. "And I don't think Bob Dozier's gonna stop runnin'."

Another month had passed, and Bob Dozier was still running. Bass Reeves was still chasing. For close to three months, Bass had been dogging Dozier's trail. And now, finally, he felt it in his bones that the trail was about to end.

"Damn your miserable black skin, Bass Reeves, this ain't fittin' weather to be out of doors!"

Erskine Jones pulled his water-logged hat lower, and clutched his coat, hunching over in the saddle as his mule slogged through the muddy trail.

" 'Bout time you had a bath," Bass said.

"Mighty funny. Why don't we just ride

back to Grove? Let this storm pass? I'm soaked to my bones, Bass. We'll catch pneumonia iffen we don't get out of these wet duds."

"It won't be pneumonia that kills us." Bass pulled the reins of his horse, leaned forward, listening. He could see little beyond the white walls of rain. The skies were pitch black, though it must have been barely 2:00 in the afternoon. Water cascaded over the brim off his hat, and the wind whipped his face. July, but the rain and wind felt like October. Thunder rolled. A flash of lightning momentarily lit up the tree-studded Cherokee Hills. His hand reached for the Winchester, but he decided to leave it in the scabbard, which offered some, though slight, protection from the rain. After he straightened in the saddle, he pressed his spurs slightly to the horse, and rode deeper into the woods.

An hour passed. Then another. The first storm had moved on, but no sunlight appeared, and now another storm unleashed its wrath. Lightning streaked across the darkening skies, and the wind howled, bending the treetops, blasting their faces with hard, pelting drops of rain.

He gave his horse plenty of rein, letting it pick its own path down the slippery slope, looking over his shoulder to make sure Erskine Jones followed safely. The mule stumbled the last few yards, but kept its feet and Jones kept his seat.

"I can't see a damned thing, Bass!" Jones snapped. "And I got no hankerin' to get struck by lightnin'. Let's quit this damned foolishness and find a cave, or some place that's reasonably dry."

"That might be hard to find." Yet Bass nodded. "But you're right. Best call it quits for the day."

They moved down the ravine, its sides thick with forests, the wind moaning through the trees, the rain never slackening. Frequent lightning showed them the trail.

Suddenly weary, Bass slumped in the saddle. So close to Bob Dozier. He could almost feel it, taste it. Yet the skies darkened with every passing minute. Tomorrow, he made himself believe. *Tomorrow. . . .*

The bullet clipped the crown of his hat.

Bass never heard the shot. More from instinct, he pulled the Winchester from the saddle as he leaped off the horse. "Erskine!" he yelled.

The mule screamed. Jones cursed. Hoofs splashed.

Lightning flashed, and Bass saw Jones whipping his horse with his hat, heading down the ravine, then being swallowed by darkness. Bass's own horse ran in the opposite direction.

"Jones! You gutless . . . !"

Bass heard the second shot. He ran to the edge. Slipped on the wet rocks. Felt a third shot slam into a tree. Thunder echoed. Bass pulled himself into the thicket, thumbed back the Winchester's hammer, and stared into the dark.

Lightning streaked across the sky, and he saw the figure of a man diving behind a tree. He brought up the rifle, aimed, waited for the next flash. When the lightning struck again, the man was gone. Yet Bass fired. Jacked another round into the chamber. Pulled the trigger again. He couldn't see. Didn't have to. He knew he would draw Bob Dozier's fire.

A gunshot exploded, echoed by rolling thunder, and Bass felt the slug tear through his coat. He let out a little yip, pitched the rifle into the dirt, and tumbled out of the thicket, landing on the hard, wet rocks of the ravine's floor. Rain water soaked him. He lay still, but, when the next wave of thunder rumbled, he drew his Colt and thumbed back the hammer.

The water, the night, the wind chilled him. He lay in the open, unmoving, playing 'possum. It was a gamble, but he thought he knew Bob Dozier well enough. After two years chasing that bastard, he should know the man.

Dozier had a clear shot at him. All he'd have to do is wait for the lightning to flash, draw a bead, pull a trigger. Bass was willing to bet, however, that Dozier wouldn't fire, wouldn't waste a shot on what he assumed had to be a dead man.

Five minutes passed. No sound but the rain and wind. He wondered how far Erskine Jones had run. He began to doubt that his assailant was indeed Bob Dozier. He smelled mud. A puddle of water began forming under his nose.

Great, he thought. *I'll drown waiting for this guy.*

A spur chimed, and Bass held his breath. Someone laughed, and Bass knew he had been right. It was Bob Dozier. The trail was about to end, for one of them. Lightning flashed. Thunder crackled. Footsteps splashed. The laughter grew nearer. The footsteps halted.

"I warned you, lawdog," Bob Dozier said.

It marked the first time Bass had ever heard Dozier's voice. Bass rolled, came up to his knee, extending the Colt in his right hand. "Drop your gun, Bob. You're under arrest!"

Lightning revealed the surprise on Bob Dozier's face, flashed long enough for Bass to see the outlaw dropping to his knee, desperately working his rifle's lever.

Darkness. The Colt boomed, the flash almost blinding Bass. He dived to his right, thumbing the hammer, pulling the trigger again. Landed in thick, cold mud, then scrambled to his feet, cocking the revolver, but holding his fire.

He waited. Lightning flashed again, but he couldn't see anything, still half blinded by the muzzle flash of his own weapon. He stood, letting the rain fall, until the next flash of lightning streaked almost directly overhead, as if God held a lantern for Bass Reeves to see.

Bob Dozier lay ten feet away, Winchester across his chest, a bullet in his throat, raindrops bouncing off his face and unseeing eyes.

Chapter Twenty-One

I found Bass hunched over a bowl at Little George Thomas's Chili Joint.

Before joining Bass at the corner table in the café, I shed my slicker, for it had been misting rain all morning, and hung it, along with my hat, on the rack by the door.

Bass nodded at a steaming bowl as I sat across from him. "Ordered you some chili," he said, and picked up a hunk of cornbread, using it to mop up the remnants of his dinner.

As I unfolded a napkin and dropped it on my lap, he asked: "You check with the doctor?"

"Doctors," I corrected. "There are four in this town. Not a one treated a Negro, or anyone else for that matter, for a bullet wound over the past few days." I spooned hot chili into my mouth. "I even checked with the barber," I said while chewing.

267

"Figures," he said.

The chili tasted like fire. I picked up a glass of water to dose the flames in my mouth.

"We just going to wait here?" I asked.

Bass and I had arrived in Grove the previous afternoon, putting our horses up at the livery, and spent the night in an empty stall there. The livery man, a tall Osage, hadn't seen Cherokee Bob or anyone in town — or so he had claimed. No one else said they had noticed Cherokee Bob or any strangers in town, so we found a place to eat — Little George's place had been closed for the day — and turned in early. The next morning, instead of lighting out with hopes of picking up the trail, Bass had announced that we would stay in Grove for a spell. That's when my brain finally started working, and I had suggested calling on the doctors to see if they had treated the wounded outlaw.

"You probably ought to have a doctor examine you," I suggested.

He picked up his cup of coffee to wash down the last of his dinner.

A Seth Thomas wall clock chimed once.

"It's paining you," I said. "You were tossing and turning all night. Could barely walk this morning."

"You ain't gots to remind me." He looked

around for a waitress, but we were alone in the hard-scrabble picket building. He forced a smile. "But it ain't achin' so much now."

I decided on another attack. "If you're right about Cherokee Bob, my guess is that he'll be waiting for us in that ravine where you killed his father. What'd you say that was . . . four, five miles south of here?"

"Somethin' like that. It's been ten years. I don't know where Little George or that waitress got off to. Why don't you find a coffee pot, Dave. Pour yourself a cup while you're at it. Little George don't just make the best chili in the Territory, he brews up a good cup of coffee."

When I'd finished acting like an employee of George Thomas, I sat back across from Bass, and turned to look out the window. The rain fell a little harder now. I reached for the cup of coffee. "Shouldn't we be getting to that ravine?"

He shook his head. "Not sure even I could find it after all those years. It was stormin' something fierce that night. Nothin' like that little drizzle today. Besides, I ain't sure Dozier's son knows where his daddy bit the dust. More'n likely, they'd be waitin' for us along the road."

"I don't see any point in keeping those gents waiting."

"I do." He drained the coffee, wiped his mouth with the back of his hand. "I spent three months chasin' Bob Dozier. How long've we been after his boy? A week? Eight days?" He shrugged. "I figure to make Cherokee Bob come after me." He tapped a thick finger on the table. "Right here."

Leaning back in my chair, I studied Bass. My expression must have bemused him.

"He ain't got no patience, Cherokee Bob. Not like his daddy, and Bob Dozier didn't possess the temperament of an oyster. He'll be along directly."

"And Bennie?"

Bass's face saddened. "I don't know," he said with a heavy sigh. "Reckon I don't know my son at all."

His head shook, and I regretted my question.

So we spent another day in Grove. The rain stopped around 1:30, and I walked north from Tenth Street all the way to First, then east to Cherokee Street and west to Center. Pretty much covered the entire town. Nothing looked suspicious, and I recognized no horses.

Dr. Drummond, the first sawbones I had interviewed that morning, was stepping out of Aunt Jane Longmire's Boarding House after I had made my rounds, and I decided to act.

"Didn't expect to find you still in our fair city, Marshal," he said, and finished picking his teeth with a toothpick, which he tossed into the mud.

"Didn't expect to be here myself." I paused long enough to summon courage. Bass was going to kill me. "Wonder if you'd mind looking at a friend of mine."

"What's his ailment?"

"Bullet in his thigh."

He stared.

"And a contrary nature," I added.

Dr. Drummond smiled. "Let me fetch my bag at my office."

"When Marshal Adams said you had a contrary nature, he wasn't kidding." Exasperated, Dr. Drummond shook his head, and poured medicine over the wound in Bass's leg. Bass cussed the doctor and me, and fell back on the straw.

"Hold still!"

"You try holdin' still," Bass grumbled, "with somebody tryin' to tear your leg off."

I leaned forward, held Bass's shoulders. His eyes met mine, revealing pure hatred.

"Nobody's taking your leg off, Marshal Reeves." Drummond brought a scalpel from

271

the lantern. "Yet." He sliced.

Bass spit in my face. Not intentional. Just from the pain, I think.

The doctor squeezed the thigh, brought up a rag, and wiped the wound. "What in blazes did you put on this wound?"

"Ask Dave. He done the doctorin'."

Now I looked into Dr. Drummond's eyes. I shrugged. "Boiled pine pitch."

The doctor shook his head, opened a jar, and applied some smelly salve to the wound, then wrapped it up with fresh bandages. "I'd have to operate," he said, "to get that bullet out. And I did not attend the medical school at the University of Michigan to perform surgery in a livery stable."

"You ain't cuttin' no more on me," Bass said.

"Either that bullet comes out, Marshal" — the light banter of the doctor's tone had disappeared — "or that leg comes off. Eventually. Either way, you'll be walking with a cane or wooden leg for the rest of your life." Drummond reached into his black satchel, and pulled out a bottle. He uncorked it, took a pull, and passed the bottle to Bass.

Bass sat up, accepted the bottle, and drank.

"I'm serious, Marshal. That wound isn't

infected yet, but only by the grace of God. That bullet will have to come out. Or you'll die."

Bass took another sip of clear liquor, then passed the bottle back to the doctor.

"Cherokee Bob might make it all moot, Doc."

"Well, you're not going after him. You wouldn't last thirty minutes in a saddle."

"Don't plan on it. Plan on Cherokee Bob comin' here."

Dr. Drummond paused, stared hard at Bass, then at me. Realizing Bass was serious, the doctor brought the bottle to his mouth and drank. He started to cork it, thought better, and tossed it to me.

"When?" he asked.

Bass shrugged.

I coughed. "Damnation! This is pure grain alcohol." I tossed the bottle back to Drummond.

"Tomorrow, maybe," Bass answered. "Day after. All I gots to do is walk out onto the street, Doc."

Dr. Drummond stared, then began gathering his tools and medicines, piling them into the open bag. "Tomorrow you might be able to walk," he said without looking at Bass or me. "I'm not sure about the day after."

Bass pulled up his pants.

"I can give you some codeine," Drummond said. "Deaden the pain."

"Reckon I'll pass, Doc."

The doctor pursed his lips for a moment, then said: "I guess you don't want laudanum, either."

Bass slipped the suspenders over his shoulders. "Need my brain to be clear. Eyes focused. For Bennie."

"Bennie?" Dr. Drummond snapped his grip shut. "Who's Bennie?"

Neither of us answered, and the doctor took a half eagle for payment, tipped his bowler, and left Bass and me in the livery.

For a long while, we just sat there in silence. The only sound came from the horses swishing their tails in the other stalls. Finally Bass cleared his throat.

"When Cherokee Bob comes, you stay out of the fight, Dave."

"Can't do that, Bass."

"The hell you can't. This ain't your fight."

I tapped the badge. "This says otherwise."

Bass looked up, and slowly fingered his own tin star pinned to his vest. He turned from me, and stared out the open livery door. "He'll be here tomorrow," he said. "Figured he'd come today. But tomorrow."

"Maybe Bennie won't be with him, Bass," I said.

"Maybe."

Both of us knew better.

Dr. Drummond brought a cane the next morning, and we hobbled over to Aunt Jane's for breakfast, and then spent the remainder of the morning mostly cleaning our weapons, waiting. Town had turned unnaturally quiet, the streets practically empty, and I wondered if Drummond had spread the news, warned everyone what might — *might* — happen this day.

When dinnertime came around, the citizens of Grove must have decided that Bass Reeves was an idiot, for the boardwalks became a trifle more crowded, and wagons and horses journeyed down the streets. Bass and I found ourselves back in Little George Thomas's Chili Joint, wondering if Bass had guessed wrong.

I was topping off our coffee cups when a voice called from out on Third Street: "Bass! Bass Reeves!"

Bass pushed himself to his feet, grabbed his cane. I fetched my hat from the rack, and stared out the window, my heart sinking as Bass hobbled toward me.

Cherokee Bob stood in the center of the street, his boots in a mud puddle from yesterday's shower. Beside him stood Bennie Reeves.

Bass whispered an oath, and tucked the Winchester under his arm. "You ain't got to walk out with me. . . ."

"Hush now." I ran my hand over my jaw. "If that colored guy Grant shot isn't dead. . . ."

"He's with 'em," Bass finished the thought for me.

We stared at each other.

"His arm was likely busted," Bass said. "Left arm, but he was left-handed."

"Means he won't be good at long range," I said.

"Scatter-gun," Bass said.

I nodded.

"From behind us," Bass said.

My head bobbed again, and I looked out the window. Across the street, an alley ran between the Sequoyah Mercantile and Martha's Millinery. Close enough, I figured, for the black man to do some damage with a shotgun. I pointed, and Bass grunted.

"Bass Reeves, come on out here, you yellow dog!" Cherokee Bob looked nervous. Bennie took a slight step back as Bass pushed open the door.

"You take the shotgun," Bass said. "I'll handle Cherokee Bob." He swallowed. "And

276

Bennie."

We stepped into the street.

"You're under arrest, Robert Dozier, Junior," Bass said, relying on the cane, rifle still under his arm. "For the robbery of the Katy and too many other crimes to mention."

The young Negro laughed, and hooked his thumbs on his gun belt. "Serve your warrant, old man."

We walked, Bass limping, me slowing my gait to match his. Kept on walking, too, forcing the smirk off Cherokee Bob's face.

He took a step back, said: "You two laws stop right there. Stop!" He and Bennie backed up again, and the outlaw put his hand on the butt of one of his guns.

Bass and I stopped ten yards in front of the two. Yet we had covered enough ground that the Negro with the shotgun would have to step out of that alley to get a clear shot at us.

The Winchester felt clammy in my hand. Always did before a gun battle. Cherokee Bob wore two Remington revolvers, butt forward; his right arm stretched across his stomach, hand gripping a Remington butt. An old Navy Colt was stuck in Bennie's waistband, but Bennie's hands hung loosely at his side.

"I. . . ." Bass stopped. He let the cane fall into the mud.

I didn't look at him, kept my eyes trained on Bennie and Cherokee Bob, and kept my ears open for the sound of the other Negro coming out of that alley. Yet I could sense Bass shaking his head, sadly.

"You were ten years old last time I saw you."

At first, I thought Bass was talking to Bennie, but I knew that couldn't be right. Then I remembered the story he had told me about Marshal Yoes's posse at the Dozier farm, with that ten-year-old boy shaking with rage on his front porch. That kid had grown up into a man, a big man with a mustache and beard stubble on his face, a man who had tortured and murdered whiskey runners, who had ambushed a federal posse on the Illinois River and in a rugged pass east of Vinita. Worse than his father by a long shot. Yet Bass must have seen a little boy watching his world turned asunder.

I found myself staring at Bennie, realizing that he was not much older, if even older, than Bob Dozier, Jr. This was a boy I had watched grow up. A man who had murdered his wife, yet I saw the kid barber, the teenager playing marbles with other coloreds in Muskogee. Then I saw the scab on his head, where he had tried to kill himself after murdering his wife.

"This is like something right out of one of those dime novels," said Cherokee Bob, the calmness, the cockiness returning. "Reckon one of them boys will write about me."

He was right about that.

"About how I killed Bass Reeves." There was something in Cherokee Bob's eyes. Something dangerous, something insane.

"Son," Bass said, "this is all my damned fault. I. . . ." He spit.

Bewilderment masked Cherokee Bob's face.

I listened, watched, waited.

"Might as well have been me killin' that wife of your'n," Bass said. "I never was good at nothin', Ben. Horses I knowed. Marshalin' I knowed. But I never knowed how to be a good daddy, a decent husband. Always let my job take me from where I should 'a' been. I don't blame you none, Ben. I want you to know that. I'm sorry, Son. Sorry I was always comparin' you to Robert, sorry I wasn't there for you, or your ma, or all your siblin's. Sorry what I told you I'd 'a' done iffen that had been my wife cheatin' on me. It's all my fault, Ben. I want you to know that, Son. Want you to know . . . I love you, boy. I've always loved you."

Chapter Twenty-Two

June 18, 1902

Keeping his hand on the Remington's butt, Cherokee Bob moved his left hand off the belt, raised the arm, pushed back his hat, and asked: "The hell's this big nigger to you, Bennie?"

For practically a decade, I have tried to piece together what happened on that early afternoon of June 18th in Grove. Yet eighteen years riding for the federal court taught me a few things about criminal investigations. Ask two witnesses to a crime to tell what they saw and you'll get two stories that vary widely. The truth likely falls somewhere between. Ask ten people, and you'll get ten versions. Even experienced lawmen might not agree on events that transpired before their very own eyes.

When men are shooting at you, your mind plays tricks. It blocks out some things, imagines others. It's hard to say if this is exactly the way things happened, but I dare say it's as close to the truth as we'll ever know in this lifetime.

Cherokee Bob repeated: "I asked you what's that nigger to you, boy?" Never taking his eyes off Bass, however.

Bennie's Adam's apple bobbed. Up the road, a door slammed shut, and I noticed how the streets and boardwalks had suddenly emptied. Maybe I could see a few brave faces peering from behind curtains in the stores along the street, although that could have been my imagination. Behind me and to the left, I thought I heard a step. My thumb scratched the hammer of the Winchester.

"He's my father," Bennie said, and drew his revolver.

I only glimpsed that, seeing Bass as he tilted up the barrel of his big rifle. I only glimpsed that because I was spinning, dropping to my knee, earing back the .25-35's hammer. Cutter Beckham — his body would be identified by Little George Thomas and two other Grove residents — had stepped out of the alley. A woolen scarf held his shattered left arm in a sling close to his chest, but his hand still gripped the forearm of a sawed-off 12-gauge, the stock braced against his crotch, right hand against

281

the grip, fingers on both triggers. That's not all I saw.

"Son-of-a-bitch, Bass!" I bellowed. "There's three of them!"

The Negro with the shotgun stepping out of the alley, we had expected. Yet another man, a long-haired Indian in buckskins and moccasins, had braced a rifle against the wooden column at the corner of Little George's small restaurant, and a third — who I recognized as Henry Black Dog, the big Osage who ran the livery stable — stood on the roof of the Sequoyah Mercantile, levering a Henry rifle behind the wooden façade.

The rest, as I have conceded, is a blur.

I pulled the Winchester's trigger, and dived into the mud, jacking the lever while moving, coming up, putting another slug into Cutter Beckham. His shotgun unleashed both barrels, but the buckshot only riddled the water trough in front of him as he staggered backward, dropping the gun, reaching for a holstered pistol with his right hand. It was an awkward movement, for he was left-handed, and had two .25-35 slugs in his stomach. I sent a third bullet chasing him, but missed. It didn't matter.

Cutter Beckham never got the Merwin Hulbert .44 out of his holster. He crashed through the plate-glass window of Martha's Millinery, and fell backward, dead. A scream came from inside the dressmaker's shop. The Negro's boots dangled out of the broken glass and splintered wood.

Before I had even pulled the trigger, Bennie Reeves had drawn his Navy Colt and shot Cherokee Bob in the back. The bullet tore through the outlaw's buckskin jacket and his shell belt, just behind the hip, and Cherokee Bob dropped onto both knees in the mud. Bennie's gunshot kept the killer alive for a few more minutes because Bass had sent a round from his big rifle that would have killed Dozier immediately. Instead, it knocked off the blackguard's hat.

"Behind you, Daddy!" Bennie cried, and jerked the trigger, aiming at the Indian with the rifle. The bullet whined off the metal rim atop a trash barrel down the boardwalk.

"Shit!" the Indian cried.

Bennie thumbed back the hammer, fired at Cherokee Bob again — and missed. By then, Cherokee Bob had recovered, was drawing both of his Remingtons, screaming out profanities lost amid the roar of gunfire. Horses tethered to rails and posts up and down the street snorted and stomped their hoofs, tugging at reins, halters, and hobbles. Somewhere, a bullet shattered a glass. The dressmaker kept screaming. A dog howled.

Seeing Cherokee Bob dropped by Bennie's first shot, and hearing my warning, Bass had turned, stepping to his right.

"Roof of the mercantile!" I shouted.

Meanwhile, I drew a bead on the Indian in front of the chili joint.

Having recovered from his shock at Bennie's actions, smoke and flame belched from the Indian's rifle as he shot at me, but the bullet didn't come close. I fired, but saw only splinters fly from the door to Little George's place. My shot had gone as wide as the Indian's.

Our next shots plowed up mud. I squeezed the trigger again. The wooden column shuddered. The Indian backed away, worked the lever, fired from his hip. Once. A miss. Twice. Another miss. We were two experienced gunmen, forty, no more than fifty feet from each other, shooting long-range rifles.

That's another thing I learned during my career as a peace officer in Indian Territory. When a man is trying to shoot you dead, and you're trying to kill him, your aim is likely to be just as bad as his.

I moved toward him, trying to steady my arms and see through the blinding smoke. A bullet tore off my hat. That shot hadn't come from the Indian, but from my right.

Cherokee Bob. His second shot knocked me off my feet.

What had happened during all this ruction was this. Guns drawn, Cherokee Bob Dozier scrambled to his feet, charged after Bennie. Bennie pulled a trigger a fourth time at pointblank range, yet missed. His fifth try resulted in a misfire, a common malady for antiquated Navy Colts. Then Cherokee Bob, hobbling from the bullet Bennie had put in his back, smashed Bennie's face with a Remington's barrel. Bennie dropped into the street like a sack of potatoes. He lay there, if not unconscious then half dead, blood gushing from his nose and lips, two broken teeth.

Cherokee Bob leveled his pistol, aimed at Bennie, then remembered who he really had come to Grove to kill. He turned, sent a shot at Bass, saw me, and, for some reason, changed his aim, pulled the trigger once, twice. His second bullet hit me just above the knee, and down I went.

Bass focused on Henry Black Dog. Also likely distracted by Bennie's shots, the Osage rushed his first shot, and the .44 slug clipped the top of Bass's suspenders. The top of the façade splintered from Bass's shot, and both men levered their rifles. Black Dog fired, but jerked the trigger.

Bass's shot took off Black Dog's left ear, and the rifle slipped from the Osage's hands, clattering on the façade, falling onto the awning above the mercantile's front doors, and bouncing onto the boardwalk. The Indian reached for a Colt tucked in his waistband, but he never found the revolver. Bass's round went through Black Dog's hand, tearing off the middle and ring fingers, through his stomach just above the belly button, and traveled upward, blowing a fist-size hole out of the middle of his back. The impact sent him to his knees, and he leaned over the rooftop, vomiting blood, then falling, headfirst, landing on the boardwalk. I doubt, however, if he felt his neck snap.

Cherokee Bob fired again and again. One bullet cut a furrow across Bass's arm, and Bass turned, jacking a cartridge into the Winchester, shooting from the hip. Cherokee Bob dropped the Remington, tossed the revolver in his left hand to his right, thumbing back the hammer, squeezing the trigger once, twice.

We assumed that the outlaw thought his first pistol was empty, but, in all the commotion, he must have become confused and miscounted his shots. For, after the carnage, when Dr. Drummond picked up the nickel-plated revolver, he found two unfired .44-40 shells in the cylinder.

Bass sent a bullet that grazed Cherokee Bob's neck and dropped him onto his hindquarters. He sat there, legs outstretched, bleeding profusely from the wounds in his neck and back, looking as if he was struck dumb. Bass fired again. The bullet hit the big, brass, oval belt buckle, knocking Cherokee Bob onto his back, but the outlaw still held the revolver, jerking the trigger, the bullet barely missing his own foot.

Seeing me on the ground, thinking me dead, the Indian in front of the chili eatery turned his attention to the back of Bass Reeves. He squeezed the trigger, but the bullet went through Bass's leg, the same leg that still had a chunk of lead in it from the ambush at the pass a few days earlier. It was a clean shot, missing the bone, but it upended Bass. The Winchester flipped out of his hands, landing in the mud between him and Cherokee Bob, who was trying to sit up.

Bass landed face down in the street. He pushed himself up, spit out a gob of mud, rolled, drew the Colt, but ignored the Indian who had shot him. Instead, he tried to finish off Cherokee Bob. Both Cherokee

Bob and Bass fired, and both missed.

The Indian pulled the trigger, but the hammer snapped. Empty. He pitched it aside, pulled a little Smith & Wesson from behind his back.

By then, I had rolled over. I didn't know where my rifle was, and pain flamed up and down my leg. Still, I found my .44 revolver, and I pushed myself back against the water trough that was leaking water from Cutter Beckham's buckshot. I pulled the trigger just as fast as I could. It was a self-cocking double-action, and I had loaded six bullets in the cylinder — instead of the usual five for safety reasons — before eating dinner at Little George's. None of those bullets came close. One shattered the window to the restaurant. Yet I must have put the fear of God into that Indian, because he dropped the .32 on the boardwalk, and took off running, north, around the first corner. He stole the first horse he could find, and galloped out of town toward the Missouri border.

Who he was, we never learned. The Indian was never caught, and nobody would be left alive who could have identified him.

Bass tried to stand, but his leg would not co-operate, and he pitched into the mud, but pulled himself up. Cherokee Bob still sat in the mud. They pulled the triggers. Missed.

I dropped my empty Smith & Wesson into a puddle of water — not enough time to reload. Spotting the Henry rifle near Henry Black Dog's dead body, I jumped up as best I could with a bullet in one leg, desperate to get that rifle. That was the last thing I remembered for a while.

It's embarrassing to admit, but, when I leaped up, my head struck the handle of the trough's water pump. As fast as I shot to my feet, I dropped into the mud, a knot the size of a revolver's butt forming on my skull.

I was out cold.

Bass sent a bullet through Cherokee Bob's chest, knocking the outlaw back onto his back, but, again, the kid raised his pistol, pulled the trigger, and Bass Reeves spun, fell to his knees, and toppled over on his side.

Echoes of gunfire died. The only noise came from the occasional shriek from the dressmaker, and dogs now barking all across town.

The entire fight had lasted scarcely more than one minute.

Groaning, Cherokee Bob pushed himself to his feet. He slipped, caught his breath, stood again, weaving. Bass's last bullet had cracked a rib, but miraculously missed any vital organ. It was still a serious wound, but he bit his lip, blocking out the pain.

A groan rose behind him, and he saw Bennie lying there, moving his head sideways. The outlaw turned his gun on the lad, aimed, and squeezed the trigger. A loud metallic click told him his gun was empty.

"Lucky bastard," Cherokee Bob said, and staggered toward the body of Bass Reeves, emptying his cylinder, feeding fresh bullets from his shell belt into the chambers.

"Daddy. . . ." Bennie's voice sounded haunting. He was alternately trying to push himself up, then holding his head, too stunned for his body to function. "Daddy . . . ," Bennie choked out, sobbing. "Daddy . . . Daddy . . . Dad. . . ."

Cherokee Bob stood over Bass, spit on him, and snapped the chamber gate shut on his revolver. He put the toe of his boot under the lawman's side, and sucked in a deep breath. He managed to laugh.

"You ain't so tough after all."

He rolled Bass over . . . and saw the Colt in Bass's hand.

"No!"

They say Cherokee Bob's scream even silenced the hysterical dressmaker. He tried to cock the Remington, but Bass's Colt boomed, and Cherokee Bob Dozier flew backward, landing spread-eagled in the mud.

He didn't move.

Bass crawled through the mud, keeping his eyes and the Colt's barrel on the dead outlaw. When he reached his Winchester, he shoved the pistol in its holster, and used the rifle to push himself to his feet. He limped, blood soaking his pants leg, a splotch of crimson spreading down his shirt from where Cherokee Bob's bullet had carved a ditch across his ribs. Briefly he paused to look into Cherokee Bob Dozier's lifeless eyes.

"You're as ignorant as your old man was," Bass said, and walked through the mud, muck, blood, and empty brass casings toward his son.

Chapter Twenty-Three

January 18, 1903

"All rise."

I pushed myself up off the hard, uncomfortable bench, leaning on the cane I still relied upon six months after Cherokee Bob Dozier's bullet had torn through my leg on the streets of Grove, Cherokee Nation.

Judge Charles W. Raymond entered the court stroking his close-cropped, salt-and-pepper beard. "Be seated," he said, but he kept standing.

In his early to mid-forties, Raymond was an Iowan by birth but had grown up in Ohio, Illinois, and Indiana, his father having been killed while fighting to preserve the Union in the battle of Nashville. Raymond had been admitted to the Illinois bar in 1886, and in 1901 President McKinley had appointed him judge of the U.S. Court of Indian Territory, a commission President Roosevelt had reaffirmed a year later.

Everyone worships the late Isaac C. Parker, but I don't believe that you could find a better judge that C.W. Raymond. Of the thousands of trials he oversaw, only five decisions were ever reversed, and he wasted no time in getting down to business, especially on that morning in the Muskogee courthouse.

"The purpose of an evidentiary hearing," he began, "is to determine if there is sufficient evidence to require a trial. Commissioner Leckley has filed a criminal complaint against the defendant. For a trial to happen, I must find there is probable cause that a crime has been committed. That is why we are here this morning."

I knew all this, of course, as did the lawyers, bailiff, and stenographer, naturally. The judge was speaking to the newspaper reporters and spectators. This wasn't even an actual trial, and the courtroom was packed. People stood against the back wall, and more people waited outside in the upstairs hallway. After eyeing the courtroom, Judge Raymond cleared his throat, and continued.

"The defendant may be assisted by counsel, as in an actual trial, and the court will recognize that Mister Andersen of the Fort Smith firm, Kyser, Day, and Goodman, has been appointed as the defendant's attorney. That said, there are differences between the proceedings that will begin shortly and the rules for a criminal trial. Most importantly hearsay evidence is allowed in an evidentiary, or preliminary, hearing. What we must determine before we can proceed, if I so rule to a criminal trial, is . . . one, if the crime, rather alleged crime, occurred within the jurisdiction of this court, and, two, as I have previously mentioned, if there is probable cause to believe that the defendant committed said crime. This does not mean that the defendant is guilty, and the newspaper journalists gathered here should not convict the defendant if this case goes to trial. All it means is that there is enough evidence for a trial to be held."

He stopped again, examined the courtroom, and said: "Very well, let us dispense with the preliminaries and get to the bread and butter. Mister Leckley, you have the floor."

U.S. Commissioner Harlow A. Leckley ran a finger under his paper collar, rose, and began spouting and pontificating and speechifying. I rubbed my knee, and glanced over at Bass, who sat behind his son, his hands on Bennie's shoulders. Despite the chill of the winter morning outside, it was hot in this chock-a-block courtroom. Sweat trickled down Bass's cheeks.

Dr. Drummond had managed to patch up my leg, to get the bullets out of Bass's, to wrap up Bennie's head, and to perform a coroner's inquest that determined that Robert Dozier, Jr., Henry Black Dog, and Cutter Beckham had died in a gun battle with federal authorities while resisting arrest. Bennie could not identify the Indian who had fled. According to his testimony, he didn't even know the Osage livery man or the Indian were part of Cherokee Bob's outfit until he saw them that afternoon outside of Little George Thomas's Chili Joint.

The evidentiary hearing being held in Muskogee had nothing to do with that shoot-out, and Bennie had already been indicted and arraigned for the murder of his wife — that trial was scheduled to begin January 22nd. This hearing was to determine if Bennie should be tried for the murder of George Littledave during an ambush at Ketchum's Gap that had also led to the death of posse member Wes Bushyhead and wounded Deputy U.S. Marshals Grant Johnson and Bass Reeves and posse member Erskine Jones.

Harlow Leckley called the prosecution's

star witness.

Wearing an ill-fitting suit, Erskine Jones strode to the chair, and took the oath. The doctor in Vinita had been forced to cut off Jones's ear when infection had set in. His left sleeve was pinned up above his elbow. The doctor had amputated his arm, too.

He took the stand, and stared, not at Bennie, not at the solicitor, not at me, but at Bass Reeves as he began his testimony.

His testimony follows here as transcribed from the court records:

COMMISSIONER LECKLEY: *Where were you, Mister Jones, on the Fifteenth of June last?*

JONES: *I was riding with a posse after Cherokee Bob Dozier in the northern region of the Cherokee Nation.*

LECKLEY: *And what happened at Ketchum's Gap on that day?*

JONES: *We got bushwhacked.*

LECKLEY: *By whom?*

JONES: *Cherokee Bob Dozier was there. So was that boy. A few others on the scout.*

LECKLEY: *By "that boy," do you mean the defendant, Benjamin Reeves?*

JONES: *Yep.*

LECKLEY: *You saw the defendant?*

296

JONES: He run down the hill, crossed the road, got on a horse, and hightailed it. Got away. But iffen you ask me, Bass Reeves let his son get out of there alive.

ANDERSEN: Objection, Your Honor. This is not testimony.

JUDGE RAYMOND: Sustained. I will allow hearsay, Mister Jones, but not your opinion, sir.

LECKLEY: You are absolutely sure that you recognized the defendant during this shooting scrape?

JONES: I said so, didn't I? Yeah, he was there, all right.

LECKLEY: Did you lose your arm while performing your duties as a member of the federal marshal's posse during that ambush?

JONES: Yep. My ear, too. Taken some buckshot in my leg.

LECKLEY: Who else was injured during that fight?

JONES: Bass Reeves got shot in the leg. Wes Bushyhead was shot all to pieces and got killed dead. Grant Johnson, another federal lawman, was hit in the arm. And George Littledave, an old Cherokee scout, got killed deader than dirt.

LECKLEY: Did George Littledave identify his killer?

JONES: He did so. Yes, he did. He told Deputy Dave Adams that Bennie Reeves done it.

ANDERSEN: Objection, Your Honor. The witness did not hear that alleged declaration himself.

JUDGE RAYMOND: This being a preliminary hearing, Mister Andersen, I will allow this.

LECKLEY: Thank you, Your Honor. For the record, Mister Jones, let me get this straight. Deputy Adams did tell, in your presence, that George Littledave, in a dying declaration, said Bennie Reeves had killed him.

JONES: He done so, yes. I heard him. Told me and Bass and Uncle Bud.

LECKLEY: By Uncle Bud, you mean?

JONES: Bud Ledbetter. He's a lawman, too, up in Vinita. Was part of our posse.

LECKLEY: How many years, Mister Jones, have you been engaged on posses in the Indian Territory?

JONES: Don't rightly know. Probably fifteen, twenty, maybe more, first out of the Fort Smith court. Usually as a translator or scout. Then after the court got moved to Paris, Texas. Finally when they made this here court. Been a while. Been a scout and a translator and lately I been driving the tumbleweed wagon. Been a guard and the likes for them prisoners.

LECKLEY: By tumbleweed wagon, you mean the wagon that is used to transport felons arrested by federal deputies to the jail in Muskogee?

JONES: Yep.

CROSS-EXAMINATION

ANDERSEN: First, Mister Jones, let me commend your duty over these years. You were shot during the ambush, and the results of those wounds resulted in the amputation of an ear and your left arm.

JONES: Yeah. My leg aches, too. Got hit with buckshot. But that ain't why I limp so. Hoss rolled over me oncet when I was in my cups.

(JUDGE RAYMOND WARNS COURT-ROOM SPECTATORS THAT NO ONE SHOULD FIND HUMOR WHEN A MAN'S LIFE IS AT STAKE, AND WARNS THE WITNESS TO ANSWER ONLY THE QUESTION HE HAS BEEN ASKED.)

ANDERSEN: You must have been in considerable pain?

JONES: Hurt like a son-of-a . . . hurt like blazes.

ANDERSEN: With four to six men shoot-

299

ing down at you from the ridge top? Is that right?

JONES: Lead was flying thicker than thieves, certain sure.

ANDERSEN: From reports I have read, Wes Bushyhead was dead, and Marshal Bass Reeves wounded, taking shelter behind a dead horse. Is that correct?

JONES: Yep.

ANDERSEN: Where were you?

JONES: I . . . I taken shelter, too.

ANDERSEN: You were hiding!

LECKLEY: Objection.

JUDGE RAYMOND: Phrase questions, counsel.

ANDERSEN: Were you not hiding?

JONES: I taken cover. Wasn't hiding. No, sir.

ANDERSEN: Did you return fire at your assailants?

JONES: I . . . well . . . don't rightly recollect.

ANDERSEN: Be that as it may, you were grievously wounded, in considerable pain, and taking cover while "lead was flying thicker than thieves." Yet you could identify the defendant running across the road? Come now, sir.

JONES: He was there, damn it. Nobody ain't going to deny that. Even that boy. And

*George Littledave, in his dying words, said
that boy killed him.*

*ANDERSEN: Isn't it true, Jones, that you
blame Marshal Reeves for the injuries that
have crippled you? Isn't that why you have
made up these shameless falsehoods?*

*JONES: I'm telling the truth. That boy
killed George Littledave. Murdered his
wife, too. Took to the scout in the Cherokee Nation. Got my mules killed when
Cherokee Bob busted him out. I'm honest
as the day is long.*

*ANDERSEN: Honest as the day is long
indeed. I'm finished with this witness, Your
Honor.*

The prosecution rested after only one witness. It sure seemed enough, but then
Malcolm Andersen called me to the stand
to testify for the defense.

"You heard Erskine Jones's testimony,
Deputy Adams," Malcolm Andersen began,
smiling, trying to put me at ease, and maybe
I was a tad nervous. As a federal lawman, I
had never been called to testify for the
defense. "How accurate was his testimony?"

"Not very," I said.

Jones shot out of his chair. "You callin'
me a liar, Dave?" Judge Raymond's gavel
fell. "You was there. You know what hap-

301

pened." The gavel fell again, harder, and a bailiff made his way toward the angry Choctaw. "You know that boy kilt poor old man Littledave. You was up there!"

Raymond fined Erskine $10 for contempt of court, and had the bailiff lead him to the jail for the duration of the hearing.

Once order had been restored, Andersen asked me again what had happened at Ketchum's Gap, then changed his direction.

"Before we get into the ambush, how long have you known the Territory's witness, Erskine Jones?"

"He's been around since I've been marshaling here."

"Do you know any reason he might have to perjure himself?"

The commissioner objected, but Judge Raymond said he would allow the question.

"Well, Erskine Jones has always been a hardcase, often bickering at Bass Reeves, that's Bennie's father. Bass is a federal deputy, too. Erskine was partly responsible for Bennie being at Ketchum's Gap that day." I explained how Bennie had gotten Jones's pistol, which Jones had been carrying against orders, and how Bass had mentioned to me later that Erskine Jones had deserted him during a shooting scrape with Cherokee Bob's father.

The commissioner glared at me like I had just stabbed his mother.

"Now," Andersen said, "what happened at Ketchum's Gap?"

"We were ambushed. We had expected it. I climbed up one ridge with George Littledave, and we engaged in a running fight."

Trials, testimony — they sound so indifferent, so distant. It's not like the memories, the nightmares. Words, written or spoken, can't capture the emotion of being shot at, of shooting to kill another human being.

"What happened on top of the ridge that you and the late George Littledave climbed?"

I took a deep breath, slowly exhaled, and said: "Bass and I shot a Creek outlaw . . . Bass was down on the road, shooting up. Bud Ledbetter and Grant Johnson were on the top of the other ledge, shooting at Cherokee Bob and others. Cauley, that was the Creek's name Bass and I fired at, was killed. There was another outlaw there, an Osage half-breed, Big Thom was his name. He was killed on the road, trying to make it to the horses. You see, they were trying to ambush us, but we had expected that, and surprised them a bit. That took the fight out of most of them, and they fled."

"Bennie Reeves, the defendant, he was on

303

that ridge, too?"

I nodded. Judge Raymond scolded me that I knew better than that, and I answered orally for the court record.

"What happened to George Littledave?" the attorney asked.

My head shook. "I don't know. There were a lot of bullets flying. After everything had cleared, I found George. He had a bullet hole in his stomach, and was bleeding profusely. There was nothing I could do for him. That wound was mortal. George said . . . 'It was him. It was him.' . . . and then he died."

"He never identified the defendant, Benjamin Reeves, as his assailant?"

"No, sir. He just said 'It was him.' Twice. Maybe three times. I'm not altogether sure. But that's all he said . . . 'It was him.' That's what I told Bass and the other deputies when I went back down onto the road. That's what Erskine Jones overheard me say. George Littledave never said Bennie Reeves killed him. He just said . . . 'It was him.' "

"How long have you been a federal deputy?"

"Since 'Eighty-Nine."

"I commend your service, Marshal Adams, and your honesty. I pass the witness."

Leckley shot out of his seat, came right up to me, and spoke harshly. That's a solicitor for you. In the last trial for which I had been a witness, U.S. Commissioner Harlow A. Leckley had praised me as the greatest lawman since The Three Guardsmen of Oklahoma.

"The defendant was there, was he not?"

I could smell coffee and cigarettes on Leckley's breath. "He was up on that hill."

"Firing his weapon, was he not? Did he not fire his weapon in an attempt to maim or kill you and George Littledave?"

Here's where things got a mite ticklish for me. I looked over at Bennie, but mostly at Bass sitting right behind him, and I found myself shaking my head.

"I never saw Bennie Reeves pull a trigger," I answered.

It wasn't perjury. Not really. I remembered seeing Bennie bringing up his pistol, but I was diving behind a tree or boulder or some sort of shelter. Maybe Bennie had fired a shot. I, however, couldn't honestly say I had seen that happen.

"Come on, Deputy Adams!" the lawyer roared. "You're a longtime friend with Bass Reeves, a federal deputy who happens to be the defendant's father. You saw the defendant pull that trigger. You saw him kill. . . ."

305

Malcolm Andersen objected, but Harlow Leckley went right on screaming in my face. "You saw Benjamin Reeves shoot! You heard George Littledave say . . . 'It was him.' I have read Se-la-gwo-ya Johnston's account in the Tahlequah newspaper, sir. I can summon that reporter to testify as well."

Malcolm Andersen voiced his objection again, longer, shouting something about my long-standing service to this court and that I was not on trial. Judge Raymond, however, never reached for his gavel.

"Dave Adams is not on trial, yet!" Leckley thundered, turning away from me and pointing a long finger at Andersen. "But he might face a perjury charge if he doesn't speak the truth." He faced me again. "Now let's have the truth, sir. You know, as God is your witness, you know that Littledave meant the defendant when he said 'him.' Isn't that the truth, Deputy Adams?"

Silence. Like the whole world waited for my answer.

Judge Raymond said: "Answer the question, Deputy Adams."

I wet my lips. "As far as I know, George Littledave wouldn't have known Bennie Reeves on sight. I don't think they ever met. When Littledave said . . . 'It was him.' . . . he could have meant Big Thom. Or, half out of his mind, he could have been seeing death coming to carry him home. Se-la-gwo-ya Johnston, that ink-slinger in Tahlequah, well, sir, he wasn't at Ketchum's Gap. I don't think newspaper reports are accurate to begin with, for the most part, and I know that one wasn't. Johnston never asked me what happened. Didn't ask Bass, or Grant, or anyone, except maybe Erskine Jones." After letting that settle, I finished. "And the only time I personally ever saw Bennie Reeves pull a trigger came a few days later on the streets of Grove when he shot Cherokee Bob Dozier. Likely helped save the lives of Bass and me that day."

CHAPTER TWENTY-FOUR

January 24, 1903

They found Bennie Reeves guilty of murder.

Oh, not for shooting down George Little-dave. Judge Raymond dismissed that charge, but on January 22nd, Bennie Reeves had appeared in Raymond's court again — for the crime everyone knew he had committed.

Murder trials are quick affairs. A day, two days at the most, is typical. Bennie's trial lasted a day. He sat there, listened to Commissioner Leckley's questioning of John Wadly and Emma Solomon, and Malcolm Andersen's cross-examination. When he took the stand, Bennie said he killed his wife. Said he ran. He didn't cry, didn't plead for leniency, and never really explained why he had killed her. Maybe he was trying to protect her reputation, although John Wadly's testimony had pretty much tarnished the late Mrs. Reeves as a trollop. The jury took twenty-two minutes to come back with a guilty verdict. Now, it was time for sentencing, but Judge Raymond asked if anyone would like to comment before he pronounced sentence.

Bass Reeves rose.

"Beggin' the court's pardon, Judge, I'd like to say a few things."

"Bennie done wrong." Bass looked old, tired. Those bullets had taken much of the starch out of him, and, he would walk with a cane for the rest of his days.

"He tried to make that marriage work. Worked hard at it. Changed jobs. Don't get me wrong. I ain't layin' the blame on his wife. I think Bennie deserved a better woman, but she didn't deserve to die. Before you pass sentence on this boy, however, well, I think I bear some responsibility for that gal's death."

He held his cane in both hands, twisting it as he sat in the witness chair, squeezing it. A tear ran down his face. Even Commissioner Leckley did not interrupt.

"A few nights before Bennie done what he done, we was sittin' over at my house. Ain't gonna hide nothin' from you, Your Honor. We was samplin' some forty-rod whiskey. I know that's illegal. We wasn't gettin' drunk. Just sippin' John Barleycorn, smokin' a cigar, discussin' his problems. Well, Bennie, he asks me what I'd do iffen it was my wife cheatin' on me, and I said . . . 'I'd shoot hell out of the man and whip the livin' God out of her.' So, I dunno. Maybe Marshal Bennett will want my badge. Maybe Commissioner Leckley will want to prosecute me. 'Cause I . . . how you say it? . . . I instigated that crime."

No more words. The clock ticked. Bass stopped spinning the cane in his hands, and started to rise, then said: "I'm a hard rock, but I believe in givin' a body a chance. Reckon I gave Erskine Jones more chances than I should've. Never give Bennie much of a chance, though. And, well, iffen not for Bennie, my guess is that me and Dave Adams would be dead now. My boy played hell in that set-to with Cherokee Bob up in Grove. I just wanted the court to know that. That's all I gotta say, Your Honor."

He limped back to the bench, sliding in between his wife Winnie and me.

Judge Raymond cleared his throat. "Benjamin Reeves," he said, "do you wish to make any statement before I pronounce sentence?"

Bennie shot his father and stepmother a quick glance before he stood. You could hear a tremor in his voice when he began talking, but soon he was speaking forcefully, and his body appeared to quit shaking.

"First of all, my father said some things. Things I appreciate. But I don't think the court should take his badge. I don't think the law should file charges against him."

"We have no plans to relieve Deputy Marshal Reeves of his badge," Commissioner Leckley said. "Or prosecute him. He is too valuable as a federal lawman."

"Thanks," Bennie said. His head bobbed. "My daddy didn't instigate nothin'. This is all my doin'. I killed my wife. Shot her down like you'd do a hydrophoby dog. Honestly I don't remember doin' it. Don't remember tryin' to kill myself. Don't remember much of nothin' after I stepped inside Emma's home that day. Daddy always told us kids that a man and a woman's gotta buck up, gotta make their own way in the world, but they gotta do what's right. Iffen they don't, he'd tell us, they gotta take what punishment comes along. I didn't shoot Cherokee Bob because I thought it might get me out of this fix I'd gotten myself in. I did it . . . well, it don't matter none. Don't matter why I did it. What matters is that I killed my wife. In cold blood. Not a day goes by that I don't regret it, but it don't matter. I killed her. Murdered her. And I'm standin' here ready to accept what punishment you say I deserve."

He didn't sit down. Just stood there.

Judge Raymond rose, and I saw Bass squeeze Winnie's hand.

Judge C.W. Raymond sentenced Bennie to life in prison at the federal penitentiary in Leavenworth, Kansas.

A light snow was falling outside the courthouse. I'd pulled up my collar, and paced in front of the hitching rail, waiting. Finally Bass and Winnie came out. The reporters were long gone to write up their stories, having given up on trying to wait and plead for a comment from Bass.

Bass gingerly descended the steps. Maybe he saw me, probably he didn't. He turned to walk to his house, but stopped when I called him name.

I tipped my hat at Winnie, and walked up to Bass. "You all right?" I asked. Damned silly question, and Bass didn't bother to answer it.

Instead, he asked me: "You been waitin' out here all this time?"

Three hours had passed since Judge Raymond had sentenced Bennie.

"Wanted to see you. To tell you something.

Back on the trail last summer, you once told me that a man wants to leave behind a legacy. Said he wants his kids to amount to something. I just wanted to say that you got a fine boy in Bennie. Most men, facing the gallows or life in prison, they'd try to influence the court, try to explain away that crime, try to evoke sympathy. Bennie held firm. Like a man."

I nodded, trying to encourage myself to keep up this speech.

"I'll be honest with you, Bass. I didn't know what to think about Bennie during that week or two we went after him. Truth be told, I didn't know what to think of you. Sometimes I thought you were letting Bennie get away. I think, now, though, that you were giving Bennie time to make up his own mind. Well, he made it up. Probably saved our bacon in Grove shooting Cherokee Bob like he did. That surprised the hell out of those other ruffians, and gave us the edge. He's a good son, Bass. Today I was proud of him. More proud than I was when he put a bullet in Cherokee Bob's back. If my kids turned out like Bennie, I'd be one proud daddy. I. . . ."

Stopped blabbering is what I did. I must have sounded like a damned fool. Here I was telling Bass that he should be proud of

313

a son who had just been sentenced to life in prison. I had planned on saying that Bennie would be a fine legacy for any father. In fact, I had mentally rehearsed a lot of other words that sounded like poetry in my mind, but not so good now. My face flushed. "I gotta go." Quick as I could move I tried to make it to my horse.

"Dave."

Stopping, I made myself turn around.

Bass limped over, and did the strangest thing. He held out his hand.

Odd. I'd spent eighteen years riding for the court out of Muskogee, Indian Territory. I'd accomplished a lot, I like to think, and have been honored with a solid gold Waltham chronograph watch with my name engraved on the hunting case and a sentiment and the years 1889–1907 etched inside. Street and Smith Corporation published a dime novel titled *Killing Cherokee Bob; or, the Heroic Marshals & Nefarious Scoundrels of the Indian Nations,* which had me shooting down Cherokee Bob, and depicted Bass Riley, not Reeves, as a white deputy marshal. That penny dreadful was published four months after our gun battle in Grove, and I immediately began trying to set the record straight, writing principal characters, interviewing others, spending hours upon hours in the dusty basements of federal courthouses. You have been reading the results of my research, my quest.

I have spoken to churches and libraries about my so-called adventures in lawless Indian Territory. Children ask to hear me tell tales of the olden times before Oklahoma became a state. Olden times! Men and women, boys and girls, black, white, and red . . . they always seem shocked, even ask me if I'm joshing, when I tell them that my proudest moment as a federal peace officer happened on a snowy winter morning in January 1903 when Bass Reeves, the greatest lawman I have ever known and the best friend I ever had, reached out and shook my hand.

David Adams
Muskogee, Oklahoma
July 25, 1911

Legend, and many non-fiction accounts, say that Bass Reeves demanded the arrest warrant and took off after his son Bennie killed his wife. Two weeks later, the story goes, Deputy U.S. Marshal Bass Reeves returned with his son. That's the story based on Richard Fronterhouse's 1959 interview with Bass Reeves's youngest daughter Alice Spahn (who died in 1966), and the recollections of Reeves's great-nephew, Paul L. Brady. That's the legend.

The reality — at least according to the Muskogee *Daily Phoenix* of June 8, 1902 — isn't quite as dramatic. The newspaper reported that after Bennie killed his wife, he began walking to town, where he was met by his father, who arrested him. In the Trusty Prisoner's Agreement unearthed by historian and Bass Reeves biographer Art T. Burton, Bennie Reeves said he was arrested in Muskogee by his father.

Burton writes: *The exact sequence of events is probably somewhere in between all three reports.*

Obviously I opted for the legend.

I don't know when I first heard about Bass Reeves, but I do know when I decided I wanted to write a novel about him. It was 2006, and I was reading Burton's biography, *Black Gun, Silver Star: The Life and Legend of Frontier Marshal Bass Reeves* (University of Nebraska Press, 2006). Later, I interviewed Burton for a magazine Q&A about Reeves, and in 2009, in a hotel bar in Midwest City, Oklahoma, during a Western Writers of America Convention, I told Burton I had been wanting to write a novel about Reeves.

Honestly I expected to be discouraged, if not outright dismissed. "You can't write about Reeves. That's my story!" . . . "Are you kidding me? A white guy can't write about a black man." . . . "I wish you won't. I plan on writing a novel about Bass."

Instead, Burton turned out to be overwhelmingly encouraging. "You should write that novel," he said. "You might be able to get to the heart of the matter."

I don't know if I've accomplished that, but I do know that I never would have been able to write this novel without the help of

Burton. His biography of Bass Reeves, as well as two other histories he wrote: *Black, Red, and Deadly: Black and Indian Gunfighters of the Indian Territory, 1870–1907* (Eakin Press, 1991) and *Black, Buckskin, and Blue: African-American Scouts and Soldiers on the Western Frontier* (Eakin Press, 1999), were incredible sources. Nor would I have likely ever tackled the story had Burton not proved so gracious and encouraging. Burton also helped me maneuver around stumbling blocks I came upon while writing this novel.

In addition to Burton's books, other sources include *Muskogee: City and County* by Odie B. Faulk (The Five Civilized Tribes Museum, 1982); *Oklahoma: A History* by W. David Baird and Danney Goble (University of Oklahoma Press, 2008); *Law West of Fort Smith: A History of Frontier Justice in the Indian Territory* by Glenn Shirley, 1834–1896 (University of Nebraska Press, 1957); *Hanging Judge* by Fred Harvey Harrington (University of Oklahoma Press, 1951); *"Let No Guilty Man Escape": A Judicial Biography of "Hanging Judge" Isaac C. Parker* by Roger H. Tuller (University of Oklahoma Press, 2001); *And Still the Waters Run: The Betrayal of the Five Civilized Tribes* by Angie Debo

(Princeton University Press, 1940); *Crazy Snake and the Smoked Meat Rebellion* by Mel H. Bolster (Branden Press, 1976); and *Historical Atlas of Oklahoma, Third Edition* by John W. Morris, Charles R. Goins, and Edwin C. McReynolds (University of Oklahoma Press, 1986).

I should also thank David Dary, *emeritus* professor of journalism at the University of Oklahoma, and Michael "Cowboy Mike" Searles, professor of history at Augusta State University in Georgia; as well as the staffs of the Oklahoma Historical Society; the Five Civilized Tribes Museum in Muskogee; Fort Smith National Historic Site in Arkansas; the Vista Grande and Santa Fe public libraries in New Mexico; and the African-American Resource Center at the Tulsa City-County Library.

Cherokee Bob Dozier and his gang are fictional, though loosely based on actual criminals in Indian Territory during Bass Reeves's reign. The fictional Cherokee Bob's father, however, Bob Dozier, was an outlaw who Bass Reeves tracked down and killed, much as depicted in this novel, *sans* the fictional Erskine Jones, of course. In fact, most, but not all, of the stories told in flashbacks relating Bass Reeves's life are, for the most part, true or based on facts from

Burton's books. For instance, Bass Reeves in fact did arrest the minister who baptized him, but that event actually happened in 1907, not in 1901.

Bennie Reeves arrived at the federal penitentiary in Leavenworth, Kansas, on February 13, 1903. Burton tells me that he has found newspaper articles published in the years after Bennie's conviction that say Reeves guarded prisoners being transported to the Leavenworth penitentiary. "I am sure," Burton says, "it gave him an opportunity to visit his son."

On November 13, 1914, Bennie's life sentence was commuted by the Department of Justice, and he returned to Muskogee, where he worked as a restaurant's dishwasher and later as a barber before fading from history.

At age thirty-six, Isaac C. Parker, the legendary "Hanging Judge," was the West's youngest federal judge when he first held court in Fort Smith in May 1875. He spent more than twenty years on the bench before his death on November 17, 1896, having tried thirteen thousand four hundred and ninety cases, including three hundred and forty-four capital crimes. More than nine thousand four hundred of those cases ended with guilty pleas or convictions, and Parker sentenced one hundred and sixty men to hang, although only seventy-nine were executed. Other sentences were commuted or appealed, and some convicts were pardoned while others died in jail before their execution date.

Judge C.W. Raymond would be appointed chief justice of the Indian Territory Court of Appeals. After his retirement, he hung his shingle in Muskogee and turned down appointments as U.S. Civil Service Commissioner and U.S. Circuit Judge. He became a successful farmer, ran an unsuccessful campaign for Congress in 1924, and died in Watseka, Illinois in 1939.

United States Marshal Doctor Leo E. Bennett was elected mayor of Muskogee in 1908. He died in May, 1917, while visiting Mineral Wells, Texas. U.S. Marshal Jacob Yoes died on February 6, 1906, and was buried at the National Cemetery in Fort Smith.

After spending eighteen years working for the federal court, David Adams resigned as deputy marshal on April 15, 1907. He remained in Muskogee, dying in the summer of 1922.

The Okfuskee County, Oklahoma, town of Paden is named after Paden Tolbert, who, as far as history tells us, wasn't shot in the lung while chasing my fictional bad guy. Tolbert left the U.S. marshal's service for a job as special officer of the Fort Smith and Western Railroad, but his lungs became congested, and he went to Hot Springs, Arkansas, in hopes of recovering. He didn't, dying on April 24, 1904. Any racial friction or animosity between Tolbert and Bass Reeves was my own invention for the purpose of this narrative.

Grant Johnson and Uncle Bud Ledbetter, who both undoubtedly played no part in the capture of Bennie Reeves, feuded in the years after this novel's setting. Ledbetter apparently thought Johnson wasn't rigid enough in enforcement of liquor laws. Johnson was dismissed as a federal lawman early in 1906, but found work as a Eufaula policeman. His son John was awarded a Purple Heart while serving in France during World War I, and Johnson died in Eufaula on April 9, 1929.

James Franklin "Bud" Ledbetter served as chief of the Muskogee police force and Muskogee county sheriff before retiring in 1928. He died, at age eighty-four, in Muskogee on July 8, 1937, and it was Uncle Bud, a white man, who was caring for Bass Reeves when the famed black marshal was dying.

Bass Reeves remained a lawman almost to the end. At age sixty-nine and walking with a cane, he was serving as a beat officer on the Muskogee police force. He spent two years on the police force before illness and age forced him to retire. On January 12, 1910, Bass Reeves died at age seventy-two of Bright's disease and complications.

He had fathered eleven children, though some died young. His heirs included his widow Winnie Reeves, who apparently moved to Los Angeles after his death; daughters Sallie Sanders of Fort Smith, and Alice Spahn of Muskogee; sons, Bennie, still in prison at the time of his father's death, and Ed, of Independence, Kansas; and two grandchildren living in McAlester, Oklahoma — Mary and Rother Reeves. Bass Reeves's funeral drew hundreds of family, friends, and admirers — black, Indian, and white.

Perhaps the most fitting tribute to his legacy came from the Muskogee Phoenix — a white newspaper.

Bass Reeves was an unique character. Absolutely fearless and knowing no master but duty, the placing of a writ in his hands for service meant that the letter of the law would be fulfilled though his life paid the penalty. In the carrying out of his orders during his thirty-two years as a deputy United States marshal in the old Indian Territory days, Bass Reeves faced death a hundred times, many desperate characters sought his life yet the old man even on the brink of the grave went along the pathway of duty with the simple faith that some men have who believe they are in the care of special providence when they are doing right.

Bass is dead. He was buried with high honors, and his name will be recorded in the archives of the court as a faithful servant of the law and a brave officer. And it was fitting that such recognition was bestowed upon this man. It is fitting that, black or white, our people have the manhood to recognize character and faithfulness to duty.

ABOUT THE AUTHOR

Johnny D. Boggs has worked cattle, shot rapids in a canoe, hiked across mountains and deserts, traipsed around ghost towns, and spent hours poring over microfilm in library archives — all in the name of finding a good story. He's also one of the few Western writers to have won four Spur Awards from Western Writers of America (for his novels, *Camp Ford,* in 2006, *Doubtful Cañon,* in 2008, and *Hard Winter* in 2010, and his short story, "A Piano at Dead Man's Crossing", in 2002) and the Western Heritage Wrangler Award from the National Cowboy and Western Heritage Museum (for his novel, *Spark on the Prairie: The Trial of the Kiowa Chiefs,* in 2004). A native of South Carolina, Boggs spent almost fifteen years in Texas as a journalist at the *Dallas Times Herald* and *Fort Worth Star-Telegram* before moving to New Mexico in 1998 to concentrate full time on his novels. Author of dozens of published short stories, he has also written for more than fifty newspapers and magazines, and is a frequent contributor to *Boys' Life, New Mexico Magazine, Persimmon Hill,* and *True West.* His Western novels cover a wide range. *The Lonesome Chisholm Trail* is an authentic cattle-drive story, while *Lonely Trumpet* is an historical novel about the first black graduate of West Point. *The Despoilers* and *Ghost Legion* are set in the Carolina backcountry during the Revolutionary War. *The Big Fifty* chronicles the slaughter of buffalo on the southern plains in the 1870s, while *East of the Border* is a comedy about the theatrical offerings of Buffalo Bill Cody, Wild Bill Hickok, and Texas Jack Omohundro, and *Camp Ford* tells about a Civil War baseball game between Union prisoners of war and Confederate guards. "Boggs's narrative voice captures the old-fashioned style of the past," *Publishers Weekly* said, and *Booklist* called him "among the best Western writers at work today." Boggs lives with his wife Lisa and son Jack in Santa Fe. His website is www.johnnydboggs.com.